W9-BST-121

*the*

# second chance
# boutique

*the*

# second chance
# boutique

*a novel*

LOUISA LEAMAN

sourcebooks
landmark

Copyright © 2019, 2020 by Louisa Leaman
Cover and internal design © 2020 by Sourcebooks
Cover design by Lisa Amoroso
Cover images © Elizabeth Ansley/Arcangel Images, Anna Ivanova/Alamy Stock Photo

Sourcebooks and the colophon are registered trademarks of Sourcebooks.

All rights reserved. No part of this book may be reproduced in any form or by
any electronic or mechanical means including information storage and retrieval
systems—except in the case of brief quotations embodied in critical articles or
reviews—without permission in writing from its publisher, Sourcebooks.

The characters and events portrayed in this book are fictitious or are used
fictitiously. Any similarity to real persons, living or dead, is purely coincidental
and not intended by the author.

All brand names and product names used in this book are trademarks, registered
trademarks, or trade names of their respective holders. Sourcebooks is not
associated with any product or vendor in this book.

Published by Sourcebooks Landmark, an imprint of Sourcebooks
P.O. Box 4410, Naperville, Illinois 60567-4410
(630) 961-3900
sourcebooks.com

Originally published as *The Perfect Dress* in 2019 in the United Kingdom by
Transworld Publishers, a division of Penguin Random House UK.

Library of Congress Cataloging-in-Publication Data is on file with the publisher.

Printed and bound in the United States of America.
VP 10 9 8 7 6 5 4 3 2 1

# chapter 1

THE WHISPERING DRESS IS NO ORDINARY WEDDING DRESS SHOP. There are no oversized *Pay Here* signs. No mass changing rooms crammed with seminaked brides, all eyeing the same white satin fishtail while stealthily noting the merits and pitfalls of one another's body types. No pitiless sales assistant pressuring for a stretch of the budget or a buy before it's gone. Above all, there are no rails of white upon white, all dresses squished together, flopping off their hangers, same but different, a monotonous rack of matrimonial sardines. At this shop, every gown sits apart. Every gown is different. Every gown has its story. After all, the most important dress of a woman's life should surely have something distinct to say.

Outside, a new customer lingers. She stares through the glass panels of the quaint Victorian bay, her eyes wide at the sight of the window display—antique lace, satin slippers, and old leather suitcases signifying honeymoons of old: a drive along the Amalfi Coast in a 1950s Aston Martin or the duplex suite of a 1920s ocean liner. Her thoughts soar, finally hopeful that she might find a dress of character, one that feels special, personal, particular to her. The One.

The interior of the shop convinces her. Everywhere she looks, there is something to admire, an Aladdin's cave of wedding parapher-nalia: veils, tiaras, silk slippers, and jewels. They hang from the walls, drip from the shelves, or sparkle on dressers, each item carefully dis-played to announce its full splendor. The wooden floors are crowned with a faded Afghan rug, aping the atmosphere of a bohemian country retreat. The beamed ceiling appears to sway with strings of dried white roses and orange blossom flowers, while an enormous art deco chandelier illuminates the central space, its geometric crystal swirl conjuring images of palm courts and jazz quartets. The light bounces from wall to wall, aided by several floor-length mirrors, each one draped with pearls and ribbons and bows. The main stars, however, are the dresses themselves. They occupy their space with such intensity, it's as if, at any moment, they could spring to life and dance across the floor.

The customer is no expert, but immediately she recognizes a few tropes of twentieth-century fashion. There is the ballerina cut of the '50s, its nipped waist and white tulle puff promising fairy-tale femininity, then something tall and slinky behind it—she'd like to say ivory satin—echoing the glamour of those Golden Age cinema stars whose names all end in *a*: Rita, Ava, Mara, Maria. Her eyes fall next on an extravagant '80s princess gown, an old-fashioned corset-and-bustle affair, then a feathered number in red (which, to her mind, looks barely qualified to be a wedding dress), and finally, within the glow of a lava lamp, she spots something distinctly '60s, a tiny mini dress with a silver plastic collar...for a wedding? Her mind cartwheels, thrown by the sight of all these twists of wedding dress history, somehow forgotten within the ceaseless full-length-and-strapless-big-gown obsession.

"Welcome," says a voice, "to the Whispering Dress."

The shop's owner, Francesca Delaney, red hair sculpted into an immaculate chignon, ivory skin, floral tea dress, plum lips, and a certain sparkle in her sea-green eyes, steps out from behind a tray of tiaras and smiles warmly.

"I may be making assumptions here, but my guess is you're looking for a wedding dress?"

The new customer sighs, almost melts with relief. "Oh yes," she says. "You don't know what I've been through. Street after street. Shop after shop. Meringue after meringue. I thought I'd never... Oh, this is wonderful." She moves through the room, mesmerized, stroking each dress in turn.

Fran watches and smiles. "The horrors of mass-produced tulle?" she says sympathetically.

The customer nods. "Don't get me wrong. Some of those dresses were lovely, but they weren't for my figure...or my budget. The good ones were extortionate. The average ones were, well, average. The sizes never seemed to be accurate. And then there were the sales assistants, with their judgy eyes and good manicures, who said we could only have a free glass of bubbles if we registered online. In one shop, the assistant insisted I try on this monstrous froufrou thing with an encrusted bust that I barely had the bones to fill, let alone the flesh, then tried to tell me it was perfect. She was so desperate for her commission, when I told her I didn't like the style, she lost the plot and told me I'd never get the dress I wanted because I was too picky!"

She sighs, defeated.

"I hated it…the whole thing of it. Then a friend told me about your shop and something clicked: The Whispering Dress, Vintage Bespoke Wedding Gowns. The thing is, I liked the idea that, with your way of doing things, you'd pick the dress and I'd just have to go along with it. I had this feeling that you'd know what I need better than me, like that's what you do."

"Yes," says Fran, delighted. "That's exactly what I do!"

The customer smiles. "To be honest, I've never bought vintage before. I get my clothes cheap on the high street like everyone else. Nothing lasts, but it doesn't matter when a T-shirt costs a few quid, does it?"

Fran frowns, masks her annoyance with a nod.

"I was a bit nervous you wouldn't want to help me. With your reputation…I don't imagine I'm your typical customer."

"My shop is for everyone," says Fran, eyes twinkling. "Call me Fran. What's your name?"

"Ella."

"Okay, Ella, tell me about yourself. Anything you think might help me decide what you need in a dress."

Ella looks down at her legs. "Well," she says, somewhat self-consciously, "I'm a size 8, flat chested. I take a size 4 shoe."

"No, no. I mean *you*, tell me about *you*—what you like to do, why you're getting married, the things you hope for, the things you dread."

"Um…"

Fran sees it in her face, her body language—Ella is unsure of herself. A shy one. Shy with a twist.

"Your fiancé," adds Fran, helping the flow. "Where did you meet him?"

"Work…which is boring, I know. Appleby Electronics. We're in different departments. I do finance. He's in quality control."

"So an office romance? A bit of playful eye contact across the watercooler? Stealing a kiss at the Christmas party?"

"It was a team-building day. I twisted my ankle on the assault course and he helped me to first aid. Now look at us, two years on and we're getting married! The only thing is"—Ella shrugs, looks down at her feet again—"I'm dreading the attention. My work colleagues are ultra-catty. The thought of walking up the aisle with them all staring at me… Every time I picture it, I break out in hives."

"Oh dear, no," says Fran. "There's no need for hives." She takes Ella by the arm and leads her through the shop. "So what is it about the staring that bothers you?"

"That none of them think I'm good enough for their Alex. That I'm boring. That I'm dull."

"One wonders, then, why they're invited to your wedding."

"Alex is friends with everyone. He's super kind. He wants everyone in the office to celebrate with us. They don't have a problem with him. Only me."

"And should you tolerate their opinions? *Are* you boring?"

"Well…no, I don't think so. I might come across as a bit shy because I don't take part in the office pranks and all the tiresome conversations about reality TV and hangovers."

"Because you have other interests—"

"Exactly," says Ella appreciatively. "I love dancing. Latin and ballroom. In fact, that's how Alex and I got together. When I twisted my ankle, I started to cry and Alex thought it was because I was in pain, but actually, it was because I knew I'd miss my competition that weekend. A few weeks later, he turned up at one of my classes. We've been together ever since. He now loves dancing as much as I do. He knows the real me."

"And so should the rest of the world," says Fran, brightening. "What better time than your wedding day to show them your inner dazzle? I've got just the dress."

"I like the look of this one," says Ella, reaching toward a demure crepe '70s maxi with full-length leg-of-mutton sleeves.

"That one's lovely," says Fran, "but it's too quiet for you. For you, I have something…extraordinary." Her eyes flash with excitement. "I've been waiting for a bride who has the right kind of spirit to carry off this little number—"

Ella nods, smiles nervously.

"If you don't like it—although I think you will once you've tried it on—then we can consider other options, but personally, I believe it's the one for you, the dress you need."

She steps forward, full of all she has seen and experienced, takes Ella's hands in hers, leads her toward a powder-pink chaise longue, and asks her to sit while she prepares the dress in question.

"Just a minute," she says, diving behind a damask curtain. "I only finished the repairs yesterday. Merely a bit of bead rethreading. Nearly ninety years old and it's in amazing condition."

"Ninety years!" says Ella.

"Ready?"

"I guess."

Fran throws back the curtain, revealing an ivory 1920s flapper dress, knee length with a scalloped hem and drop waist, its front bodice shimmering with glass beads, sequins, and silver threads. Even on the mannequin, its dancing energy pulses, every thread eager to shimmer and shake in the quake of a leg flick, a hip twist, or a hand flutter. A dress for moving in. A dress with zest.

Ella gasps, clasps her hands to her mouth, the sparkle of sequins dazzling her eyes. "You—you actually think I could wear *that*?"

"I think you're the perfect person to wear it. In my world," says Fran, "a wedding dress that brought joy to a bride of the '20s can transfer its pleasure to a bride of today and maybe, just maybe, it can impart something of its wisdom too. A whispering dress isn't just a yard of trimmed and stitched fabric, you see. It's a story, a legacy, a lesson from history. You might even call it a talisman. The woman who first wore this incredible gown was a dancer like you. Here."

Fran goes to a bulletin board and returns with a faded sepia photo of a woman and man, smiling as their bodies lean together in a dance embrace.

"Looks like a fox-trot," says Ella, curious.

"Meet Phyllis Noble and her husband, Harry."

"You mean—?"

"The dress's original bride. She and Harry married in 1926. A very lively occasion, I believe. There were more than three conga lines and an awful lot of Charleston. The guests drank juleps and Manhattans, ate turbot and peaches, and everyone got a slice of the five-tiered wedding cake. The honeymoon was in Majorca, in a newly built villa overlooking the sea. Phyllis and Harry were dance partners, pretty well-known I gather. Once married, they toured all around Europe."

Ella shivers, visibly amazed. "Are they still alive?"

"No, but the important thing is they had a long, full, and happy life together, doing what they loved. Phyllis's granddaughter donated the dress. She knew how much happiness it had brought her grand-mother and thought it might do the same for another bride."

"Can I...can I try it on?"

"Of course."

Barely able to undress fast enough and with no thought for who else might be in the shop, Ella strips down to her underwear and, with Fran's help, climbs into the dress. The weight of it shocks her, but as soon as Fran fastens the back and adjusts the straps, it feels right for her skin. Fran turns Ella toward a large gilt-framed mirror, where she meets her wedding-day self for the first time. The result is instant tears, studded with rounds of delirious, delighted laughter.

"Oh my goodness! I can't believe it! After all those awful, disap-pointing, swamping, great big meringues, I can hardly believe this is it! And to think it's been right here all along—"

"Waiting for you," says Fran as she hands Ella a veil, a swathe of tulle attached to a simple cloche-style headdress. "This will set it off perfectly. Did you know it became customary in the '20s for the bride to throw back her veil at the end of the ceremony, then walk out unveiled, a proud married women?"

Ella ponders this, then takes the edges of the veil and flings it away from her face.

"You show them," says Fran. "Show them who you really are."

"Hey, are you married?" says Ella, catching her eye. "I bet your wedding dress was *amazing.*"

Fran startles. "No," she says hastily, smiling to mask her inner panic. "No, I'm not. I—I guess I haven't met the right person yet."

*Please*, she thinks, her thoughts drifting to places she doesn't like to go, *change the subject.* She looks out through the bay window, feels a sudden urge to flee, to leap out and fly away into the clouds... With a blink and a sigh, she snaps herself back to Ella.

"Just let the dress speak for itself," she whispers, "and I promise you'll have your own wonderful, dance-filled marriage."

"I will," says Ella.

*And she will*, thinks Fran. *Phyllis Noble will make sure of it.*

Brides aren't hard to find. Throw a bouquet into a crowd, and they'll be there, clinging to one matrimonial ideal or another. Finding dresses, however—brilliant dresses, *whispering* dresses—now that's the challenge. There are dresses around if you know where to look, on internet buy-and-swap sites, charity shops, and flea markets, sometimes donated, sometimes sourced from vintage dealers, but Fran has to choose with care. One great dress, hard-won, is better than ten average ones. Her work is bespoke, her mission to sweeten the trial of modern romance with the careful matching of dress to bride. She sees it as her duty to take her time and get to know both, then find a pairing that fuels the fire of love.

Each of her gowns is painstakingly researched, its backstory teased from the shadows of the past. "Field work" she calls it. And this, she believes, is what makes her service so unique: the forensics of vintage clothing. Some gowns come primed with stories, their donors only too eager to relay memories and share photos, videos, and wedding day keepsakes. Others are more mysterious, but as long as Fran has the original bride's name, with a little research, she can usually uncover its truths. Dresses tend to fall into one of four categories: the "family" dress, handed down through generations, usually offered up when the latest daughter rejects it for something fresh and contemporary; the "joy" dress, from the woman who likes the idea of her beloved gown bringing happiness to others instead of gathering dust in a suitcase; the "basic" dress, from the unsentimental woman who is on a mission to declutter; and the "dead" dress, the venomous outcast of doom, disillusionment, or divorce. Fran meticulously steers clear of this latter category—its energy is rarely conducive to happiness. After all, she's in the business of improving brides' lives, not saddling them with the echoes of past disasters.

She has three simple rules:

1. Never covet your own stock.
2. Never sell a "dead" dress.
3. Never say no to a wedding invite.

The Phyllis Noble flapper was one of the finest she'd had in a long time, the perfect combination of style, condition, and story. She knew it was special the moment it arrived on her doorstep, wrapped in brown parcel paper with a bundle of photos and a charming letter from Phyl's granddaughter, who'd learned of the Whispering Dress after her best friend had found nuptial joy with a wonderful Norman Hartnell brocade two-piece rescued from a junk shop in Muswell Hill.

Every now and then, a dress of true distinction comes Fran's way. There was the 1970s wedding kaftan that had belonged to a well-known folk singer; the fairy-tale French couture gown that had been worn by three generations of brides from the same family; and then the wine-stained Lacroix sheath dress—Fran had managed to remove the stain and had consequently received interest from scores of brides, but had eventually sold it for half her usual fee to an impoverished, pregnant fashion student. Not the best price, but the match was compelling: the ensembles' original bride had also been pregnant and had rushed a marriage to avoid public shame, yet through hard work, patience, and the invaluable art of compromise, she nevertheless created a happy, lasting union, resulting in four children and a thriving wallpaper business. Good energy to pass down the line. Integrity is everything. Fran has no qualms about turning away business if she cannot find the right gown for a bride. There is nothing to be gained from sending a woman down the aisle in an offering that doesn't speak from the heart—that's what the high street is for.

Today, however, Fran feels under pressure, distracted from her capacity to cherish old fabric and fire Cupid's arrows. Success has overwhelmed her. Her remaining good gowns are earmarked for sale, and she hasn't had time to hunt for new stock. Whispering dresses take time to evolve. They cannot be rushed on a conveyor belt. There are a few '80s romantic numbers waiting in the wings, but synthetic taffeta isn't great for the soul, and she fears the world isn't ready for a puff-sleeve revival. It is a relief therefore that her assistant and long-time friend, Mick Haigh, has suggested the gift of a house clearance:

"Says here: 'Dryad's Hall, six-bedroom country retreat in Epping Forest, needs prompt and discreet clearing. No valuables remaining. Mattresses, some furniture, general waste, and clothing. Contact Rafael Colt 07972472678.' Some rich old girl probably croaked it and now her kids want a quick sale, take the money and run, buy a new yacht, pay for little Farquharson's school fees and what have you. So how about it? Try our luck? Epping Forest isn't far. We could have the van there in a half hour and if there's nothing vaguely bridal in sight, I'll at least find a few bits I can upcycle and stick on eBay. And at the very least it's a trip to the countryside."

Mick, a one-time Camden Market stallholder with an eye for restorable bric-a-brac, an obsession with Victorian gentleman's tailoring, and a hand-drawn calligraphy font to his name, waves the newspaper advertisement under Fran's nose. Fran eyes it suspiciously, bothered by memories of all those dispiriting probate clear-outs, the 1930s houses with their smoke-stained walls, moldering food in semi-warm fridges, smelly carpets, mottled net curtains, and garbage bags of unwashed clothes.

"Oh, I don't know, Mick. So often these clearances turn out to be a waste of time. Auctioneers will have claimed the best stuff."

Mick twiddles the extremities of his well-groomed handlebar mustache (inspired by a favorite portrait of Lord Frederic Leighton). A long-standing companion/substitute for a boyfriend, he knows

Fran well. He can tell that, even in protest, her curiosity is crackling. The thrill of finding a dress, even just the slimmest chance, among the detritus of other people's unwanted junk, is impossible for her to resist.

"I guess if it's a six-bed country retreat," she says ponderously, her gaze shifting around the shop, "even the leftovers could be interesting."

"Excellent," says Mick. "I'll buy you a full Englishman's breakfast on the way."

Epping Forest, a slim but stately strip of wilderness on the outskirts of Northeast London, offers greenery, peace, and birdsong to those wishing to escape their urbanized environs. The woodland is ancient, dense with the gnarled trunks of beeches, hornbeams, silver birches, and oaks. Fran is surprised by how quickly she feels immersed, the cocoon of nature concealing all trace of grime and traffic and city noise. She likes the sensation, the getaway feeling. Mick has lots of stories about secret pond-side raves and trees he's climbed and smoked in. He also claims he was confronted by a stag on the same stretch of road they are driving on.

"Regal, it was. Right there. Stared at me, then walked on."

Fran isn't paying attention however. She is lost in an idyll of woodland wedding bohemia with moss on the tables, tea lights in jam jars, an arch woven from twigs and a gorgeous empire maxi dress in soft gray lace, paired with bare feet and bluebells. In her reverie, she nearly misses the entrance to Dryad's Hall. The sign is all but consumed by flora. Mick reverses, then shunts his minivan between two ivy-clad gateposts and continues up a meandering willow tunnel drive. The house emerges in a glade ahead, an arts-and-crafts masterpiece, its hive of nooks and corners rising out of the earth, surrounded by flower-studded rhododendrons. It is picture-book perfect, twee old England with a deep russet roof, three tall chimneys, leaded windows, and wooden beams.

"It's everything I love," says Fran, delighted. "Heart, history, and that tantalizing hint of untold stories."

"Told you," says Mick. "Not all house clearances are alike."

"But it's so hidden away," says Fran, gazing in wonder at the rising chimneys. "You'd never know it was there from the road."

Another van is already on the drive, a clean one, with a burgundy spray job and gold signage: *Luckmore's*. Mick scowls, recognizing the name of one of the established London auction houses. He once applied for a job there as a trainee valuation clerk but failed the interview on account of being too "excitable." *No matter*, he thinks. Now he has Fran and the Whispering Dress and exquisitely tailored frock coats. They watch as two men in matching burgundy dust jackets load a baroque dresser into the back.

"Careful, boys," says Mick, glaring from his window. "Don't drop that corner now."

"Bring on the leftovers," says Fran. "Although, are you quite sure this is bona fide?"

"A hundred percent. I spoke to the chap earlier. Rafael. Posh boy. Says he wants the whole house cleared by midday. No dawdling."

"I guess we better get on with it then."

In the distance, she sees him, his back to her and the sun behind him, straining through the window dust. He doesn't belong here. Judging by his crisp suit and neat, pale shirt, his world is a million miles from the arcane quirks of this crumbling forest retreat. Tall and slim, his stature is elegant, but his shoulders bunch. His neck bows in an uncomfortable arc, straining toward the phone in his hands, fingers furiously typing, messaging, actioning.

Mick coughs. "You must be Rafael." He bows forward to offer a handshake. "Mick D. Haigh, secondhand furniture restorer, professional dandy, and part-time assistant at the Whispering Dress, at your service. And this, the delectable vintage dress expert and all-around good egg, Ms. Francesca Delaney."

Mick grins, clearly pleased with the pomposity of his introduction. The man—Rafael—stares at Mick's homburg and waistcoat, slightly raises one eyebrow, then shifts his focus to Fran. For a moment he gazes at her, then he blinks, sighs, gives an emotionless nod.

"Take it all," he says. "There's a dumpster at the side for whatever you don't want."

No hello. No welcome. And definitely no handshake.

"Is there anything we shoul—"

"I'd like you out by midday."

"Right you are," says Mick, backing away.

He and Fran burrow into the rest of the house, through wood-paneled hallways and interconnecting receptions rooms, inglenook fireplaces, carved doorframes, and hammered pewter handles and rails—the handcrafted hardware of a long-gone era. Such a trove of past treasure would normally set Fran's vintage instincts alight, but she is distracted, locked into a small infuriation of etiquette.

"Never mind 'take it all,'" she mutters. "What about *take the hint*? Evidently we're not wanted nor worthy of basic courtesies such as 'hello' and 'thank you.'"

"Ah, suck it up, girl," says Mick. "We're not here to make friends. I'll forgive him his lack of manners if I can make my fortune from his family castoffs. Talking of which, what have we here—"

They come to a large, high-ceilinged kitchen. Save for the main units, the butler's sink, and the cooking range, the contents have been stripped. Fragments of a broken dinner plate are strewn across the terra-cotta floor. Fran bends to pick one up.

"Delft blue. Pretty old by the looks of it."

"Better be the only plate those Luckmore's fools have smashed," grumbles Mick. "Check the cupboards."

They begin opening doors. Luckmore's have been thorough. Most of the cupboards are empty apart from a few items here and there: tea towels, jam jars, wooden spoons, jelly molds, and a dusty mug tree. There is nothing of worth, yet Fran feels eerily tense about these utilitarian leftovers and all the emotion that lives in them. *Everyday objects*, she thinks, handling the box from a 1980s blender, *say so much more about a person than their ostentatious showpieces, their grand pianos, antique sofas, and glorious artwork*. There is honesty in the mundane. She likes honesty. And manners. She really likes manners. As she and Mick begin boxing up the scraps, she is compelled to keep venting about the rude and abrupt Rafael Colt.

"I mean, the basics take no effort, Mick. And what about glancing up from your phone screen for more than a heartbeat? It doesn't hurt to make eye contact." She opens a shopping bag of folded cotton tablecloths. "Anyway, they say we've evolved from Neanderthal, but I say we're evolving back. David Passemore would never have been so rude. Or Harry Noble. Or James Andrew Percy. In fact, Percy would have charmed the pants off us. According to Meryl's journal, on their tenth wedding anniversary, he surprised her entire family with a hot air balloon flight over the Serengeti."

"A bunch of dead grooms, Fran. Not really a fair comparison, is it?"

"Maybe not, but I'll stick with my dead grooms if modern man has to be so unpleasant. At least dead grooms aren't permanently attached to their smartphones. I mean, who did he think he was? *Take it all…out by midday.* Miserable, modern sod—"

"Ahem."

Fran looks up. The subject of her mockery is standing in the doorway.

"Ah, hi," she says, flustered. "Um…we're just…um…you know…sorting…"

He has heard her, no doubt, but his face is devoid of reaction. He stands motionless, watching as she tries, through embarrassment, to shovel a pair of soiled red gardening gloves into a slippery bin liner.

"She loved to garden," he says wistfully.

"Oh, then you should have these." Fran offers up the gloves.

"No."

"Keepsake?"

"No," he presses, and then, as though to prove his manners, adds, "no *thank you.*"

She pulls the gloves back, hugs them to her chest, feels they should at least have love from someone. "If you don't mind," she ventures, "who was she?"

"My mother, Alessandra, the woman whose mortal possessions you're currently rifling through"—he catches Fran's eye, gives a small, wry smile—"not quite a dead groom, but…she was a bride once."

"Yes, um, sorry about that," says Fran. "I didn't mean…"

But her words are wasted. He has already walked away.

Florid-cheeked, Fran leaves Mick to finish the kitchen and starts searching the upstairs rooms, now eager to get the job done and get away, if only to spare herself the embarrassment of her gaff. The few piles of boxed-up clothes offer nothing more rousing than a mound of brown wool and plaid jackets, which will no doubt be appreciated by someone, but not by young brides. Finally, Fran goes to the last room, its door beckoning from the end of a long, wood-paneled corridor.

"Come on," she whispers, turning the handle. "Just give me a veil or a slipper or *something.*"

The door creaks. The room inside is gloriously large with double aspect windows and views across the forest, yet its immediate emptiness kills it, a sad shell of degraded wall coverings and broken floorboards, bare and fruitless. Seduced by the treetops, Fran goes to the nearest window. Beneath her is a garden surrounded by a screen of dense forest, with a terrace and a lake and an ornamental waterfall. There are signs of neglect—rampant growth and untamed boughs—but the garden is in a better state than the house, richly planted with miniature trees and shrubs, the project of a keen and knowledgeable gardener. The frisson of curiosity takes hold, and she turns back to the room, conjures an idea of Alessandra, unravels a vision in her mind of a young, bright woman pinning her hair in a dresser mirror, preparing for a dance or dinner. Was she feisty? Glamorous? Quiet? Proud? So many questions, but the bare walls won't speak. Fran smiles to herself and pushes away from the window, then wanders through to the smaller adjoining dressing room, which prompts a holler to Mick.

"Quick! Up here. Look at this!"

Her shout rattles through the empty rooms, but Mick doesn't appear. Impatient, she goes forward to admire her find, a ladies' armoire, early 1930s perhaps. It is in a dismal state, but Fran knows Mick will appreciate the exotic wood carcass and brass fittings.

"If I didn't know better," she whispers, running a finger down the ebony and mother-of-pearl inlay that adorns the door panels, "I'd say French, early deco, handmade. I'm surprised those so-called Luckmore 'experts' didn't spot you!"

The reason behind the experts' rejection becomes clear the moment she tries to open the armoire. The doors fall away like dominoes. As she struggles to hold their weight, the rest of the armoire collapses in a heap, a final declaration of defeat. Fran, meanwhile, finds herself staring down at a large faun-colored holdall. It emerges from the splinters like a hidden relic. She stares in silent wonder, then hoists the holdall up, immediately tipping backward, stumbling to the floor as its weight overwhelms her.

"Money stash?" she whispers. "Doesn't feel like small change."

She pushes the holdall off her chest, hunkers onto her knees, and dives at the zipper, wiping away the dust. She's heard all the stories about house-clearance gold mines—the thousands in notes stashed under the floorboards, the ten-carat diamond rings wedged inside armchair cushions. People have such funny ideas about hoarding and storing. Houses up and down the country must be groaning under the weight of their long-forgotten booty. As the sides of the holdall fall open, however, her curiosity takes another twist. There is no money. Instead, there is something squishy wrapped in dull layers of tissue paper. Fran gives the paper a prod. It takes a moment for her eyes to catch up with her brain, but when they do, a new excitement arrests her. She's seen paper of this kind many times. Colorless, odorless, acid-free, it is the type used to store and preserve valuable fabrics. In fact, there are companies online who specialize in it. She'd once thought there might be profit in teaching people how to correctly package their best dresses, their wedding dresses.

Fran stills, anticipation overwhelming her. She knows it without seeing it. The moment seems to expand, fill the room, steal the air. She lifts a corner of paper, throws her face skyward, blows the hair from her face, then grins and gives thanks to the universe.

Meter after meter, a swath of fine white silk overlaid with lace slips through her fingers. Its form: full length, nipped waist, sweetheart neck, elegant lace sleeves, a dramatic full skirt, and a train that goes on for over four meters. She sits motionless for a minute, the dress spread across her arms, barely able to see straight, barely able to think. The lace overlay is impeccable. French, surely? Its dense and detailed flower pattern is hypnotic to the eye. Both the bodice and train are exquisitely decorated with embellished appliqué—pearls, glass beads, bugle beads, silver sequins, gold threads. They shimmer and sparkle, creating rhythmic scenes of hummingbirds and lilies. Each bird is different, its own little character fluttering from the silk, bringing life to the surface. Such attention to detail, such hand-stitched care—one of *those* wedding dresses. In fact, it is more than that. This one is exceptional, once in a lifetime. Fran's eyes well with tears. She clasps the dress to her body, runs her hands down its folds, feels the weight of the embroidery. Her gaze catches the little hand-sewn label at the neck, and a shiver runs through her limbs.

"Garrett-Alexia! The House of Garrett-Alexia!"

A shaft of sunlight enters the room, illuminating the beaded wingtips of the hummingbirds. Two real-life pigeons flurry at the window. Fran snaps to her feet and lifts the dress to her shoulders. It has aged gently, despite being stuffed in a dusty holdall for any number of years. The silk is a little yellowed in parts, and there are loose threads throughout the lace, a few missing pearls and beads, but other than that, it flourishes. With the bodice pressed against her chest, she crosses the floor and imagines a sea of swirling dancers in a grand ballroom with palms in bronze tubs, lacquer tables, marble columns, and gold leaf scrolls, a full band onstage playing Gershwin and a league of penguin-suited waiters serving trays of champagne in crystal coupes. She, Alessandra, the presumed original wearer of the dress, is in the center of it all, with her upstanding groom, who is surely an echo of the son, with those coat-hanger shoulders, that arch profile, those dark eyes. A new groom, she wonders, who might one day earn his spot on the fabled Wall of Dead Grooms. Perhaps he will even replace sweet James Andrew Percy as her favorite dead groom of all time.

"And one day," she says wryly, scooping the skirt up and letting it flop between her hands, "I might even find myself a *living* groom."

Her curiosity is piqued. She never tries on her wedding dresses. Call it superstition, the never covet rule, but this one…she cannot resist. The urge consumes her. In the soft light, shadows flickering on the walls, she slips off her jeans and top and steps inside the white gown's voluptuous well. She pauses a moment, feels its sensuous mass all around her, then lifts it over her hips, reaches behind, and tightens the corset ribbons enough to feel its form, how it moves, how it supports, how it gives. The cut is sublime. The V at the back creates the most perfect bloom of skin, bone, and muscle she has ever seen. The shape around the décolletage makes even her small chest seem sensuous and feminine. The cinched waist and draped train form such a picturesque silhouette, the effect is transformative. She has entered the realm of the ethereal bride. Should she? Could she go there again? A twist to the left, a glide to the right, back arched, arm dipped, a glance over the shoulder…

A shadow flickers.

Someone has seen her.

"Mick?"

But instead of Mick's familiar features, her eyes meet with

Rafael's. Across the room, their gazes interlock—a standoff, a show-down, yet somehow, she feels it, a *union*. She gasps, caught by the intensity, struck by emotions she doesn't understand. He hovers in the doorway, face half-hidden in darkness. He seems as startled as she is, his otherwise crisp demeanor tousled with surprise.

"I—I heard someone calling out," he says eventually, words rippling into the silence.

Fran feels the heat in her cheeks, her breath heavy as her ribs expand inside the dress's stiff bodice.

"That was me," she whispers. "I—I was looking for my friend, but…I got distracted—"

"Yes, I can see that," says Rafael.

Fran cannot tell his state of mind. His mouth is a frown, but his eyes seem to sparkle. She presses her hands to the dress. "I found this in the wardrobe. It's very, *very* beautiful."

"And it fits you…perfectly."

Her heart thuds. Should she say more? Should she explain herself? Is he shocked? Offended? Intrigued? "I guess it must have been your mother's."

"Yes."

She pitches forward, hands outstretched in a peace gesture. "I'm sorry," she whispers, knowing how emotional a family wedding dress can be—all those memories and resonances tied inside. "I didn't mean for you to—"

"No matter," he mutters, stiffening, turning away as though to avoid further discussion. "If you think you can find a use for it, please…take it."

Then he walks away, leaving Fran alone with the dress, alone to stand and wonder.

Mick is still in the kitchen, sorting old cutlery. He has a habit of overabsorbing himself with unnecessary details, which makes him a careful but slow worker. Fran presents him with the dress.

"You're not going to believe this. It's House of Garrett-Alexia."

Mick gives a vaguely approving nod.

"They were legendary! They specialized in richly embellished evening gowns during the '50s. They were among the most sought-after couturiers of their day. They clothed royalty, not to mention every movie, theater, and music star. And then, at the peak of their success, everything collapsed. There was a fallout, some kind of argument. They suddenly stopped designing, and that was the end of their reign. No more dresses made. Quality of design combined with extreme rarity, Mick, means anything with a Garrett-Alexia label is highly collectible. I've seen evening dresses crop up at auctions—they create an instant frenzy because they're so unusual, but a wedding dress?" She gathers the train in her hands, tries to absorb its energy. "Honestly, I don't know if there's anything out there like it."

Fran stares and thinks. "What do I do?"

"Take it," says Mick, as though there is no other option. "Patch it up, get it valued, and sell it to the best bride."

A complex chain of ifs and buts takes over. "But I can't just walk out with it—"

Mick balks. "Why are we here then? I mean, we came looking for a wedding dress. We found a wedding dress. Result. And let's not forget, our dear, charming friend said, I quote, 'take it all.' Fair square."

Fran dithers. She is tempted, *so* tempted, but wedding dresses—like love itself—are a test to her moral compass, too precious, too important to mess with. She stiffens, shakes her head.

"I can't. It feels wrong. A dress like this, it's—it's family history. Not to mention fashion history."

"Do you really think that man will care? He doesn't strike me as a fashion history buff, or for that matter someone who gives a damn about his old ma's backstory—"

"No, but…" Fran pictures his face, his gaze upon her. Something about the way he looked at her—as though, in that moment, his thoughts were more charged, more potent than he was prepared to let on.

"Do what feels right for you," says Mick. "I'll finish loading the van with my haul, give you some time. Meet you out front, dress or no dress."

Alone, Fran walks a circuit of the room, clasping the dress to her body, dragging the train behind. It would have taken the assistance of several bridesmaids and pageboys for the original wearer to move with any grace—a procession of extravagance, bursting with glamour and status. Clearly there is more to Alessandra than a love of gardening and mug trees. Every detail of the gown is exquisite, from the pearl inlay to the fine lace sleeves and the cinched waist. Weeks of work, possibly months, everything hand stitched, everything perfect. The one Fran has always dreamed of. How could she let it go?

Hastily, she stows the dress back in the holdall, stuffing and pushing and squishing to get its bulk contained. With a determined sweep, she hoists the holdall over one shoulder and creeps into the corridor. She passes the rows of empty, silent rooms, the echoing ceilings and dusty windows. She is almost at the front hall when she catches sight of Rafael again. He is standing alone, arms folded, staring into a cold inglenook fireplace. There is an air of melancholy about him now that makes her nervous to speak. A creaking floorboard gets his attention. He looks toward her, the blacks of his eyes catching the light, then the holdall.

"I think," she says, "you should consider this more carefully." She opens the holdall to him, tugs out the silk, tries to smile, but her offering is met with immediate disdain.

He barely lowers his gaze, almost as though he won't deign to acknowledge what is in front of him. "I'm happy for you take it," he says crisply.

"But—"

"Well, I'm not going to wear it, am I?"

"No, but I feel like I ought to tell you…" Fran cannot help herself. The excitement fizzles within her, so much that her hands start to tremble. She digs into the holdall, pulls out more fabric, presents beaded hummingbirds and embroidered lilies. "This is a very extraordinary dress."

No reaction. If craftsmanship and sentiment don't move him, maybe money might.

"And I believe it could be very valuable. I research and sell vintage wedding dresses."

Rafael sighs and huffs, looks impatiently to the ceiling, the sinews of his jaw bulging with tension. But Fran persists.

"Trust me, this dress is special. It's House of Garrett-Alexia, which is very rare couture in case you're not… Well…anyway…the point is, there are brides all around the world who'd love to get their hands on a dress like this. I could sell it no problem, but my method of working is…particular."

Finally, his curiosity prickling, Rafael graces her with a side glance.

"I find brilliant dresses," she explains, "then match them to brides. It's niche work, but I've been rather successful. The thing is, in order to make good matches, I need to understand my dresses as much as I understand my brides. You see, the best dresses—and I believe this could be one of them— don't just bring their beauty to the occasion; they bring their energy, their *truth*. And I think this one," she suggests, eyes alight, leaning forward with enthusiasm, "is capable of something close to magic. The ultimate life-changing statement dress. It needs life. It needs love."

"Love it then," says Rafael, turning back to the fireplace.

Right. Okay. She should be happy. The dress for her, above-board, without any subterfuge, but the way he speaks, it doesn't feel like generosity. It's a patronizing slight and the fact that he could be so disregarding about something so magnificent…

"You don't appreciate what this represents, do you?" She snaps, her passion overcooking.

"Forgive me," he says. "I forget how we must always cherish outdated, moth-eaten matrimonial regalia…because the other alternative"—he suddenly grabs the holdall, the fabric spilling out, cascading onto the floor—"is dumping it in the trash."

"What?"

With Fran at his heels, fury in his eyes, Rafael snatches the bundle and hurries it out of the front door, into the sunshine, to where a dirty yellow rubbish bin is being loaded with garbage bags. Despite Fran's pleas, he lobs the holdall and dress over his shoulder, into the mire. Fran cannot speak. She is too stunned, too offended by this cruel, erratic action. Without a care, Rafael brushes his hands, turns, and walks back to the house. When he is out of sight, she dives to rescue the dress. If anything can reassure her that it should now rightfully and respectfully become hers, this is it. Moments later, however, she is disturbed by the sound of screeching breaks. A battered blue Corvette swerves into the drive, stops suddenly at the front porch. A young woman tumbles out of the passenger door, a gravity-defying nest of dreadlocks piled on top of her head and an armory of piercings along her eyebrow and ear.

"Hi," she says cheerfully, eyeing Fran, who has one leg in the dumpster and one leg out. "You here for the clear-up?"

She thrusts out a hand, a friendly shake. Reluctantly Fran relinquishes her grip on her corner of the wedding dress and obliges.

"Nice threads," says the woman, nodding toward Fran's 1970s kimono, which she has taken to wearing with an old pair of Levi's. "So where's the prodigal son?"

"You mean Rafael?"

"The very one. He inside? Oh wait, here he comes—"

From the doorway Rafael appears, feet marching quick, face stern. He pays no attention to Fran but goes straight to the woman.

"What are you doing here?" he asks, his tone scolding.

"Nothing," she cries. "Just having a conversation, all right? Being polite. Calm yourself down."

The pair start arguing, right in front of Fran. She sees the dress twinkling from inside the dumpster, but they are distracting, locked into their mutual fury, bodies tense, voices loud. She has no desire to get caught between some uncomfortable family domestic. Mick starts beeping his horn. He is in her periphery, waving to her from the van. She looks at the dress again, then at the arguing pair, then back at Mick.

*Let's go*, he mouths as he starts the engine.

Fran is urged to grab the dress, but just as she moves forward, the argument erupts into full-on yelling.

"Get yourself together for once in your life!" Rafael bellows.

The anger in his face is almost tangible. The veins at his temples throb, as his cheeks suck tight around his clenched jaw and his eyes narrow to slits. He looks wild, dangerous, a cornered wolf.

"Fuck off!" the woman shouts in return, spitting the words. "Stop telling me what to do! You know what you are? You're a nasty, selfish, pigheaded womanizer who nobody likes!"

It is too much, too difficult. Fran has no choice. She backs away and returns to the van, to the security of the passenger seat.

"Should we do something?" she whispers.

Mick shrugs, then opens his door. "Hey," he calls, never one for confrontation. "There's no need for hostility, sir!"

Rafael ignores him and marches the woman toward the house. She shouts and swears. Neither of them looks back.

"Ah jeez," says Mick. "Let's leave them to it. Old money, old problems."

"Tell me about it," says Fran. "I mean, that's one cold, emotionless example of human nature. Honestly, Mick, is it any wonder I've given up on the chance of finding love in the twenty-first century? Modern men are fuckwits."

"Ahem."

"No good. You bat for the other team. Plus your imagination spends a peculiarly large amount of time in 1892."

"True."

They laugh a little, breathe the relief of their escape, but as they speed through the forest, the canopy of beech trees blanketing them, Fran is hit by a sudden and overwhelming sense of despair. The thrill of the dress, the mass of it somehow weightless in its glory, she'd had it in her arms, such a fortune of love, the answer to all of the problems in the world.

And now it is left in a heap in a dumpster.

# chapter 2

RAFAEL COLT BREATHES SLOWLY AS HE PULLS ON HIS VELVET DINNER jacket and adjusts his cuff links. He craves a sense of stillness, something that has been lacking since six o'clock that morning. He is minutes away from stepping onstage and delivering the biggest speech of his year. The venue, the grand glass atrium of the Royal Opera House, is full to capacity—a celebratory gathering of London's great and good, there to network and pose and claim their own invaluable connection to the prestigious family name. The Colt Foundation annual black-tie ball has steadily established itself as one of the top events of the London social calendar. Saturated with old wealth, smart, refined, and unfathomably stuffy, Rafael dreads its annual arrival. As chairman of the foundation, however, he understands he has to break out of his private persona and play the hero. He knows what's at stake, the difference his money makes to those who need it.

The guests—a curious blend of charity leaders, corporate kings, and London's richest—are waiting for him, fingers poised around thin-stemmed champagne flutes, eager to offer their whitened smiles and gushing praise. Hasn't the foundation had a brilliant year? Marvelous. Superb. He knows he'll be loved, aggrandized, flirted with, gossiped about, damn near sainted. Year after year, it's the same. In fact, on this occasion, he's made a little game in his head, a checklist of inevitables: General Marvin, his late father's aged golf buddy, will collar him for a lengthy discussion about the state of the Edinburgh links. Dame Felicity Pollinger, in disgusting fur, will force him to dance, then whisper vile things in his ear. Three trays of canapés will be upturned. Two accountancy firms will argue during the raffle and Hannah Atherton-Rhys will cry. A point for each hit, and if he gets every point, well, whatever—as in life, no reward, just a little self-amusement now and again.

"You have one minute, Mr. Colt," says Mimi, his loyal assistant, handing him his speech.

He doesn't look through it. The words are firmly fixed in his head. Every time he tries to focus, however, intrusive images rush in and take over: those empty rooms, that cold fireplace, his mother's gardening gloves, the dress…the wedding dress, brought to him in a bundle by a stranger, by Francesca Delaney. He sees her now, swan-like in his mother's gown, her perfect pale skin, the shine in her eyes, the little bump in her nose and the bow of her lips, those lips with so much to say about the hell of weddings. Overexcitable. Wedding fanatic. Two traits he cannot abide. Why, *why* is she pestering his thoughts so much?

"Five seconds," says Mimi in her perfunctory way, hand outstretched for the countdown.

Out of all the assistants he has had, Mimi is the best, which is why he has paid double to hold her for another year, keeping her from her studies but nonetheless well paid. She arrived in London two years ago, an overseas student from a wealthy Canadian family. She is—or has been—studying European culture. She loves opera and tea. She is smart, methodical, cold as ice, possibly a little ruthless, and an expert verbal minimalist. Her phrases are never longer than they need to be. He likes that. No chitchat. They don't pretend to be friends, yet they manage to spend most of their waking hours meshed together in acceptably professional silence.

"Three seconds, two, one, go."

Rafael takes the deepest breath he can, then pushes the whispers of his mind back inside. An explosion of flashbulbs and applause fills the hall. Through the dazzle, the white-haired master of ceremonies takes his arm and artfully guides him toward the microphone stand. Hush fills the room. *Just say the words,* he tells himself, *play the part. Look dignified. Make everyone feel good. Say the words and be done with it.*

"Good evening. It is with great joy that I'm able to say that the Colt Foundation has had its best year yet."

A burst of applause as the shock of his voice, normally so soft, is now mega-amplified, bouncing off the iron pillars and the barrel-vaulted glass ceiling. He lurches for the next line.

"We have given a record amount of money to a record amount of causes, which means more support where it is most needed."

Another round of applause.

"Through our grant program, we have been able to educate thousands of disadvantaged children and young people, rolling out our Colt Community Learning Schemes in the north, southeast, and now southwest of England. We have financed an ambitious program of building works, providing state-of-the-art schools within the country's poorest communities and given thousands in grants to public health concerns."

This triggers a massive round of applause. He feels the glory wash over him, soak him, drench him, then drain away into the gutter. He is many things and not all of them good, but he isn't deluded. *If they knew the truth*, he thinks, *they would know when to cull their adulation.* Through the glare of the stage lights, he senses their darkened faces, bodies wrapped in silk and satin and diamonds and gold, staring up at him, hanging on for the next rousing statement. He straightens his speech notes.

"In 1955," he says, forcing the words out, "my grandfather Lord Samuel Anders Colt had an idea. He decided that the wealth bequeathed to him should be used to enhance the lives of others. Over the past five decades, my late father and myself have striven to grow the seed of his vision and make the foundation what it is today. But we haven't done it alone. It has been through the efforts of all of you, our tireless employees and supporters. So if there is any more applause to be had, it's for you."

He used to say more—the crowds love a dose of Colt family history, all the pomp and stateliness of the old money—but since his father's death, he has revised the lines. He likes to think that one day the foundation will outgrow its ancestral origins and come to exist in its own right, valued for all the good that it does rather than the name—the *name*—it carries.

"Marvelous, Rafael, as always. You definitely have your father's gift for public speaking."

A florid-faced man shakes his hand vigorously. Rafael doesn't recognize him, but smiles as though he does.

"My daughter's single you know," says the man, with a jovial wink-and-nudge, "and I think it's high time she settled down. You wouldn't be in the market for a wife by any chance?"

"I'm afraid not."

"Found someone already, have you?"

"Not even looking."

"Are you homosexual?"

"No. Just…playing the field."

"Right ho, can't say I'm not envious. Why commit yourself when you can have all the fun of the fair?"

"Absolutely."

Rafael flatters the man with an old-boys' locker-room wink, then eyes the room for Mimi, who is immediately on hand to steal him away to another crowd, for more quips and compliments. *One more circuit of the room*, he thinks, *then* please *let me end this charade, let me slip away quietly.*

After the sixth round of priority greets, Rafael is weak with hunger. He tracks a team of waistcoated attendants as they glide around the hall, bearing trays of delicately rolled rare beef and horseradish, caviar blinis, and miniature pavlovas, but the thought of these polished, diminutive offerings depresses him. His mind and body ache for pizza, dirty, sloppy take-out pizza with extra pepperoni, the kind that makes you sweat pure salt. Another night, perhaps. In another life.

When no one is looking, he heads for the exit.

"Raf! Don't you dare go without saying hi to your best friend's girl."

Kate Michaels. Someone he genuinely likes talking to at last. Kate is the partner of one of his oldest friends and sound for an LTG (long-term girlfriend), despite the fact that she has denied him the last of his single friends. He leans in, kisses her on both cheeks.

"Nice to see you, Kate. Tell me you're here to save me from the clutches of social despair."

"Great speech, Raf. Rick and I are so impressed by everything you've done with the foundation. You've worked so hard."

"Thank you."

"Sorry Rick couldn't make it. He's on a booze cruise to Calais, stocking up for the nineteenth—"

"The nineteenth?"

"Ha ha, Raf."

"No, seriously. What's the nineteenth?"

"Er…I believe you've been recruited by the groomsmen squad. Just the small matter of a wedding in Scotland. Rick and I tying in the knot in Loch Lomond."

"Oh—oh yes. I hadn't forgotten. I just—"

"Blocked it out?"

Rafael winces.

"You'll be there won't you?"

"Of course. Honestly, I'm…hugely looking forward to seeing you two lovebirds have your…special moment. Can't wait."

"Bullshit."

"Will there be whisky?"

"Obviously. There'll also be a ceilidh."

"Good god."

"Oh, don't panic, Raf. Who knows? Maybe a chapel in candle-light will soften your hard heart."

"I wouldn't count on it."

On the cab ride home, the pressure unwinds. As Rafael sinks into his seat, the lights of the Embankment twinkling through his window, he thinks of her again—how she'd had the nerve to force the dress upon him, like he should want it. Like he should *care*. Okay, so throwing it in the trash was perhaps a little harsh, but what else could he do? She'd pushed him to it. Francesca Delaney. What was it she said she was? A vintage wedding dress expert. Please. Is that even a job? As for the dress, he had no idea that his mother had kept it, that, after all she'd been through, she hadn't thought to cast it out. He sighs. *Letting go of the house will be healthy*, he thinks. *No good can come from nostalgia.* A severance from history, a restart, fresh and untainted. He is tired now; his eyelids grow heavy as he slides into the cocoon of the back seat. He wants pizza. He tells the driver to stop at the first cheap takeaway he can find, which isn't obvious in such an exclusive part of London.

"We're nearly at your home, sir—are you sure?"

Rafael can see his block, the smooth white shield of marble across the walls, the neat chrome balcony rails, and the black Thames glistening in front. He considers the comfort of his bed, but then

aches inside—not just to eat pizza, but to live, to release, to *feel*...
something...anything...

Everyone around him is in love. Everyone is getting married.
Everyone has someone.

"Actually, I could do with one more drink."

"Seekers?"

"That will do."

After twenty minutes, the driver pulls up outside a bar in Old
Street, its discreet neon sign announcing *Seekers*. Rafael hands the
driver a bundle of twenty-pound notes and tells him to wait, then
removes his jacket and tie, climbs out of the cab, and nods at the
doorman.

The black walls and low ceiling make it difficult to see, but
the club is busy. As Rafael approaches the bar, the barman greets
him.

"Old-fashioned?" he says, anticipating the favored drink choice.

He mixes bourbon, sugar, and soda in a stout glass, while Rafael
leans back and scans the room. If he buys enough drinks and talks
enough crap, he knows from experience, the charm will work. He
downs the drink, warm and sweet, and sets his sights on a table.
Three women laughing in a corner, leaning over an empty cocktail jug, each attractive in their way, stylishly dressed, professional
looking, probably lawyers or accountants. He orders another jug of
whatever lurid cocktail is on special and carries it over.

"You can't sit there with empty drinks," he says, smiling smoothly.

The women look puzzled, a little wary.

"Humor me," he says. "It's been a long day, and you all look like you're enjoying yourselves. It's a refreshing sight, that's all. So…have a drink on me."

The women glance at each other, then back at Rafael.

"Uh, thanks," says the one nearest to him.

"Why don't you join us?" says the second.

"Always room for one more," says the third, eyeing him up and down. "Pull up a chair."

"Sure."

Within less than an hour, the third woman is in his bed, or more precisely, the bed of room 206 at the Park Lane Hilton. The sex is mediocre. It scratches an itch but doesn't satisfy on a deeper level. And in the night, the moonlight shining through the window, Rafael wakens. She—Francesca Delaney—is in his head again, and the sight of another unnamed Seekers girl snoring in the bed beside him feels more lonely and hollow than ever.

The sisters and cousins of bride-to-be Melissa West, in comparative efforts of denim, have gathered at the Whispering Dress to aid Melissa in her wedding dress quest. Amid a furtive discussion about penis straws, they grapple inside their shopping bags, eager to demonstrate an array of bachelorette paraphernalia: inflatable sunglasses, synthetic boas, and miniature chocolate dildos. Ever resourceful, one of them produces four bottles of prosecco and a sack of chipotle corn snacks. She has, however, forgotten the disposable plastic flutes.

"They were those screw-in ones—don't laugh—the ones that screw together, top and bottom."

"Don't worry. We'll just drink from the bottles. We're classy like that."

A round of raucous cackling. Melissa herself has been ushered to the opposite end of the shop, to a secluded area in front of a mirror draped with beads, pearls, flower garlands, and fragments of Honiton lace, a shrine to the goddess of wedding accessories. Melissa giggles sweetly, a foil to the coarseness of her entourage. *Where do they come from,* Fran wonders, *these women, all hooting and crowing and claiming their own little piece of Melissa's sacred moment? Here for themselves no doubt, for an excuse to drink and gossip, under the pretense that their tell-it-to-you-straight responses will help their girl find the wedding dress of her dreams.* Fran tries not to judge too harshly however. Their vulgarity won't outwit the dress, and besides, she likes a buoyant, happy energy when she works.

The dress itself sits in wait behind a damask curtain. It hasn't, as yet, been seen by its new bride, which perhaps explains some of Melissa's nervousness. Fran invites Melissa to take a seat. She chooses the velvet pouf over the louche, oversize Moroccan floor cushions or the battered Winchester. She perches, hands on lap, knees stiff. *Poor thing,* thinks Fran, sensing she is more worried about the judgment of her entourage than her own future life and happiness.

"So, are you ready?"

The moment, the magic, the chance to witness a whispering dress make its first potent impact on its new bride—time for all that painstaking research and resonance to come out and breathe, take form, find purpose.

"This dress," urges Fran, eyes glinting, "is going to change your life. You have my word."

Melissa, smothered by her own meekness, merely shrugs.

"I just hope everyone likes it," she says. "When I walk down that aisle, I want them to turn around and think, *Actually, you know what? She isn't so bad.*"

Fran pauses, because such naked self-doubt requires attention. "Or perhaps," she says encouragingly, "they'll think, *My goodness, she's radiant!*"

Melissa shrugs again. "You know how it is though." She leans forward, stares at herself in the mirror. "I probably shouldn't be so hard on myself, but sometimes I look in the mirror and…I feel hideous. If I could lose a bit of flab around the middle, tone up my belly, get my nose fixed, my teeth. I try to keep up. You wouldn't believe the amount of squats I did yesterday, but it's never enough."

Fran nods. She has experienced this many times, the monologue in front of the lace-draped mirror, a final pummeling of premarital insecurity. So many of her brides seem to find verbosity in the space between sitting and seeing the dress, as if the anticipation itself is an amplifier of all their hopes and fears. *It is good*, she thinks, *cathartic.*

"Just so you know," Melissa confesses, "I had four takeaways last week, so if it doesn't do up at the back—"

No more. Fran dives behind the damask, pulls it back, and reveals the magic. Melissa blinks, shifts, then blinks again, her mouth falling open in a perfect O.

"So?"

"It's...it's..."

"Perfect?"

"*Red*. It's very red. I mean, um, it's redder than a wedding dress usually is."

"But you like it?"

"I...like the skirt bit, but what are those?" She points to a froth of marabou trim.

"Ostrich feathers. Aren't they fabulous?"

"They're a bit—"

"Delicate?"

"Scary."

Unperturbed, Fran lifts the dress from the hanger and offers it to her bride.

"Just touch them," she says. "Feel the way they bounce."

"Are they dirty?"

"They've been steamed and dyed and trimmed by feather professionals. They couldn't be cleaner. They're over seventy years old yet in perfect condition. You won't find an equivalent on eBay."

"I've never looked for feathers on eBay."

"Don't. I've tried. They're beastly."

"What kind of red is it?"

"I'd like to say scarlet."

"As in the actress?"

"As in the color."

"Does it come in white?"

Fran sighs. This is a little too much, even for her.

"White is merely a modern Western convention," she says,

railing. "All around the world, and throughout history, dresses of color have held equivalent matrimonial status."

"But in Streatham, white is normal. Everyone will expect white."

"Why be normal when you can be...extraordinary? Think of this dress as a statement, a colorful exclamation mark pledging independence from all those tired and overdone assumptions about purity and virgins, which are only as old as Queen Victoria. And *she* only chose a white dress because it matched a fancy piece of lace that she wanted to show off. In fact, it was a business decision, her secret plan to give a boost to her country's flagging lace-making industry. Yet somehow we've gotten stuck with the idea that a big white ball gown is the only way to say 'I'm a bride!' Honestly, Melissa, a white dress can be fabulous, but it's by no means a rule. Plus it does dreadful things to certain complexions. This dress, on the other hand, scarlet or otherwise is bespoke vintage, a one-off, selected and altered especially for you."

Over the years, Fran has come to realize, no matter how individual her brides are, their issues are often universal. She has even considered arranging her dresses into categories: the "People Pleasers," the "He Never Talks about His Feelings" dresses, "Otherwise I'll Die Lonely," and the ever-popular "Once we're married, I'll change him" collection. She is careful not to make her judgments known however. Each bride needs to feel like her wedding is special, like she is the first, last, and only one of her kind. But the human species, Fran fears, is staggeringly inept at learning to conquer the art of the heart. Thankfully she is here to help, because bride after bride, dress after dress, the answers to marriage's uncertainties always arise in the cycle of time.

"The woman who first wore this dress," she continues, "was brilliant and fierce. She didn't stop to worry about how white her teeth were or how flabby her middle was. She married in 1942 and spent her wedding night in an Anderson shelter, where she laughed and danced and drank like she was at the Ritz. Two weeks later, she learned to drive a fuel tanker and helped restore power to hundreds of bomb-frightened homes. I can tell you anything you want to know about her, but the one thing you actually need to know is that she knew how to love another human because, and this is the important bit, she knew how to love herself."

Melissa leans away. "Is she...still alive?"

"She died two years after her husband in 1977, but I like to think she lives through this, her wedding dress."

"Creepy."

"Don't think of it that way. Think of it as a gift. This dress—now your dress—it's had a life, one that it carries within its fibers, like an echo passing from wearer to wearer. Try it on. You might sense it."

Melissa finally rises from the pouf, ventures toward the dress, and begins to investigate the detail of the fabric.

"Is it tight? It looks tight."

"Find out. And remember, there's good tight and there's bad tight. This tight will fit and flatter you to perfection."

She lifts the gown from the satin boudoir hanger and holds it against Melissa's body.

Melissa enlivens instantly. "It *is* a good color on me! I never thought I'd get away with pink...scarlet, I mean."

"Find out more," whispers Fran.

Melissa slips behind the curtain and begins to change. As Fran busies herself with her antique accessories, acquired to aid her brides in their wedding day vision—satin slippers, tiaras, brooches, beads, laces, sprigs of dried flowers, ribbons, and diamond hair clips—a sense of satisfaction creeps over her, for she knows, she *knows* she has found Melissa's perfect dress. The curtain parts. Already Melissa seems taller, straighter, brighter. Fran ushers her forward and encourages her to twirl—a sparrow now transformed into a flame-bird, as strong and striking as the scarlet dress itself.

The cut is simple, a column of shin-length red chiffon with a neat belt and a marabou stole—a bit of fun to lighten the austere mood. Its original owner had been clear about the design from the very beginning: nothing predictable, no white, no veil, no train, no sprig of orange blossom. A bold, self-assured dress for a bold, self-assured woman.

"How do you feel?" asks Fran, because it is never about how a bride looks, but how she feels.

"Amazing," says Melissa, a laugh on her lips, eyes moist with tears, captivated by the way the feather trim flutters and settles in rhythm with her movements. "This is it! You found it! I can't believe it! I just know…this is the one!"

She begins to waltz—or a variation of it—around the space, snaking her arms and tipping her head, surveying the beauty of her sumptuous décolletage. Fran senses she doesn't look at her reflection very often, at least not in a favorable way—she's a scrutinizer, a faultfinder, a worst self-critic. But to Fran, it is simple: If you look for ugly, you find ugly. So look for beauty.

"I swear it makes me look thinner!"

"It makes you look like you."

Pulling and pinning, Fran makes deft adjustments to the sleeves. As she works, she offers a little more of the dress's history. Just a little though. It has to feel like it belongs to Melissa.

"The chiffon came from France. The designer dyed it himself. It was the bride's wish that it was scarlet, her favorite color. It caused a few raised eyebrows at the reception, but she didn't care. She was a very self-assured woman, some might say wayward."

"What was her name?"

"Meryl Percy."

"What did she do?"

"She liked cars. She became an engineer. She won a global prize for services to her industry. I found photos of her and her husband at an award ceremony."

Fran glances up at her bulletin board of dead grooms. There he is, Meryl's husband, James Andrew Percy, applauding his wife as she collects her prize. The photo is of poor quality, but his pride is obvious. *How he loved her*, thinks Fran, *how he looked upon her with such deep, unfolding admiration, remembering the sight of her on their wedding day, in scarlet, striding up the aisle. Where are they now*, she wonders, *those noble, bighearted grooms like Mr. Percy?*

"Mel! *Mel!* Let's see you, love."

At the other end of the shop, the sisters and cousins are growing impatient. They have to be faced. One of them careers across the rug, brandishing an open bottle of prosecco.

"Wait!" says Melissa, desperate to hold on to the soulful intimacy of just her, Fran, and the scarlet dress.

Fran takes Melissa's hand, gives it a gentle squeeze. "Go and show them," she encourages. "Own it."

Together they pad the length of the floor to the tune of the wedding march—six drunk voices all at different speeds, tempos, and pitches, creating the ugliest version Fran has ever heard (and she's heard many).

"Eyes closed," she says, announcing her charge above the din.

To her surprise, the women do as she asks.

Melissa steps forward. "Ta-da!"

Six jaws drop.

"It's red!"

"Are you sure it's actually a wedding dress?"

Fran watches for Melissa's reaction, the uncertainty in her eyes, the worry lines, the tremble. What will she say? How will she conquer the criticism?

"I like that it's different," says Melissa after a pause.

"It's different all right," sneers the cousin with the booze bottles. "And tight."

"What are the other options?" says another cousin.

Fran holds back. This is for Melissa to handle.

"There aren't other options. This is it. It's the one. Look, I know it's not traditional, but…I just know."

The sisters, clutching each other, are close to tears.

"You can't wear red, Melissa. If our mum were here today, she'd have a fit. You know she would. All she ever wanted was to see her girls go up the aisle in white. I did it. Jackie did it. And now you want to spoil the tradition with *this*. Unbelievable."

"But…you and Jackie are getting divorced," says Melissa with a shrug.

"Don't bring us into it, Mel!" says Jackie herself, flinging her arms up in fury. "It's the wrong dress, you know it is! Just wrong!"

"Come on," says Fran, leading her away.

Behind them, the alcohol-fueled outrage expands, led by the sisters and their demand to know why little Melissa has suddenly grown the balls to reckon on a "bloodred" dress, that everyone, including their dead mother and the good Lord himself, will absolutely loathe.

But despite the sniping, Melissa still smiles, the kind of smile that radiates from deep inside, the kind of smile that Meryl Percy would approve of.

The sun sets over Walthamstow, gilding the roofs of the mosques, the churches, the synagogues, and the temples. It spreads its warm glow over the cozy Victorian terraces with their glass extensions and zinc-clad loft conversions, over the refurbished Georgian mansion that was once home to William Morris, the tennis lawns of Lloyd Park, the '80s-built shopping center by the bus station, the tarmacked roads, and the mile-long market on the main street with its end-of-day litter and clanking stall poles—the ebb and flow of hundreds of years.

In the shop, working late, Fran sits among her sewing and sighs. She is hopeful that Melissa will gain both inner and outer confidence in the Meryl Percy dress. There is so much satisfaction, so much joy to be gained from witnessing others' joy, but then…spurred by one too many sips of leftover prosecco, Fran finds herself staring at the flea-market art nouveau wardrobe at the back of the shop. The doors, with their carved bronze acanthus leaf handles, pester for her attention. They have been shut for years. She can no longer bring herself to look at the dress inside, although she's always aware that it's there, drooping from its hanger like a sad phantom, the ghost of a broken heart. Urged to distract herself from bad, destructive thoughts, she opens her laptop. *The only worry worth having, she tells herself, is where to find good dresses, how to make sure that good love spreads. The hunt must go on.* She trawls through her favorite vintage clothing websites, but as nothing comes forward, the thought of the extraordinary House of Garrett-Alexia dress lying abandoned in a dumpster crushes her anew.

How could anyone throw away such a stunning and valuable creation?

Curious, she reaches for her laptop, types the name "Rafael Colt." Somehow it has resonance. The Colt Foundation website appears. There he is, in photo form—pale-gray shirt, immaculately smoothed hair, aristocratic nose and jawline, deep-set brown eyes—tagged as the foundation's chairman. The notion soaks through her, that as well as being an angry, difficult, supercilious dickhead, he also happens to be in charge of one of the biggest and best-known private foundations in the country. An inherited role no doubt, but still, the cogs and wheels of her curiosity start to turn. There is something about his face that reminds her of a deer—that regal yet strangely vulnerable gaze. Fran looks to her wall of dead grooms. Wonderful and gentlemanly as they were, none of them ever had their own charitable foundation.

So what of the dress's wearer, his mother? Her curiosity unfurling, Fran searches for *Alessandra Colt*. It seems she married Lyle Colt—presumably Rafael's father—in 1978. Her maiden name was Agnelli. Italian perhaps? A face, possibly twenty or thirty years old, appears on the screen in a grainy photograph portrait. While not traditionally pretty, there is no denying that Alessandra is striking: a long face, dark eyes, high cheekbones, olive skin, jet hair, confirming a Mediterranean heritage. It is always a thrill to see original brides for the first time. Somehow it brings zeal to the imagined life of a dress, anchors the vision. She stares at the photo, tries to read the inscrutable lines around Alessandra's eyes, that unknowable almost smile. There is an enigmatic sorrow in her gaze that seems to echo her son's.

"Who are you?" she whispers, fearing she may never find out.

She then searches *the House of Garrett-Alexia* but can find no record of the couturiers having a wedding collection. There are evening dresses in every style and color touted by private collectors or showcased in museums, dated from as early as 1951 through to 1954, when the company went into decline. There are shrugs, stoles, and capes—accessories of decadence. There is even a box of Garrett-Alexia clothing labels. But no wedding dress. Rarity will only add to its worth—and the pressure to do the right thing. On impulse, unable to contain her curiosity, she takes out her phone, dials the number from the house clearance advertisement.

"You have reached Rafael Colt. Please leave a message."

She takes a breath, waits for the beep, then launches into a tangle of broken and unplanned sentences.

"Um, hi...it's me again—Fran...Fran Delaney...who found the dress. Big, white, fancy? I'm sure you remember it, not that you were all that happy about it, but, well, to cut a long story short, I'd really like to talk to you about it. You can call me on this number... or I'll call you again...and then again...but not again because that might start to annoy you, but... Okay, bye... I'm not a stalker by the way...just a curious dress obsessive."

The voicemail cuts Fran off and she despairs, cursing herself for her erratic rambling. He will never reply now—of course he won't. She slumps and berates herself for her impulsiveness. Suddenly, however, her cell phone buzzes, announces the call returned. In her excitement, she drops it into the folds of her skirt.

"Hello?" she exclaims breathlessly after scrambling to retrieve it.

"You called this number" comes a clipped and unexpectedly female voice.

"I—I'm trying to get hold of Rafael Colt, but you're not..."

"My name is Mimi Mischler. I am Mr. Colt's assistant. All unrecognized numbers go through me during work hours."

*Work hours? But it's the evening.*

"Is there something I can help you with?"

Fran opens her mouth, surprised, disappointed.

"I—I have a question for him, about his mother's wedding dress—"

"Then I advise you contact him in writing or email."

"In writing? I just want a quick chat."

"Mr. Colt doesn't chat."

"Oh. Okay. Right, well—"

"You will find contact details on the Colt Foundation website. This is a personal line, so if you persist in calling, I will block your number. Goodbye."

Fran flops to her elbows. "And who exactly are *you*, Mimi Mischler?" she grumbles into the phone once she is certain the call has ended. "His guard dog? First line of defense? Well, I don't give up that easily."

There is only one solution. That dress deserves a second life with a bride who'll care for it and not stuff it in holdall in a wardrobe, or worse, in a dumpster. She looks at the clock on the wall—1950s, salvaged from the set of a rockabilly-themed TV pilot—and checks the hour. The sun is still high enough. There is time before dark.

Fran takes a cab to Epping Forest and asks the driver to drop her on the road. She doesn't want the car on the drive in case the property isn't empty. She is nervous about being caught; although, in her mind, it isn't trespassing—merely a righteous liberation. With the silk of her embroidered kimono billowing behind her, she makes her way through the tunnel of willow trees, their acid-green fronds tickling her head. The frogs in the lake croak rhythmically, hailing her impish arrival. A warm breeze shushes the flowers of the rhododendron bushes, purple glowing electric against glossy, dark foliage. She feels safe around nature, no matter where she happens to be.

The house is smaller than she remembers, but is even more magical in the early evening light. As she creeps across the weed-infested gravel to the porch, she can see through the windows, from one side to the other, right through the heart of the building to a streak of orange sky and the forested hills beyond. She stops for a moment and leans against the wall, the warmth of the sunbaked brick bleeding through her jeans, the thought of Alessandra Colt's wedding dress feverish in her mind. What if it's not there? What if the dumpster has already been emptied? She tenses, crosses her fingers.

Grateful for the modern-world durability of denim, Fran hastens to the side of the house, climbs over the hedgerow and dives toward the rusting yellow dumpster. As she leans in, all she can see are piles of old carpet and trash bags. She shovels through the waste, fearful she is too late, then spies the handle of the holdall beneath a mound of cardboard. Her heart beats relief. She tugs it free, unzips it, presses the white lace overlay to her cheek. A light, breezy joy fills her senses as she brushes away the grit, gathers up the fabric, holds it to her body, and breathes. With each rise and fall of her chest, the energy once woven into those graceful lilies and appliqué hummingbirds now yields to her. She has it. It is hers, the dress of dresses. *Hers?* She means hers to sell. Rule number one: Never covet.

Oh, what the hell.

Unable to resist, she shakes the dress out, then pulls it up around her tiny frame. Surely a little "fieldwork" could be useful. Fueled by those strange, uncanny impulses to tease and conjure and brighten the scenery, she looks to the house. In her mind, she hears the trace of laughter echoing through the evening air. There are Singapore slings and prewedding high jinks—a perfect night before the loving, summer send-off for the darling couple of one of the most revered families in Britain. Cradling the train in her arms, she hastens to the flagstone terrace that surrounds the back of the house. She fills the deserted space with chaise longues and planters, beds of hydrangeas, lupins, and dahlias, then conjures two maids attending a large gilded cocktail trolley—multihued drinks in highballs and martini glasses, ice buckets and tongs, trays of nuts, stuffed olives, and unctuous little pastries. The patio doors, she mentally throws open, to welcome the early summer scents of lilac and rose, the coming moonlight, the nightingale, the good things in life, and, above all, love. She aches to linger and enjoy this reverie, but with the light fading fast, she has work to do. She pulls her trusty lucky hatpin from her hair and prods the lock of the patio doors. The lock releases with ease, and like a ghost from the future, she slips inside.

She finds herself in a high-ceilinged salon devoid of furniture and carpets. Even the light fixtures have been stripped, but with some artful thinking, to her it becomes an elegant library, floor-to-ceiling shelves filled with leather-bound volumes of Shakespeare, Dryden, and Milton; a vast sofa and a grand piano in the corner, where a suited musician cracks his knuckles over the keys. Swing music floats through the air, fills the space and the rooms beyond. The entire house echoes with the melody of joy.

In the main vestibule, with its double-height leaded windows and heavy oak staircase—where Fran first saw Rafael Colt—she imagines a pair of young boys in sailor suits, chasing each other up and down the lower steps, crouching against the thick, carved banister. Along the upstairs corridor a repeating pattern of silk-curtained windows, family portraits and miniature palms alleviates the heavy oak paneling. The rows of doors hide bedrooms and dressing rooms and private quarters. Some of these doors still bear brass name plaques, but it isn't until Fran reaches the very end of the corridor, the room where she found the dress, that she finds the name she is looking for: Alessandra.

She turns the handle. The catch releases, and with a little push, the door gives way. Inside there is stillness, a secretive peace to mollify the jazz and laughter downstairs. A tangerine sky blazes through the window. With the dress shifting around her, she places teak dressers where she thinks they would fit, a wicker-and-bamboo-cane rocking chair, a dressing table, and then a bed—a solid four-poster heirloom made up with orange-and-brown floral drapes because the 1970s are in her head. She pictures a bout of prewedding pampering. Face masks and nail painting or perhaps a final private gaze in her mirror for the bride-to-be on the eve of her wedding.

Fran tiptoes to the collapsed armoire. She stands in front of the broken door, which has been left propped against the wall, its mirror cracked from corner to corner, presumably from when it fell. With a shiver of anticipation, she stares at her reflection. How does she feel? Excited? Nervous? Extraordinary? Through herself in the dress, she sees Alessandra now, sees her face forming, those dark eyes, that uncertain smile, hand hovering over the lace of the skirt, daring herself to cherish it, adore it, *possess* it. She shuts her eyes and—Fran feels it—has The Moment, the ultimate bonding of a woman to her dress, herself refigured as a bride. The wedding, the marriage, the love, it is all ahead of her, a future of happiness and strength and heartfelt companionship.

And yet…

Something is wrong.

The mood sours.

All the joyful energy of the dress collapses.

There is Alessandra, a faint imagining within Fran's reflection, the dress shrouding her, shrouding them both. Fran stares wordlessly, feeling, *fearing* that Alessandra is frightened, scared by the sight of her marital form. The pair are still for a moment, then the torment surges. With a howl, Alessandra lurches forward, smashes the mirror with her fist. Red rivulets of blood stream down her arm and drip onto the dress.

Fran stumbles back in fright, shuts her eyes, and blinks away the scene.

Her visions have never been any more than daydreams, the hopeful vestiges of an overactive imagination, a way to bring fullness to the dots and dashes—the wedding certificates, old photos, and paper documents—of her research. But now, here, the intensity overcomes her. She scrabbles to loosen the dress, then steps out of it as eagerly as she'd stepped into it. And so it sits in a crumpled heap, pulsing with malignant energy. Not a dead dress, but something else—something she doesn't yet understand.

A thud breaks the trance. Someone is moving around downstairs. The slam of a door followed by footsteps brings the fear right into the moment, into real time. There was no one in the building when she'd entered—or so it had seemed. She scoops the dress up, heart pounding, palms sweating, and prepares to run. But the clumsy pattern of the footfall, heavy on bare floor, suggests more of a stagger than a walk—someone without grace or composure. She goes to the corridor, looks down through the banisters, and sees a dark silhouette heading toward the stairs. Moments later an almighty *thud-thud-thud* reverberates through the hall. Whoever—or whatever—has come to the stairs has now fallen down them. She listens again.

Silence. Tense relief. What now? Does she flee undiscovered or check the situation? Oh why does she get herself into these scrapes in the first place? Curiosity killed the cat and the dressmaker—and her sanity.

"Only I," she whispers to herself, "could find an intruder while intruding."

Breathing deeply to induce bravery, she dismisses the shadow world of Alessandra and her prewedding anguish and creeps down the stairs. In the dim light, she sees a hump of a body, the person out cold on the hallway floor. When she realizes the body is a slight-built woman, her fears are quashed. The instinct to help takes over. She races down the last few steps and tries to stir her, but as she strokes a clump of dreadlocked hair, her memory spikes: Rafael Colt's unwelcome visitor, who now has a nasty gash on her left temple and likely black eye. Fran checks her pulse, sighing with relief as she feels life within the woman's painfully thin wrist. She then smells the odor of alcohol. Gingerly, she searches the duffel bag that is still slung across the woman's limp shoulder: a half-empty pack of cigarettes, a bashed-up phone, rolling papers, a corkscrew, sunglasses, hair bands, pliers, and baby wipes.

The woman stirs, eyes flickering, gathering awareness.

"Raf," she murmurs. "Where's Raf?"

"I'm afraid you fell down some stairs," Fran explains, knowing she can't leave her despite it being the simple answer. "You've hit your head."

"You're not Raf," groans the woman. "Where's Raf?"

"I—I don't know. I can call him for you? Do you know his number?"

The woman moans, shuts her eyes, then Fran remembers his number is still in her phone from earlier. Triumphant, she calls it, but as she waits for an answer, she questions herself: Is Rafael really the person to speak to, given the previous scene she'd witnessed between him and this woman? And will he even answer, or will she get the frosty assistant again?

"Hello?"

"Is—is this Rafael?"

"Yes."

*How to say this?* Fran takes a breath… "Sorry to bother you, but I'm at your late mother's house, Dryad's Hall—which I can totally explain, so don't think I'm crazy or anything—but the important thing is, your girlfriend or wife or whoever she is, the one you argued with, she's here too. And it looks like she's fallen down the stairs and knocked herself out. She's quite badly hurt, and, well, she's asking for you."

Fran has already made up her mind that if he isn't interested—which seems likely given his general hostility—she will go to plan B and find a way to get the woman in a cab, then send her wherever she wants to go, but to her surprise, Rafael's response is quick and concerned.

"Where is she? Is she bleeding? Is she conscious?"

"I'm with her. Don't panic."

"Oh thank god."

"She's coming around, but… Look, I don't mean to be nosy, but is she…on anything? She's not really with it, like she's really drunk and—"

"Who is this?" he demands.

"Um, Francesca. Francesca Delaney. I helped at your house clearance the other day. The wedding dress, the one you threw in the dumpster—"

"You?"

"In a word, yes…me."

"Wait there," he says. "Stay by her side, won't you? Don't let her out of your sight. You *mustn't* let her out your sight. I'll be straight over."

With that, Fran stares down at her dreadlocked charge. "Oh boy," she whispers, amazed at her capacity to find trouble in the unlikeliest of ways.

As Rafael emerges through the doorway, he isn't interested in Fran's whys and wherefores. He rushes to the woman, kneels beside her, cradles her head in his arm—so tenderly, so differently from the way he treated her before.

Fran doesn't speak. She just looks on, lets them have their moment.

The woman stirs. "Wha—? Where am I?"

"Janey, I'm here."

"Raf. Oh, Raf…"

He holds her face, almost smiles, strokes her forehead, then his expression tightens. He starts rifling through her bag. "What are you on?" he demands.

"Nothing."

"Don't lie."

"Vodka."

"And?"

"Codeine."

Rafael throws his gaze to the ceiling.

Fran shuffles uncomfortably—this isn't a conversation for strange ears. She contemplates slipping away, but he catches her in his sights, looks straight at her.

"Thank you," he says. "Thank you for calling me. Um…do you have a tissue or a handkerchief, something I can wipe her head with?"

"This?" says Fran, fishing a vintage Liberty print scarf from her bag—one of her prize possessions, but it seems like the right thing to do.

Rafael dabs the blood around Janey's eye and encourages her to sit up. Her head lolls and droops as she grins in her daze. He attempts to stand her up but struggles under the intoxicated recklessness of her limbs.

"Here, let me help," says Fran. Despite her slight frame she bears the strength of the determined, courtesy of her mother, who raised her in the costume departments of various London theaters, working extreme hours with extreme people. She steps forward, takes Janey's other arm, and hoists her into an upright stance. Together they semi-walk, semi-drag her through the front door to a gleaming silver Jaguar E-Type.

"Nice ride," whispers Fran wistfully.

They bundle Janey into the back seat, where she flops, arms folded, bottom lip pushed out like a sulky teenager.

"Will she be all right?"

"Will she ever be all right?" growls Rafael.

They stand opposite one another, feet grinding into the gravel.

"Hopefully she'll feel better in the morning," says Fran, filling the silence, unsure of the next move. "Is she…your wife?"

Rafael laughs. "She's my sister."

"Oh, I—"

"Her name is Janey. It's okay. We don't exactly look alike…or behave alike."

She feels bad for him suddenly, that she misread the situation, that perhaps he can't help the hardness of his shell for the burden of his wayward sibling, who clearly he cares for, despite the brittleness between them.

"It's fortunate you were here," he says. "Otherwise she might not have been found for days, but"—he looks confused—"why *were* you here?"

"Good question."

"The clearance is done. You had no need to come back. This is private property you realize?"

Fran lowers her gaze and winces. "I—I came back for the wedding dress," she admits. "I got the gist you really didn't want it, so I came and pulled it out of the dumpster. In fact, I need to go in and get it. I let it go once. I can't let it go again. It's in the house still—"

Rafael glares at her now, a moonlit flash in his eyes. Is he angry? It's hard to tell. His general demeanor seems to be fixed on angry of one level or another.

"Trust me," urges Fran, "I don't go to this kind of trouble for any old dress. This one is special. I—I can't get it out of my head. I believe there's a bride out there whose world will be...*transformed* by it. Your mother, her story." She pauses, spooked by the thought of Alessandra's anguish in the mirror. "My hunch is there's a *lot* of history in those fibers, a lot that needs to be said. Honestly, a dress like this, it's worth so much—"

"My mother's wedding dress isn't worth anything to anyone," says Rafael coldly. He eyes Fran, as though he is puzzling over her, trying to decipher her intentions. "We're a private family," he warns. "I'm responsible for a large charitable foundation, and I protect its reputation at all costs."

*I know*, thinks Fran, realizing this probably isn't the time to mention the research she's already done on him.

"I can't have strangers digging around in my history. Do you understand?"

Fran nods, slighted by his patronizing tone.

"Our work is the reason why two million children get a decent school education. Any misrepresentation could put that at stake."

"I hear you," says Fran, affronted. "I can't compete with that, can I? Wedding dresses are just frippery by comparison. Hell. You can keep the dress." She marches off.

"Wait," says Rafael. "You can't just wander into the night." He hesitates, sighs, shakes his head. "If you want the dress that badly, go and get it. I'll give you a lift. I have to drive three-quarters around the North Circular to get Janey checked out at the hospital first, but then I can drop you where you want."

"Really?"

"Go. Before I change my mind."

"Thank you," she says. "You won't regret it."

The bright moon casts leaf-fringed shadows across the dashboard as they drive, mostly silent, through the forest lanes. Janey sits slumped in the back, spitting the occasional cuss word, too messed up to take more aggressive action. Quite how Francesca Delaney has become embroiled in the never-ending wild-child sister saga, he cannot fathom, but here she is, perched on his passenger seat with her silk and beads, the wedding dress piled at her feet. Dumpster diving, breaking and entering, plus all that near-mystical nonsense about bridal wear—as if more weddings are what the world needs. Possibly she is not of sound mind. He checks his pocket for his phone, wonders whether his security team might need an alert. He's known his fair share of troubled individuals, and she bears a few hallmarks. Yet, something…something about her…those sparkling green eyes, that beguiling half smile. She fills the air with grace and light. Her perky energy is magnetic. He blinks, steels himself.

"So you sell wedding dresses?" he says, trying to make a connection but only succeeding in sounding more patronizing.

"Not just wedding dresses," she asserts. "*Whispering* wedding dresses."

"Rrright. So you like clothes?"

"Doesn't everyone?"

"I've never much considered it."

He senses the coming judgment as she stares him up and down, eyes assessing his tastefully bland shirt and trousers, the same most days. Gray and black are his preferred colors. He finds Selfridges very reliable for shirts, but his best suits come from a tailor on Savile Row, where his father and grandfather were customers.

Fran sits forward, eager to claim his focus despite his responsibility to concentrate on the driving. "You may think you don't consider it," she says, pestering him, "but your shirts, that tailoring, those silk socks…they're all a choice. You've considered it more than you realize."

"It's work wear, what's expected of me."

"And if you turned up in dirty jeans and trainers?"

"It wouldn't be appropriate."

"No. Because clothes matter. People think they're frivolous, but they say more about our lives than anything else. Throughout history, our fashions have embodied the changes around us, our shifts in class, status, work, style…attitude. Whatever you wear, from your filthy, comfortable robe to your polished best, you're displaying a decision that represents you, your state of mind, your hopes, your doubts, your insecurities, your ambitions."

"Okay," says Rafael, intrigued. "But let's be clear, I have never owned or worn such a thing as a filthy, comfortable robe."

Fran laughs heartily and it takes him by surprise. Laughter is not a common occurrence in his life. He hadn't intended to be funny, but clearly she enjoys his mannered snobbery. And he enjoys the sight of her enjoying it.

"I mean, does anyone own such a thing?" he adds with mock disgust, playing along.

She catches his eye. "Are you always this stuck-up?"

"No, I—"

"Yesss," slurs Janey before falling asleep.

"Because the other day"—Fran ventures—"when we were clearing the house, you were pretty rude to Mick and me. Not to mention very forceful with your sister. We thought—"

"I realize it looked bad, but trust me, I've had ten years of this. Ten years of trying to save her from herself. I love her more than anything, but she's on a one-way self-destruct mission. I ran out of patience years ago, but I won't ever give up." He sighs. "She's all I've got."

They sit quietly for a moment, then out of the darkness, he speaks again.

"This is a routine we know too well," he says. "The drunken messes, the angry rants. She's been through rehab, had a stint in a sober house. She's had whole years where she's been fine, but then she loses focus and goes back to square one. What more can I do? I flew her to Barbados once, sat with her for a month in a hotel room overlooking the ocean. My first holiday in six years, and all I did was watch her wretch and argue her way through detox. Naively I hoped that, among all those beautiful palms and tropical flowers, she'd see that the world has beauty, that it's there regardless…" He sighs again.

Fran is thoughtful. There is more beneath the surface, she thinks, more than she credited him with. She rearranges the folds of the wedding dress and waits for him to continue.

"She gained some weight and got her glow back," he explains. "Then the minute we landed at Heathrow, she ditched her luggage and went on a three-day binge."

"I'm sorry."

"Don't be. It's not your problem."

Eventually they pull up outside a small, discreet building in Saint John's Wood, which turns out to be a hospital with a private Accident and Emergency service. Fran stares at the smart entrance, more like a hotel than an emergency room.

"No queues, no long waits, and above all…discretion," says Rafael. "I expect she'll need stitches. You can wait here while I get her checked in, or—"

"I could come in too," says Fran, hoisting aside the bundle of embroidered satin hummingbirds. "Keep you company?"

Rafael ponders the prospect. "Yes," he says, to his surprise. "Yes, that would be good."

They both exit the car hastily, self-conscious of their mutual interest in each other. Rafael coaxes Janey from the back seat. He checks her wound, covers her frail body with his jacket, then instructs her to put one foot in front of the other. His methodical action reminds Fran that he has done this—not once or twice, but possibly dozens of times before.

As Janey grows aware of what's happening, she starts swiping and clawing to get Rafael away.

Undeterred, he swings her over his shoulder and marches her to the entrance. The lobby smells of peonies.

"You don't get that at the National Health Services," says Fran.

Rafael smiles wryly. It isn't his idea of a night out and it certainly isn't a date, but somehow he is glad that this strange evening with Fran can be prolonged. They take seats in a clean, bright waiting area, with Janey wedged between them. An awkwardness arises, as though the harsh lighting and disinfected floors have exposed the erroneousness of their circumstances—like a badly lit dressing room mirror. They sit quietly, watching the clock. Fran flicks through a pile of lifestyle magazines. Rafael takes out his tablet and starts tapping the screen.

"So," says Fran, desperate to save the atmosphere, as she casts her gaze to Rafael's scroll of official looking emails, "if you weren't here now, where would you rather be?"

Rafael glances up. "Work," he says definitively. "I'm that exciting."

"Oh dear."

"The foundation is my life. My family made their money buying unwanted farmland and selling it for profit to housing developers and trailer parks. By the mid-1950s, they were sitting on a fortune. My grandfather, Samuel, decided his conscience was due a spot of philanthropy, so he set up the family foundation to support initiatives in education and public health. The responsibility for the foundation then passed to my father and now it's mine. I want the money to make as much a difference as it can. As well as making donations to various charitable organizations, we've recently developed our own school building scheme."

"Wow," says Fran. "I really *can't* compete with that."

Rafael smiles. "Well, if I make sure their minds are educated, you can make sure their hearts are full of love."

"I'd say the two are connected, wouldn't you?"

"Maybe," says Rafael, staring at her curiously.

"And how hard is it to build schools?"

"More headache than I'd like, but"—his focus drifts back to his emails—"it's a way to keep busy."

"Oh, come on," says Fran. "Don't downplay it. It sounds incredible. Do you always have to be so closed up?"

"Mostly. Do you always have to wear your heart on your sleeve?"

"Yes," says Fran. "Mostly."

"So where is it that *you'd* rather be, Francesca? Other than this peony-scented center of sterility?"

Fran thinks for a moment.

"Haworth," she replies out of nowhere. "I rather fancy running around the moors in a cotton nightgown à la the Brontë sisters, lost to the wilds and the haunting vim of Heathcliff. As it goes, I recently invested in an excellent Victorian bridal gown from rural Yorkshire. Not everyone's idea of a big dress, and, in fact, the cut of it was outdated from the start—bearing in mind this was long before Instagram, when fashion trends were slow to spread from the cities—but it's ever so lovely. Someone will adore it. Brides turn up at my shop in all states of bewilderment, mostly refugees of the chain stores. At the Whispering Dress, they get a gown like no one else, a gown with a beating heart."

"And where do you find these 'whispering' dresses? Apart from dumpsters, of course."

Fran flashes him a scolding look, still sore that he threw a Garrett-Alexia wedding gown away.

He evades her stare.

"I'm always on the hunt," she explains, "but to be honest, the hard work starts once I've found a dress. Then it's all about the research. That's where the magic is. I spend months growing each dress's history, building its narrative from fragments: photographs, diary entries, newspaper cuttings, church accounts, census records... whatever I can find. Sometimes I actually meet people, talk to those who knew the bride and groom."

She thinks of the Meryl Percy dress, how she spoke to several old Percy acquaintances who were only too happy, amid the niceties of biscuits and tea, to share memories of their dear, departed friend whose infamous red wedding dress had once been the talk of the community. She even visited the shop where the dress had been shaped and stitched, then walked the aisle of the little stone church at the top of the hill, where they married—it was like Meryl and James were there, actually there. Every detail—from the perfume mark at the collar, to the tiny rip in the hem, thanks to a tipsy attempt to Lindy Hop—she felt it all.

"My aim is to bring joy," she says, sighing. "To make brides feel great and, in turn, help them create happy, lasting marriages."

"Sweet," says Rafael cynically. "And just out of curiosity, do you have interests other than wedding dresses?"

"Well, I quite like evening gowns."

Rafael smiles and rolls his eyes. Inside, however, his interest is unfurling. *Take away the veneer*, he thinks, *get rid of all the distracting vintage wedding dress madness and there it is: that rare ephemeral brilliance, sparkling light, the essence of fairy-tale heroines and first loves. Francesca Delaney.*

Suddenly Janey perks up.

"I know you," she slurs, prodding Fran in the ribs. "You were at the house. I tell you though, you're no way his usual type—"

Rafael tenses, tries to shush her.

"Yeah, that's right. Silence the wicked little sister. Bundle her home, out of view. Make sure she doesn't spill the dirt—"

"Janey! Shh!"

But Janey gets louder, as though announcing to a crowd. "Oh yes! The illustrious Colt family, great givers of humanity, we love a good ruckus. That's because behind the altruism we're all a bunch of drunks, thieves, philanderers, and bullies—"

"Janey! Enough!"

The doctor calls her name. The relief on Rafael's face is transcendent as he ushers his sister to the consulting room. He returns twenty minutes later with coffees for himself and Fran and a decidedly frazzled expression.

"They'll patch her up and keep her overnight," he explains wearily. "I'll collect her in the morning. Let's go."

~⚬~

As they return to Rafael's car, the air between them is different. They are comfortable together. More than comfortable. They are keen. As though one intense hour in a hospital waiting room has equaled three evenings of mannered chat. When Fran climbs into the passenger seat, she feels a flutter in her stomach. The last time she experienced something similar she was…so young. She glances at Rafael, finds new interest in the details of his face, his dark, brooding eyes, the slight curl at the corners of his mouth that only shows up when he smiles. With a smile, she gathers the folds of the wedding dress on her lap. The car pulls away, and rather than being their last journey of the day, somehow she wishes it were their first.

As the city lights twinkle around them, they slip into contented chat about their favorite places to go in London. Fran remains loyal to the markets around the East End, the city churches, the elegant serenity of the Queen's House in Greenwich, and a certain secluded spot in Regent's Park where she likes to hide on a summer day, eating strawberries and reading short stories by Somerset Maugham. Rafael declares his allegiance to Saint Pancras station and to the riverside at Richmond— both of which, Fran notes, represent a means of exiting the city.

The chat then turns to their favorite films (Fran: *Top Hat* with Ginger Rogers and Fred Astaire; Rafael: *The Shawshank Redemption*), favorite books (Fran: anything by Austen or any of the Brontës; Rafael: *The Selfish Gene* by Richard Dawkins), favorite cocktails (Fran: a French 75; Rafael: a dry martini), and favorite doughnuts (Fran: classic jam; Rafael: none, far too unhealthy). Then to family matters. It seems safe to venture there again.

"Why do you think she does it?" says Fran, sighing as she thinks of poor Janey.

"She's an addict."

"Yes, but…what makes her an addict? It doesn't come from nothing. You're her brother. I assume you had the same upbringing and yet you seem so…"

"Different?"

"So why aren't you an addict too?" she asks plainly.

Rafael balks, shocked by the candor of this question. It feels like she is looking right into him. "That—that's none of your business," he says.

"I'm sorry. I don't mean to pry."

A lull follows, but to Rafael's surprise, he finds himself crawling out from his armor, willing, *wanting* to fill the silence with an answer. "If you must know, I was groomed to be the responsible one. There's no place for three-day vodka benders when my work is so intensive. Besides, I spend too much of my life keeping my errant younger sister out of the newspaper gossip columns. I don't have time for addictions of my own."

"What do they say about her?"

"'Another privileged princess turned wild child.' I'd laugh it off except it really doesn't help her recovery. And it certainly doesn't help the image of the foundation."

"I never read gossip columns," says Fran. "In fact, I try not to observe the news in general. Too depressing."

Rafael rolls his eyes. "Why doesn't that surprise me? Where do you want to be dropped, Fairy Land?"

"Walthamstow."

"The East End. Very trendy. Where all good vintage wedding dress experts reside, I suppose."

"On that note," says Fran, "I'd like to talk to you more about your mother's dress." She picks up the hem, clutches the silk to her.

Rafael stiffens. *What is her obsession with this dress?*

"Do you have the remotest idea how valuable it is?" she asks. "I could sell it to a private collector for tens of thousands."

"So do it. Cash in."

"But it's your mother's dress, your family's history. Don't you care? Its monetary value is nothing compared to its romantic value."

*Change the subject*, thinks Rafael, fixing his gaze on the road ahead.

"Well, if you're really not interested," Fran huffs, "then I'll do my thing. I'll find a worthy bride and sell it on. The only trouble is"—she pauses, checks his body language—"there's something about it that bothers me. I mean, it's radiant in every way, and yet, when I tried it on in the house—"

"You tried it on again?"

"Well, obviously. To feel its energy."

Rafael exhales.

"The thing is, it had a rotten energy…really, the worst…" Her voice trails off as she thinks of what to say next, careful words, not to disturb or freak him out. "I went into her bedroom, stood in front of that old armoire." Fran pictures it. "It was so intense, so real, like I could sense her, right there, standing in front of the mirror. Normally that's a high point for a woman—the moment of becoming, when they look and see themselves for the first time, reconfigured as the icon bride. It can be nerve-racking for some, unsettling even, such a monumental change. But it's always a happy occasion, unless of course…"

She looks down, sighs. "The things is, I could tell she wasn't happy, not at all happy, which only makes me wonder—forgive my intrusion—but were there problems in the marriage?"

"That's it!" says Rafael, astounded. "I've heard enough of this."

The engine lags as he presses on the accelerator. He wants it to stop, needs it to stop, to open the car door and flee from this facile intrusion.

"I know it sounds bonkers," says Fran, desperately trying to claw her way back, "but there you go. It was in the dress. It came from the dress. My mum—she was a costumer. She worked in all the London theaters. That was my upbringing, hiding backstage with a Chelsea bun and a sewing box. We had this guessing game we used to play. She'd bring things to me—giant bloomers, velvet bodices, Tudor robes, animatronic fairy wings…whatever she could find in the dressing rooms. We'd try them on and then make guesses about who wore them, how they felt onstage. It was like magic."

The car slows to a halt as Rafael pulls into a turnout. "Get out. There's a garage up ahead. You can call a cab."

"I'm not crazy. I promise I'm not crazy. This matters. You need to know—"

"I need nothing from you except for you to leave me and my family alone."

"She punched a mirror."

"What?"

"On the eve of her wedding, she punched a mirror and cut her hand—"

Rafael's knuckles go stiff at the wheel. His head throbs with fury.

"Am I right?"

"Just go!" he hisses. "Take the damn dress and leave me alone!"

# chapter 3

MICK LISTENS PATIENTLY AS FRAN COMPLAINS. HE DOESN'T MIND. Over the years, she has repaired an awful lot of shirt buttons for him, taught him to hem, listened for hours to his "only Victorian dandy in the village" teenage angst. Three failed relationships have left him with an alarming black hole of emotional turmoil, and she has picked up the pieces every time, kept him going. She's a diamond. He doesn't quite follow why she's so keen to pursue that tricky little family dynamic they'd had the misfortune to witness at the house clearance, but then, this is Fran, always on the trail of one wedding dress saga or another. He also has to question why she talks so persistently about the rudeness of the man she now calls "Mr. Colt," but again, this is Fran—her feelings toward men are more mercurial than the weather.

"He's hiding something," she insists, as they prepare the '60s minidress with the silver plastic collar for its final fitting. "And I'm going to find out what. Can you believe he just abandoned me on the roadside like that?" She glances at her wall of dead grooms. "James Andrew Percy would never do such a thing. And to think I was starting to like being around him, only to be reminded of what a hateful man he is."

"'Hate' is a strong word," says Mick sagely. "For someone you've met only once."

"Twice," Fran says, correcting him.

"And have you ever thought there might be more to it than hate?"

"Such as?"

"Attraction."

"Oh please."

"Seriously, I read about it in one of those psychology magazines. Hate and love are very closely linked. It's all about the brain chemicals."

"I know what you're doing," says Fran. "But honestly, I'm not interested. I don't need or want a boyfriend, and Rafael Colt, no matter how striking—"

"And rich."

"—is *not* my future. Not a chance."

"Even though you've talked about nothing else all morning?"

Fran sighs, shapes the dress, then sees Kate Michaels advancing through the shop door.

"Enough now," she whispers. "Here comes the bride." She turns to the doorway, breaks into a smile. "Kate—"

Kate spills in, snappily stylish in a tan raincoat and Jackie O sunglasses. "Hello, Fran. Hello, Mick. Lovely to see you again."

"You must be so excited," says Fran, beaming, switching on her wedding joy. "Only a few days to go."

Kate smiles. "I've dreamed of this day since I was six years old, when me and my sisters used to marry the neighbor's cat in a mock ceremony that lasted half a minute and involved copious amounts of daisy petals. Thirty years on, after a decade of artful idea implanting, I've finally gotten my wish."

"How's Rick?"

"Nervous, I think."

"And how's his kilt?" says Mick. "I do like a kilt."

"Itchy," says Kate. "But as I've told him, one can't have a wedding in Scotland without a bit of tartan." She glances around the shop, spies her prize: the '60s dress, artfully displayed in front of a floor-to-ceiling mirror. She rushes toward it, clapping her hands with glee. "Oh! Look at it! The coolest non-meringue wedding frock ever!"

"For the coolest bride," says Mick. "I mean, what's not to love about a rock and roll wedding in a proper Scottish castle, wearing a dress with a hemline as high as the sky?"

Kate grins.

Fran, meanwhile, stands back and delights in the fact that the Sandy Dorit minidress, with its edgy, exciting legacy, now has another chance to shine. Sandy, she discovered, thanks to many chats with the Dorit daughters, was something of a late bloomer. After snubbing four previous offers of marriage, she finally made her own proposal to a bohemian jewelry designer named Lars. The ceremony took place at the Brompton Oratory on March 18, 1966. Despite parental concerns about so much flagrant flouting of convention— apparently Sandy's mother had pinned her hopes on a *very* traditional gown—Sandy and Lars forged a happy union, traveling the world and photographing rock stars. So when Kate Michaels first walked into Fran's shop, sassy and smart, yet worried that, at forty-two, she'd look like the oldest bride on the block, Fran knew that a good match was in the ether.

"I've taken in the waist a tiny bit, as we discussed, just to get the perfect silhouette. Try it on, then you should be good to go."

Kate slips behind the damask curtain with the Sandy Dorit dress in her arms, then emerges minutes later, the '60s cool bride in all her glory.

"Nearly there," says Fran, "just one more thing to add. I discovered this at an auction the other day and immediately thought of you."

She opens the drawer of a dresser and lifts out a short, pearl-studded veil. "It's a 1965 original," she says. "And it belonged to a well-known actress."

Kate's eyes bulge with joy. "It's amazing! Quick, put it on!"

Fran obliges, wishing all brides could be as enthusing and easy as Kate. The veil sits neatly upon Kate's thick chestnut waves, bringing brightness and youth and just a hint of playfulness to her gracious features. She catches herself in the mirror and blows a cheeky Brigitte Bardot kiss.

"Love it!" says Kate. "Now I know you've said it's hard to get away from the shop, but please won't you come to the wedding? You've played such a major part in my enjoyment of all of this. I was never destined to wear a big, daft ball gown, but I didn't think I'd have much choice…until I met you. Please say you'll come."

Mick glances at Fran, gives her an encouraging nod.

Fran twitches, feels a tiny panic rising in her stomach.

"She'll be there," says Mick, speaking up for her. "Fran always accepts a wedding invite."

"Indeed I do," says Fran.

Mick shrugs, turns to Kate. "Would you believe she's in love with love, loves dressing brides, loves everything to do with weddings, but gets the fear whenever she's invited to one?"

"It feels like an intrusion," Fran protests. "When a bride has a dress, my work is done. Besides, I hate going alone…and I can't dance…and I don't have anything to wear."

"Now that, coming from you," says Mick, "is the lamest excuse of all."

"Come on," urges Kate, squeezing Fran's hand. "Be my guest. You'll have a lovely time, I promise. The castle is stunning, and it has its own lake. My friends are great, and I expect they'll all be desperate to meet the genius responsible for finding the coolest wedding dress on the planet!"

Fran sighs. She really *would* like to see the Sandy Dorit dress make its mark in the traditional chapel of a Scottish castle—such a wicked, playful contrast.

"I'll be there," she says, heaving a sigh.

"Excellent," says Kate, changing back in to her civilian clothes. "Well, I better go. I've got a hair appointment across town, sort out the gray roots. But I'll send you all the details, okay? See you on the nineteenth!"

Just as she's leaving, she catches sight of the Alessandra Colt dress, its enormous bulk swallowing the entire sewing table it sits upon.

"That's a grand one," she remarks, kissing Fran goodbye. "Who've you got in mind for that?"

But before Fran can answer, the door opens. Another customer, a walk-in with immaculate ice-blond hair, bursts in. "I need a dress," she demands.

"Well, you've come to the right place," says Mick.

With Kate Michaels merrily on her way, the new customer is welcomed. "What's your name?"

"Rachel. Rachel Pointer."

"And how about some background? Tell us a bit about you and your wedding plans, then we can figure out what kind of dress you might need."

They are duly given a monologue. "I suppose you could say I got the proposal I wanted—one knee, big diamond, champagne on ice, New Year's Eve boat party, just as the fireworks went off. Thankfully, Elijah was paying attention to my hints; otherwise"—Rachel smiles, assassin cold—"I might not have said yes."

Fran and Mick swap glances. Every now and then, one of them gets through the door: a Bridezilla.

"And now I'm having the wedding day to match," she continues, constantly smoothing the sides of her hair. "The Cedars. Have you heard it? It's a mansion near Windsor. We've rented the whole place. We've got a harpist, a jazz trio, a funk band, two decorative swans, a five-tiered cake, a dozen classic floral displays, a bus to ship guests around, and guaranteed all-day sunshine. The only thing is"—her face falls flat—"I've been let down by my dressmaker." The flatness then turns to fury. "*Bitch.*"

Fran leaps into action. "No matter." The words burst out. "Put it behind you. The Whispering Dress is here to help. How did you hear about us?"

"A work colleague recommended you. She said your methods are unorthodox, but that you find really special dresses. And mine has to be special. I don't want to look like anyone else. I want a dress that will have people's jaws dropping. I want to be a princess. Not just any old princess. *The* princess."

Fran nods. A match is forming. "Mick," she says, "bring out the Sarah-Anne Bootle dress, will you? I think we might have found its perfect bride."

"But I like *that* dress," says the woman, pointing to the Alessandra Colt gown, which is hard to ignore since it fills half the shop.

Fran flinches, finds herself walking in front of it, shielding it. "That dress isn't for you," she says, feeling weirdly protective.

"Well, what *is* for me? I'm not sure I'm comfortable with this way of doing things. You say you can help, but I'd really like to know what you expect me to wear on the most important day of my life in precisely three weeks' time. I'm putting huge trust in you. I expect something brilliant. Otherwise, I'll have you know, I'm watching a Vera Wang on eBay."

Fran stifles a sigh. Bridezillas can be a little wearing. "Come with me," she says.

She leads Rachel to the damask curtain, where Mick is hurriedly preparing the proposed dress. She offers Rachel a seat, but the offer is declined, which isn't the best of signs. Normally by this point, no matter how demanding and high-maintenance, a bride is excited-apprehensive rather than irritated-apprehensive.

"Ready?"

"Obviously. I've been planning this wedding for ten months."

"Just so you know, I traveled the length of Britain to find this gem. It might surprise you at first, but, well, you said you wanted something different, something no one else will have. After all, it's your day. It's only natural you'd want to stand out. Anyway, it may not grab you immediately, but once you try it on, trust me, I think you'll find it will grow on you."

"Just show me."

Fran hoists back the curtain. Mick presents a simple, block-printed cotton Victorian smock dress. Its original owner, Sarah-Anne Bootle, was a laborer's daughter from rural Yorkshire, a cheerful girl who rode horses, helped her mother bake bread, and played the recorder on Sundays at her local church. In May 1849, she married her childhood sweetheart in the village that raised her. Bunting lined the streets, the May Queen gave them her blessings, homemade cider was drunk straight from the barrel, and the dancing—wild and raucous—went on all night. Of all the weddings Fran has envisaged, she'd like to have been a guest at this one.

The dress sits sweetly, its full sleeves, high nipped waist, and billowing skirt, like a blossom upon a tailor's dummy. It isn't Vera Wang, Norman Hartnell, or Lacroix, but it has a kind, innocent, softening grace. Fran can almost smell the hay in the sunshine as Sarah-Anne Bootle and her beau take a stroll through the fields—a halcyon reverie where there are no daft delusions of materialism and no perversely glamorized social media profiles to keep up with. Sarah-Anne, she imagines, took pleasure in what was right there all around her, the simple things. Regardless of whether this is the dress Rachel Pointer wants, it is the one she needs—at least her future husband will think so when he is reminded that there is more to her than the Bridezilla she's become—and that a moat full of gilded swans can be eclipsed by a pub garden, a mug of cider, and a pork pie.

"You're kidding me?"

"Do you like it?"

"I hate it." The horror in Rachel's face is startling. "I absolutely detest it. It's like something from a farmyard. I'm not wearing it. Oh, for god's sake! I should never have come here. This is ridiculous, a total waste of time."

Fran grits her teeth, fears she may have pushed the mission too far with this one. She shakes the skirt fabric, wills it to works its charm.

"Why can't I have that lovely dress over there?" Rachel points again to the Alessandra Colt gown. "That's a princess dress, but this...this is a peasant smock!"

"At least try it on. You might feel differently when you see it on your own body."

Rachel huffs and grunts and reluctantly deigns to shovel the dress over her shoulders, giving little thought to the fact that it is centuries old. The moment she catches herself in the mirror however, she quietens.

"It's—it's flattering, I suppose. Really flattering. I didn't realize my shoulders were that pretty. And I like what it does to my jawline and..." Her fury melting, she strokes her hands down the fabric, presses it to herself, smiles, and shuts her eyes, and then, out of the unlikeliest of reveals, has The Moment.

"Take your time," whispers Fran. "Let it settle. I know it's not what you were expecting, but really, it does something wonderful to you. The shape is so feminine. In fact, in that dress, I'd say you are the very essence of all that is charming and good."

"Do you really think so?" says Rachel, a smile in her eyes—and her soul.

When Rachel Pointer finally exits, the Sarah-Anne Bootle dress packed in a ribboned box under her arm, Fran and Mick sit back in vintage splendor and toast their effort with a glass of champagne.

"That was a tough one."

"Seeded by an all-too-common phenomenon: the bride who focuses too much on the wedding and not on the marriage itself," says Fran ruefully.

She knows only too well the cost of allowing all rational thought to be obscured by the giddy prospect of bridehood. How easy it is to get distracted, blinded even, by the excitement of an unfettered wedding-day plan—especially if it's a daydream that has been flowering since childhood. Never mind the rightness or niceness of the fiancé, just make the big day *incredible*. The rest will fall into place...won't it?

The sun is radiant over Regent's Park. The presentation in the boardroom, however, is not. Rafael finds himself staring sideways through the window, longing for fresh air and trees. Mimi keeps nudging his coffee toward him, a small hint to look more alert, more interested, more dedicated.

"We've been providing the elderly with a listening ear for over seven years," says the woman in the loud cerise knit, pointing to her Glynda's Listening Ear charity pin. "Our service users report a 73 percent increase in feeling happier, more energized, and less lonely."

*How do they measure so precisely?* he wonders. *With a machine? An algorithm? Do they have an app—an app that absorbs human emotions then turns them into a spreadsheet, squishing all those unfathomable layers of cruelty and deceit into a bunch of colorful pie charts, instant rationale out of something he's never in his life been able to begin to face?*

"We find that the service is particularly helpful for those who are separated from family or perhaps widowed."

Rafael nods, heaves a breath. Each time Glynda opens her mouth to speak, her enormous earrings quiver and jangle. *They are an awful distraction*, he thinks, *from the valid points she is making. Does she honestly believe her bid for money will be more appealing if she dresses fun and bubbly?* He doesn't need a clothing con. He doesn't want to be schmoozed by wacky jewelry. If he likes a project or likes its possibilities, he makes a grant for it. It's that simple. He doesn't need to be visually assaulted so early in the morning. A plain shirt would do it.

He thinks of Francesca Delaney. Somehow she has managed to make him see clothes differently. He cannot look at his staff now without questioning their choices of apparel, even Mimi, in her stiff black suit dress, its razor-sharp tailoring and understated luxury screaming, *I'm serious and deadly.*

"Mr. Colt?"

"What? Sorry?"

Mimi gives him a glare. "Glynda was asking if you'd like to visit one of her weekend Listening Camps. I said your schedule is very busy, but that you'd consider it."

"Very busy, but yes, thank you, Glynda, for the fascinating offer. And for presenting to us this morning. We'll look at the figures, then…be in touch."

"No, thank *you*, Mr. Colt. Thank you so, so, so, so, so much!" she gushes, earrings circling wildly. "You don't know what this means to me. Just to stand here in front of you…it's…awe-inspiring."

When she is gone, Mimi fixes him with another glare. "What is wrong, Rafael? You are not focused, not your usual self."

Tired, jaded, empty of spirit, no highs, no lows, just a flat wash of gray fading into the horizon.

"I need a holiday," he says, pacing over to the window. Below, he can see a group of children scooting through the park, laughing and chasing one another.

"So go," says Mimi. "I'll clear your diary, book you a flight today, wherever you like."

Rafael sighs. That isn't quite it. He studies the children, the way they swerve and swoop around each other, occasionally colliding, then falling into a happy heap. A holiday alone would be just another stretch of time spent…alone. He looks at Mimi, attempts a smile.

"Would you come with me? Where would you like to go?"

Mimi frowns. "No."

"I didn't mean anything—"

"I know, but I don't wish to holiday with you. I will do that with my fiancé."

Rafael blinks. "You have a fiancé?"

"Sure."

"Who? Where? Why don't I know this?"

"Because I didn't tell you. Because I assumed you wouldn't be interested."

"But…"

Mimi turns her attention to a pile of correspondence.

"So, tell me," he ventures, trying to embrace the matter. "Who's the lucky guy?"

"His name is Anton. He's a surgeon at King's. We get married in September."

"Oh. Well, good. Good for you."

"I hope so. I need a visa."

At this, Rafael can't help feeling relieved. The thought of his reliable equivalent, the cold fish Mimi, having a loving significant other is too disturbing. She is his. He wants her always to be his. She of all people cannot fall into the happy-clappy marriage trap. Nonetheless, he is rattled, sideswiped by a sudden clear vista into the chasm of loneliness that has become his daily existence. That his closest ally could have a life—a marriage plan, in fact—that she didn't think he'd be interested in hearing about. Is he really that cold?

His concentration slips. He closes his eyes, and there she is again: Francesca Delaney—her face, her radiance, her romantic optimism— his mother's wedding dress bundled in her arms, more startling and alive than anyone he's ever met. He was rude, so unspeakably rude to her—all because she was scratching beneath the surface.

He needs to make amends.

❧

Later that evening, amid bundles of white silk, Fran sets to work on the Alessandra Colt dress. There are other dresses that need repairs too, urgent ones, but its presence in the shop is too distracting. She feels compelled, even though she cannot imagine the kind of bride she would—or could—match it to. She stares at it draped across her sewing table, its secrets twisting and twitching within its threads. It has been a week since she brought it here. Every night, she has woken in the dark and found herself thinking about its moonlit folds, mesmerized, awestruck—and slightly terrified. Part of her wants to try it on again, but another part—a stronger part—is too scared of the awful dread it gave her, all that Colt family complication. Her conscience insists that she cannot sell it as it is, not without knowing the full story—too risky. Rule number two: never sell a dead dress.

Online, she finds endless pages about the good works of the Colt Foundation, a few tawdry gossip articles about Rafael's ceaseless bachelorism and Janey's yo-yo rehab habit, but otherwise, the family report is exemplary. Even adding the word *scandal* turns up no dirt. From what she can tell, the previous generation of Colts were bastions of all that is good in the world, role models for the rest. Their foundation is one of the queen's favorite organizations. They were regulars at the palace. Not a hint of trouble or marital disharmony.

With a cluster of photos printed from the internet, she pieces together a family tree and pins it to the wall. Among the many Colt sisters, brothers, and cousins, it seems Samuel Anders Colt, who began the foundation, married Janice Eloise Tricklebank. She gave birth to Lyle, who married Alessandra in 1978, which led to Rafael and Janey—and everyone was rich, important, and happy. On the surface at least. Despite the money, the glamour, and the pristine philanthropic image, Fran understands there is something awry in that world.

The dress beside her, its provenance emerging, suddenly seems to glow—an *it* dress, the jewel of a society wedding, which perhaps explains the extravagance, not to mention the Garrett-Alexia label—an *it* dress with a secret. It is strange to her, however, that Lyle and Alessandra married in 1978, the era of the maxi dress, the bell-bottom suit, and jersey fabric, yet this garment is unmistakably '50s in style. Wedding dresses have always had their timeless, fairy-tale qualities, but brides are not completely untouched by the movement of trend.

Fran's fingers tingle, desperate to touch, to understand. She runs her hand across the bodice, feels the rise and fall of the cluster work, its pearls and bugle beads shimmering in the honeyed light. As she allows the weight of the skirts to slip through her hands, she notices some unusual stitching on the inner seams. She pulls the lines of thread closer, inspects the work. Some neat slip stitching and some less-refined topstitching, in mismatched thread, suggests the dress has been altered. Fran scrutinizes each section. It isn't unusual for wedding dresses to require last-minute adjustments, but this looks like a major modification to accommodate a significant change in waist size. A pregnancy perhaps? Or to fit another bride?

With the dress against her, as if to test it, Fran stands bolt upright. She takes a deep breath, half shuts her eyes, and tries to dig back, to connect with what she sensed at Dryad's Hall—Alessandra's anguished cry, the smashed mirror, the blood—but there is nothing. No sorrow, no pain, just acres of fabric. The dress is quiet. Fran can only wonder if she made it up, another ruse of her fertile imagination—a touch, perhaps, of her own angst blending into the story, confusing the threads of fact and fiction.

A phone call to Mick is the answer. Mick has a friend who works for a newsreel archivist and is generous with favors on account of his love for antique radios, which Mick is more than happy to source for him. Within a few hours, the friend has managed to locate some old movie film of the "Society Wedding of Mr. and Mrs. Lyle Colt, Marylebone, July 7, 1978." He emails Fran with a download of the footage. She leans close to the screen and watches the grainy, colorized images flicker: crowds lining a London street, young men and women bearing shaggy, winged haircuts smile and wave. The reel is silent, but her imagination fills in the blanket of cheers and street noise. The camera pans and focuses on a columned, neoclassical portico with two huge doors behind it. She knows them well: Marylebone Church, where Charles Dickens baptized his son and Judy Garland married Mickey Deans. One of her favorite London wedding venues. The doors open. The bride and groom step out, Alessandra and Lyle, there on the screen, animated, moving, *alive*.

She zooms as close as she can, hovering the cursor over Alessandra's face. Through pixelated tones, she studies the creases of Alessandra's shy, self-conscious smile, her eyes peeping out from the hollows of their sockets, gaze shifting from side to side. She looks nervous, frightened almost, but who wouldn't be? A bride at the center of a public spectacle, worthy of a newsreel and several inches of society gossip—it must have felt overwhelming. Lyle looks far more comfortable in front of the crowds. Dashing in an elegant three-piece morning suit, he smiles and waves, then places an arm around his new wife's shoulders, and they proceed down the stone steps through a shower of white confetti.

Once they reach the flat of the pavement, Alessandra seems to strengthen. Her shoulders lift. She, too, begins to look out at the crowd, offering smiles and waves. *The dress*, thinks Fran, *is working its magic.* Four meters of embroidered train follow behind her, carried by a troupe of bridesmaids in powder-blue crepe maxis—the emblem of the '70s, a shapeless foil to Garrett-Alexia's feminine, fairy-tale silhouette. A bridal gown from the 1950s catapulted into a 1978 wedding? It doesn't seem right.

Fran ponders the equation and wonders if Alessandra Colt is, in fact, not the first bride to wear the dress, which only makes it a more intriguing prospect—maybe a family dress, passed down through generations, mother to daughter and beyond. The family dress has the deepest whispers, imbued with the ions and atoms of every bride that has worn it, history upon history. Rare to find, usually kept close, it is a prized heirloom, too precious and resonant with memory to be given as merchandise to a love-obsessed dress enthusiast—unless, of course, the dress in question happens to have become the inherited property of a less-than-gracious male heir. Then it's fair game.

Fran leans into the screen and soaks up the pomp of the procession. With the bridesmaids in rows behind the couple, the crowds are enthralled by the stately display. Each step makes Alessandra seem bolder, brighter, the embodiment of the wife she is becoming...but just then, Fran sees it—a slip of the truth. She pauses the footage, rewinds, and watches again. A girl in the crowd hands Alessandra a bunch of posies. As Alessandra receives them, her lace sleeve slips, revealing a thick strip of bandage on her left hand, her wedding ring hand…the hand that smashed the mirror.

Fran sits back, breath trembling against her heart, unnerved by her own acuity. She'd hoped that what she imagined that evening at Dryad's Hall had been nothing more than a flight of fantasy. But this…this tells otherwise. She watches the footage again, then lets it play out, as more flowers are thrown into the path of the couple and the screen goes blank, the rest of the day consigned to the memories of those who were there.

*It is not enough. No way.* Fran stares at the dress and realizes she is now hungrier than ever to know, to understand, to *feel* the truth. Yet she fears the pursuit is an unhealthy one, especially since Rafael has shown his true lack of gentlemanliness. She looks to her bulletin board of dead grooms. There are seventeen now, prints in various tones of black, gray, and sepia, plus a couple of color Polaroids—the husbands of the brides of the dresses she's sold. Not all of them make the wall, just the best ones. To Fran, they are the great romantics of history—real men with real charm, heart, and dignity.

"You're all I need," she whispers. "The only worthy suitors."

She unpins James Andrew Percy's photo and holds it to the light.

"It's such a shame they don't make them like you anymore. Instead, we have the discourtesy of the 'enlightened' metrosexual who thinks more about himself and his hairline and his wallet than anything else."

She plants a kiss on James Andrew Percy's sepia cheek, then pins him back.

Her contemplation is shattered by a thud at the front door. Despite the *Closed* sign being up, the knock thunders through the walls, shaking the crumbling mortar from the bricks. Her first thought is that it's kids. It isn't unusual for disturbances to occur at this time. Rishi's Chicken Shop, the fast-food restaurant down the road, has its fair share of disobedient clientele. Weekends are particularly rowdy. Yet something about this knocking makes her instinctively alert. It is purposeful. She is wanted. She swoops her silk 1920s dressing gown over her shoulders, slips her feet into the marabou slippers she liberated from a derelict hair salon, and sneaks behind one of her mannequins, cautiously peering through the shop window. She sees a silver Jaguar E-Type parked on the curb—a car she knows. She remembers the sight of it gleaming in the moonlight, speeding away, leaving her stranded.

The door thuds again.

She blinks, bewildered. Why is he here? What does he want? Has he found more anger to vent on her? She hastily pulls her Colt family tree from the wall, shovels the evidence under a dresser. He spots her in the shadows, waves her over. It is starting to rain. She contemplates ignoring him, letting him soak, but her inquisitiveness wins. As she opens the door, to her surprise, he tries a smile, his hair ruffled by the weather.

"Thank you," he says, "for letting me in."

"You're not in," says Fran warily. "This is just the porch."

"Right." Rafael bows his head, embarrassed. "I—I just came to say sorry, that's all. Sorry for the way I threw you out of my car the other night. It was rather despicable of me. I'm under a lot of pressure at the moment, but... No excuses." He sighs, relieved to have squeezed the words out. "By way of apology, I'd like to give you this."

He hands her a gift box in stiff purple cardboard embossed with the name *Liberty of London*.

She takes it, stares at him. With a nod, he urges her to open it, so she slowly tugs one of the ribbons, keeping one eye on him, then slides the lid open.

"To replace the one that was ruined by Janey's blood," he says. "It's an old design, quite rare I believe. Anyway...it's for you. I hope you like it."

Inside is an emerald-green silk scarf printed with paisley swirls in cornflower blue and terra-cotta. It gleams like a treasure, its sheen rippling as Fran touches it. Old and deep-rooted, a classic design of the 1970s. She couldn't have chosen better herself. She opens her mouth to speak but doesn't know what to say. He seems sincere, sounds sincere, but...

"Do what you like with it. I just wanted to show you I'm not a complete wanker and that I really appreciated your help with my sister."

"Thank you," says Fran eventually. "How is she by the way?"

"She's fine. For now, anyhow."

"That's good."

They stand silent for a moment, the air swirling in circles around them, until Fran's will to resist caves in. "Please, come in if you like, if you have time."

"Are you sure?"

"If only to show you my shop isn't as awful as you probably think it is."

"Why would you think I think it's awful?"

"Because it's full of wedding dresses."

He follows Fran inside. She feels every step, startlingly conscious that he is entering her territory. With his sudden humility and vintage scarf, he is crossing the threshold. And what a threshold! He has to blink three times before his eyes can tolerate the cacophony of white and all its variations, the texture and sparkle. Everywhere he looks there are veils and tiaras and pearls. His senses start to whirl and thrash. And there, in the center, is his mother's wedding dress, not so much folded but heaped. He bristles, surprised by a sudden sense of protectiveness over it.

"I know I threw it in a dumpster," he says, "but dumping it on the floor? I thought you said it was immensely valuable."

"Actually, it's lying across my sewing table," says Fran. "But there's so much of it, the table is buried. A dress of that size is a nightmare to store. A standard coat hanger won't take the weight."

Rafael ventures farther inside the shop, eyes wide with astonishment. "Where do you *get* all this stuff?"

"Around and about," says Fran. "I spend a lot of time at vintage fairs. Look at these." She passes him a pair of pale silk gloves. "Aren't they beautiful? They're Edwardian, so delicate. Can you believe women's hands used to be that small?"

"Amazing," says Rafael politely, disguising the fact that all he can see are a pair of dirty, fraying mittens, fit for a child's dressing-up box.

"And this," says Fran proudly, reaching for a halo-shaped fascinator. "This was made by the bride who wore it, Mrs. Angela Symmons. She based it on the one Wallis Simpson wore when she married King Edward. Look at the detail! Sadly, neither wedding was popular with wider family."

"Perhaps Mrs. Angela Symmons should have chosen a less controversial style muse?"

"Now you're thinking like a dress whisperer," says Fran.

"Steady," says Rafael, catching her eye, catching a smile. He walks around the room, allows himself to be feel vaguely impressed by this careful collection of matrimonial delight.

"And you really believe that items from the past can influence the present?" he says, touching the lace of a Victorian veil.

"But they're not items from the past, are they? They just happen to *have* a past. There's a difference. And in answer to your question, yes, of course. I've seen it happen time and time again. All over the country, I've matched flamboyant '20s flapper dresses to shy girls, demure tea dresses to the argumentative ones, tulle ball gowns for shrinking violets. I take great care with my matches because it's not just a dress they're getting but the wisdom of experience." Fran begins to walk between the mannequins, weaving a scenic line through her bridal parade, and Rafael follows. It's a game.

"So who would you match this one to?" he quizzes, staring at an enormous, sleeveless '80s number, blush peach with a dramatic trumpet skirt.

"A bride who needs to be reminded that there is nothing wrong with believing in fairy tales."

"Until she discovers that fairy tales are a load of patriarchal non-sense perverted to market cartoon channels."

"You're a born cynic, aren't you?"

"I prefer to say realist. How about this one?" He diverts his attention to a high-necked '70s dress with full sleeves and a slightly dizzying floral pattern.

"For the kind of bride who thinks explosive fights are akin to passion, who needs to learn to argue less, listen more, and enjoy the kind of closeness that empathy can bring."

"Fair enough," says Rafael. "So how many brides have you helped? And what proof do you have of your success? I mean, do you ask for customer feedback? Do you give out questionnaires?"

"I trust my instincts," says Fran. "I've been doing this for years."

Rafael smiles. His gaze then drifts to the wall of dead grooms. "You seem to have a lot of insight into other people's marital needs, Fran, but something tells me you're still very much single."

"My standards are high," says Fran defensively, walking in front of her bulletin board. "I like old-fashioned charm, the way men used to be."

"Because life was so much better back in the day, hey?"

"Men were chivalrous. They showed more respect. Granted, there was a lot wrong…"

"Like no votes and few career opportunities for women, homo-sexuality being illegal, colonialism, slavery…but we were all polite to one another, so it's okay."

Fran sighs. "I'm not saying I'd have all of the past back, just some of it."

"The past is a dead land, Fran. All this"—he gestures around her shop—"it's lovely, but it's a shrine to a world that has gone. How can a person move forward in their life if they hide themselves away in this whimsical little fantasy of history?"

"Tell it like you mean it," says Fran, scolded by his harshness.

They stare at each other, lock eyes.

"I'm just telling you what I see, that this seems like the realm of someone who's avoiding reality. If you think it's too tough a judgment, that's up to you."

"I think it's a judgment I didn't ask for. And for your information"—she feels her hands slide to her hips, the boss-girl stance—"I adore my whimsical little fantasy of history. It's my life, my world. I created it. It has beauty and fun and vibrancy...and heart. My world has got *heart*. If it's whimsical, so be it, because there's not a touch of whimsy about you, is there? You're a fish. An ice-cold fish—"

"A human actually."

"—who needs to find some human feelings."

"While you could do with getting rid of a few."

They stand in combat, staring each other down, until Rafael sighs and steps back. "Look, I didn't come to argue. I just wanted to say sorry and—" He shakes his head, shuts his eyes. "This isn't working," he mutters. "Good luck. Good luck with the dress and your business and...your life. There. That's it. Goodbye." He goes to the door, yanks it open and marches into the rain.

In fury, Fran snatches it before it closes. "Goodbye to you too," she yells after him, desperate to have the last word. "And for your information, you're wrong! Completely wrong! I'm not avoiding reality! I'm not avoiding anything!"

# chapter 4

"Done your online check-in?" asks Mick.

"All sorted," says Fran.

"And what time do you need to be at the airport?" he says, pestering her, knowing Fran will leave it to the last minute.

"I've booked a cab for midday. Scotland, here I come, but before that…Petra Zatakis and her mother are coming for the final fitting—"

"Ah, the Vicky Pinder gown," says Mick, brushing his mustache. "Not for the fainthearted."

Fran goes to the damask curtain where she has prepared acres of peach taffeta and lace—a bouffant, trumpet-skirted strapless dress complete with sculpted silk roses and a full church veil. It excites Fran to see it primed and ready for its new life.

Right on cue, Petra Zatakis walks in clutching a latte. Her mother, Margot, is behind her, laden with shopping bags. Having met the pair twice before, first for the initial consultation, in which Petra described her fiancé as "nice," and again at the fitting (which was dominated by Petra's work emails), Fran knows the Vicky Pinder dress has found its match. Of course, to some, such an immense

gown might seem ostentatious, but Fran has a hunch that this dyna-
mite dose of fairy-tale couture is just the thing to sweep a rather staid
doctor off her feet. Because while there is nothing wrong with nice,
if that's the only compliment you can come up with when asked to
describe your future husband, perhaps you are setting your expectations a little low. Fran fears a touch of "otherwise I'll die lonely"
resignation. But she can fix that. Or rather, Vicky Pinder's '80s
extravaganza can.

"Petra! Margot! Lovely to see you again! Everything's ready."

"Aw," says Margot. "We've been really looking forward to this,
haven't we, Petra…Petra?"

Petra gives a lukewarm nod. Although they look alike, they are
most different in character. Fran wonders how such an effervescent
woman could raise an utterly glee-resistant daughter. She also wonders
whether this wedding is actually for Petra's benefit or her mother's.
Fran gives Mick a nod, then ushers Petra to the damask curtain, sensing that this final fitting will go smoothest if there is some distance
between the pair. Mick, meanwhile, takes Margot aside to show her a
tray of antique corsages. They gush and gossip like old friends.

"When I got married for the third time—"

"The third? Goodness me, you've been greedy, Mrs. Zatakis."

"Or lucky. I tell you what, Mick, I adored all of my husbands—or
at least I did when I married them. And all of my dresses were fabulous. I'll bring them in one day and show you. But the third, my
word, it was glorious. Some women think it's vulgar to dress up for
remarriages, but I couldn't help myself. If anything, the gowns got
bigger. Maybe because I got better at choosing."

"The gowns or the husbands?" says Mick, with a wink.

"Both."

They cackle together, much to Petra's irritation.

"Please, Mother," she scolds, taking a seat in front of the damask curtain. "We can't all be as giddy as you, falling in love with every fireman that walks the planet. Some of us have other priorities."

"Oh, Petra, don't be a stick-in-the-mud," says Margot, before cupping her hand over her mouth, leaning toward Mick and whispering. "I was starting to think she'd never find anyone, but…she got lucky at a medical conference. He's nice, really nice. Sort of reminds me of my first husband. Not that Petra seems remotely pleased for herself. I don't know, maybe it's a generational thing—that they always feel they have to downplay everything."

Fran breaks the tone by pulling back the damask curtain. "Ta-da!"

Margot takes one look at the dress and with gasping delight, starts fanning back tears. "It's everything a wedding dress should be!"

Petra, meanwhile, is less ebullient. "Oh. I forgot how bride-y it is," she says, frowning.

"I've taken up the hem," Fran explains, "so it should sit just upon the floor, giving you that perfect princess sweep without being a tripping hazard."

"But I'm not sure…seeing it again…I'm not sure whether I've got the guts to carry this off…"

"I think you've got the guts," says Fran carefully. "But perhaps you're lacking the enthusiasm. So let me remind you of Vicky Pinder."

"The bride who first wore it?"

"That's right. Vicky had it specially made, spent every penny she had on it. And with good reason. She fought for five years to convince her family to give her and her fiancé their blessing. With Vicky being the youngest daughter of a wealthy car dealer from Newcastle and her intended being a thirty-eight-year-old fisherman from a tiny village in Kerala, they had everything going against them: age gap, geography, culture, status, religion. They had to work so hard to prove their love and be accepted as a couple, but despite all the hurdles, they never questioned their adoration of one another. When the family finally came around, Vicky Pinder knew she had to go all out on the dress."

Petra stands up, walks toward the gown, and strokes one of the satin roses.

"Sometimes," Fran continues, "we watch a couple walk down the aisle and think, *Well, isn't that lovely? Don't they look happy together?* But really, we have no idea what it took to get them there. Marriage isn't something to take for granted or just go along with because everyone else is doing it. Wearing a wedding dress is not a right." She catches Petra's eye. "It's a privilege."

Petra nods, and it is clear to Fran that she is making the connection between Vicky's plight and her own. "Should I try it on?"

"Absolutely."

She helps Petra slip out of her suit and climb into the bodice. They lift it around her shoulders, and then Fran begins lacing the corset ribbons, chatting as she works.

"You say he's nice, and your mum clearly approves. That counts for more than you realize. It may not be sparkles and unicorns right now, but give it time. People grow. He might surprise you. Many of the best marriages are slow-burners. All I advise is that you respect your decision to wear this dress and to say 'I do.' Don't act like it's nothing."

Petra runs her hands down the ruffled skirt, looks in the mirror, and smiles—genuinely. Her face relaxes. "It will be fun, I suppose," she says, swishing the skirts, admiring her form. "I mean, I can't deny I didn't daydream about this sort of gown when I was a little girl."

"If you're only going to do it once," says Fran, "you might as well do it properly."

"Tell that to my mother," says Petra wryly.

The two of them sit and talk through ideas for shoes and accessories. Petra gets excited by the thought of a tiara and even stops to ponder what impact it will have on her future husband.

"He's going to be blown away. He's so used to me being dismissive of everything. This will show him I care about becoming his wife—because I do care, deep down."

"I know you do," says Fran. Suddenly, she is disturbed by the beeping of a car horn. She glances at her watch. "My cab! Is that the time already? My apologies, I have a wedding to get to."

"Wow. You must live, eat, and sleep bridal wear. Don't you ever get tired of it?"

"Never," says Fran. And in a whirl of excitement, she leaves Mick to finish up with Margot and Petra, scoops up her luggage (a vintage leather suitcase with matching attaché case), and hurries out of the door, calling behind her:

"Respect the dress, Petra! You look radiant!"

⤜⟿⟾⤛

Crowley Castle is everything one would wish a castle to be—solid stone turrets and crumbling battlements boldly claiming the land, promising echoes of sieges, homecomings, and medieval feasts. Surrounded by hills of pine trees, a fine lake at its foot, and now run by a charming host with an eye for detail, it is the perfect Highland getaway for a raffish London wedding party. Inside, the huge stone fireplaces smolder and the beamed ceilings hum with the drone of the castle's very own bagpiper, as the last of the guests arrive and take their seats in the candlelit chapel.

Fran delights in the coming and goings. From her seat at the back, wearing her favorite 1916 Paul Poiret–inspired harem gown, happy to be anonymous, a quiet cupid in vintage couture, she watches the reunions unfold. Old friends wave across the pews, briefly comparing the passing of five or so years—the job promotions, house moves, and children they've borne. The thrill on their faces is obvious, the point where they realize, having lived in separate worlds since leaving university, they are about to spend an entire weekend together, rekindling old joys, old drinking games, and perhaps, a few old heartaches.

As she waits, Fran gazes up at the vaulted ceiling and bright-colored remnants of stained glass. She has always loved churches, aisles especially. Although she has never found comfort in faith herself, she has learned to respect the role of religion in marital custom: all those brides who believe their wedding day is not just for them, but for their faith as well. Every wedding needs a sprinkle of magic, she thinks, godly or otherwise. When the big moment finally comes, the air is tremulous. The groom, Richard Fugle, or Rick as he prefers to be known, rocks nervously on his toes. *What is going through his mind?* Fran wonders. *How sure is he? How ready?* She shuts her eyes for a second, can't quite bear to look.

The music starts, a harpist's riff on Pachelbel's Canon, as the front doors creak open. Kate Michaels (soon to be Fugle) takes her first steps up the aisle. The whole chapel gasps as the '60s minidress, incongruous in such traditional surroundings, makes impact. The bride advances and, through the wisp of the pearl-encrusted veil, catches Fran's eye.

Fran smiles. The stress of attending is worth it for this, being here in the moment, seeing her bride, seeing her confidence, seeing that wonderful dress take flight once more—new chapters, new chances. The joy of it all catches in her throat, prompts a prickle of tears, the pleasure immediately tainted by the pain of regret.

The great hall is an explosion of red-and-green tartan, with silver cutlery, twinkling crystal, gleaming dinner plates, and white roses. Fran finds herself assigned to the odds-and-ends table, the place for guests who have no clear allegiance with any other. While buttering a bread roll, she makes polite conversation with an orthodontist, a dairy farmer, and a couple with four children whose sole mission, since they are "child-free" for the weekend, is to drink and dance and stay up until 3:00 a.m. Youthful waiters serve crayfish and prawns, followed by roast beef with "neaps and tatties," and Cranachan in tall dessert glasses. The food is rich and generous and the wine flows.

By the time the speeches are announced, the atmosphere in the hall is jubilant.

As the guests are called to quiet, Fran turns her chair, leans forward to try to get a better look at the top table, at Kate in her dress, snuggling up to her new husband. The father of the bride speaks first, a slim man with a wry sense of humor, just like his daughter. He talks fondly of Kate's wild school days, her first car, her appalling student digs, her devilish laugh, and her love of punk rock. Then it is over to the best men, not just one, but a squad of them, boarding school buddies, complete with props and slideshow. Everyone sits up. This should be good.

The first of them speaks, offers the usual best man opening banter: "Loyal, caring, sincere, honest...but that's enough about us. We're here to talk about our good friend Rick." He pulls out examples of rubbish mix tapes that Rick used to give to girls he fancied at school, then projects a series of cringe-inducing photos—bad haircuts, paisley shirts, and stone-wash jeans—before describing the many antics that went on during a French exchange trip. He wraps up his speech with a joke about rugby balls, then looks down the line.

"So, over to my compadre, who has a lot more to say about the naughty side of Rick, since they used to be each other's wingman. Introducing the only singleton left in our group, whose appetite for indecent, no-strings sex will leave you appalled and retching into your coffees."

He hands the microphone down the line, as the guests cringe in anticipation of the upcoming gags. Fran sits back—she's heard it all before. The next best man steps up, takes his place at the podium.

Rafael!

Fran freezes, stares at his suited form.

Everything blurs. The world spins in circles. There he is, *the only singleton left in the group.* Why now? Why here? The "indecent, no-strings sex" remark sticks in her throat. Not that she should care what he gets up to after hours. She watches, eyes wide, half-horrified, half-amazed, as Rafael raises the microphone. He opens his mouth to speak and, in that instant, spies Fran through the fanfare of champagne flutes. Their gazes meet once again, and his opening lines dissolve into a series of stutters, hijacked by the shock.

"Um…uh…hi…"

The microphone squeaks. The guests start to fidget and cough.

"I mean thanks," says Rafael, unable to take his eyes off her. "Thanks for that…*charming* introduction…for making me sound like some sleazy, shameless womanizer…which is somewhat inaccurate…in fact, very inaccurate of you, Mark, with your perfect wife and your two-point-four children…but there you go…anyway."

The first best man glares at him. "This isn't what we rehearsed," he hisses. "Do the gag about the kissing competition."

Rafael blinks, rattled, then, with the encouragement of the best man squad, manages to pull through the material, while constantly glimpsing back at Fran, checking for her reaction.

He eventually finds her on the balcony overlooking the lake, the outline of her gown fluttering in the breeze—an artful array of sage-green chiffon drapes and harem trousers, with a dusky pink appliqué sash. Everyone else is inside drinking up the free bar and enjoying the live music, but out here, it is peaceful. A mist is moving in, shrouding the water with its cold, mystic veil. They stand against the stone balustrade, pretending to admire the view, while being fiercely aware of each other's proximity.

"We meet again."

"So we do."

"If I may say so, Fran, you look lovely. An Eastern-inspired silhouette made popular at the turn of the twentieth century by innovators such as Paul Poiret. The belle epoque, right?"

Fran nods, raises an eyebrow. "Very good. So you've been reading up on fashion history?"

"A little."

"Despite so many misgivings about its worth."

"What can I say? You inspired me. Nice ceremony, wasn't it?"

"Charming. Nice, um, speech."

Rafael winces, shakes his head. "Obviously it was highly embarrassing. All that stuff…it was just…you know…gags."

"Sure. I've heard a fair few best man speeches in my time. Those 'indecent, no-strings sex' remarks are nothing new." She catches Rafael's eye, checks for a glimmer of shame.

"I've been single a long time," he responds, poker faced. "No strings, yes. Indecent, never. Like I said, it's just best man banter, designated to make fools of us all. You were responsible for the bridal dress, I suppose?"

Fran nods.

"Touché. It's very cool. Everyone's talking about it."

"Are they?" says Fran, narrowing her gaze. "Well, it's nice to know that whimsical little fantasies of history can be appreciated by *some* people."

"Look," says Rafael, "I appreciate we haven't had the smoothest of starts, but…maybe…since we're both here…we could try to… try again?"

Fran lowers her eyelids, resists that strange inner urge to stare at him, face him, connect with him. Suddenly she feels very aware of the effort she's made, in the most sensuous of her outfits. She is even wearing her lucky shoes, which are good for standing in, if not for moving. But, of course, she dresses to please herself, no one else. Not him. Not a man. Not Rafael.

"There are only so many tries," she says resolutely.

"We could at least chat."

"I think we did chat the last time we met. And it didn't work out so well."

Rafael sighs. "Okay, I'll admit I've given you a rather poor impression of myself, but if you'll give me the chance to…show you…"

"Show me what?"

"My better qualities." He stares at her, an unassailable intensity in his deep, dark eyes.

Determined not to give him leeway, Fran leans over the balustrade, feels the breeze in her hair. Her emotions turn in circles. How he fascinates her, enthralls her, yet infuriates her too. *Hate and love*, she thinks, remembering Mick's platitude, the chemicals are the same. And now she senses them mixing and twisting inside her, luring her like a magnet toward the unknown.

"Tell me about yourself," she inquires. "What's your thing? Are you into the arts? Theater? Sports? Music? Fine dining and exclusive champagne bars?"

Rafael laughs—he'd hardly call Seekers exclusive. He looks around, as if trying to latch on to a better answer than the one in his head. "Mostly I work. I'm that boring."

"Not much time for indecent, no-strings sex then?"

"Oh, please. Those comments, they were bravado. It's true I'm single, but…"

"You like your job then? I mean, it's quite a job—philanthropy."

"If I could call it a job," he says wryly. "It's a lot more than that. It's more like a duty. I guess you could say it's…"

"In the family," says Fran, finishing the sentence for him. "Well, at least you help people. You make a difference. You can go to bed each night feeling proud."

"Can I?"

Fran nods, stirs the dregs of her Whisky MacDonald.

"I am proud," says Rafael, "but it's a weight, a burden even. The world doesn't want me to say that though, because obviously I'm supposed to be eternally grateful for all my privileges. You know, when I was young, my father sent me all around the world to show me what poverty looked like, all from the comfort of an air-conditioned limousine. He talked endlessly about society's problems and how the foundation was helping to solve them, while swigging Chablis from his vintage wine cellar. It's not…" He pauses, thinks carefully about how to say this. "It's not that I'm not proud of my work, Fran. When I think about what we do for people, there's no question of its worth.

It's not the charity I doubt. It's the bullshit that goes with it. Don't assume the world of philanthropy is full of generous-hearted altruists. There are plenty who are in it for themselves, to massage their egos or to improve, or even protect, their reputation. The mask of kindness, it's a convincing one." He looks at her sharply, blinks as though startled. "But…why am I telling you all this?"

Fran shrugs. "Because you're not one for small talk."

"Yes, yes, I suppose you could say that."

He looks away, stares over her shoulder.

Meanwhile, through the swirling lights of the hall, the fiddle and drums of the ceilidh band start up. The happy couple, Kate and Rick, twirl into the center, laughing together, immersed in the kind of love that shuts out the rest of the world.

*What is happening?* thinks Rafael. Why does Fran make him feel so…outside of himself? All those years ago, he'd made the choice to forget love. And now, here he is, caught in a surge of excitable emotion, barely knowing what to do with it. Like a sunray, she has struck him, ignited some long-forgotten want, and there is no going back. He must connect, take a risk, pull her closer.

"Well, if you really don't want to chat," he says, gesturing to the dance floor, "maybe we could…?"

Fran blinks. "I only know how to fox-trot."

"I don't even know that, so…"

On impulse, he hooks his fingers around hers. The spontaneity of his touch does something peculiar to her breathing. He is actually asking her to dance, this wedding-hating, love-skeptical, cold fish of a man, who is not, it seems, such a cold fish after all. Unsure where this will all unwind, Fran shuts her eyes and accepts, the warmth of his skin, the strength of his grip, wrapping her tiny, milky palm entirely.

They run to the middle, among the cavorting couples. The fiddle and drums are at the peak of their frenzy. He wraps her in his arms, then releases her outward, then coils her back again, pressing her tiny ribs to his chest. He can, therefore, dance—enough not to tread on her toes anyhow.

As they twirl and spin, the amalgamation of disco lights, party dresses, and tartan become a kaleidoscope. Are they in time with the music? Who cares? Is the music fast, while they dance slow? Why not? They hardly notice. They are only aware of each other.

Suddenly he doesn't want to let go of her.

Yet the thought of letting her *in* is terrifying.

As his hands skim the outline of her hips, barely touching, the deepest fear grips him—that he will damage her, that she doesn't deserve the hurt he will bring. He can't. He mustn't. His heart must stay closed.

But then…

She throws her head back, laughs like the world is painted with glitter. She is so free, so weightless.

He cannot help himself. He kisses her before he can ruin it, takes her face in his hands, gives her no choice…not that she minds.

Minds? Her heart is on fire, sparking and fizzing and cartwheeling through the light. She hasn't been kissed like this since…since… She cannot look back, cannot compare. Only now. Only this. His lips are soft. He kisses her like he wants her—not in a predatory way, nor possessive, nor desperate, but in a way that speaks of love, the truth of it, all the courage and compromise and effort that drives it.

A kiss from one who knows that love is not easy.

When they finally pull apart, stunned and wordless, the music has stopped. The hall is silent. The enormity of the moment sweeps through them. For the first time in years, they have let down their guards. But then…Rafael sees it, a sudden shadow in her eyes, her stunned delight eclipsed by alarm.

She backs away, mouth open. "I—I'm sorry," she says, trembling. "I'm so sorry. I shouldn't have… I'm sorry. I have to go."

She turns and flees into the darkness.

"So you kissed him?" says Mick, fluffing the hem of an ivory swing dress. "It's not a crime, Fran. Consenting grown-ups are allowed to do that sort of thing."

Fran sighs, cradles her coffee to her chest. She has the feeling she is about to get a lecture.

"But you said it yourself," she argues. "He has a certain arsehole factor about him."

"Okay, first impressions weren't great, but he must have something going for him, given how much of your attention he's commanding. Give him a chance. Maybe a date, Fran…one that doesn't involve weddings? Romance in reverse."

"Oh, I don't know, Mick. I—I'm just not sure I'm ready."

"Ready? *Ready?*" He throws his hands up. "Fran, it's been over ten years! You deserve to find someone, someone who'll make you happy, a mate, a future. You try and try to convince me—to convince yourself for that matter—that dressing brides and fussing over other people's wedding days is romance enough for you, but I've seen that look in your eyes. I know you're lonely. I have my reservations about the guy, but honestly, I've never seen you so worked up about anyone, ever. On your own advice, girl, go for it. Take a chance."

Fran sighs, wraps her arms around her middle, squeezes herself. She wants to see Rafael again—so badly—but she is scared. She glances at the Alessandra Colt dress, its mysterious energy pulsing in the corner of the shop, then her eyes track to the wooden wardrobe with the art nouveau handles, wherein another dress lies.

"I know you kept it," says Mick solemnly.

Fran looks down at her feet. "I never get it out," she blusters. "It's fine."

"If you say so," he says, eyeing her carefully. "Come on. We've got work to do. Let's get these veils cleaned."

"Mimi, where are the papers on the water project?"

"On your desk. Why don't you look properly?"

"Excuse me. Who's in charge here?"

"Your head is in the clouds, Rafael, so at the moment, it's me."

"Thank you, Mimi. Noted. How are the wedding plans coming?"

"Like you care."

As Mimi stomps back to her desk, Rafael stretches and stares across the grassy vale of Regent's Park. It has been three days since he kissed Francesca Delaney at the insane Scottish wedding, and they haven't talked since, haven't dared. Not even a text. He could almost think it had never happened, yet its dreamlike vivacity swirls though his thoughts with uncontainable frequency. Perhaps it was the drink. Or the grip of wedding fever. Or both. Either way, in the wake of his distraction, a mountain of folders have stacked up on his desk—new bids for funding, youth groups wanting lump sums for retreat weekends, a traditional folk dance troupe hoping to tour disadvantaged schools, medical research centers begging for finance—everyone wanting something from him, from the family, from their money.

Mimi signals him, asks to patch through a phone call. "Apparently it's urgent."

"According to whom? If it turns out to be a sales call, I'll fire you."

She sighs, knows he'll be cross. "It's that reporter. He's very insistent. He claims he has some 'insights.' I think you should talk to him."

"Hell no!"

Too late. The phone buzzes. The line is poor, long distance.

"Yes?" says Rafael, unable—and unwilling—to disguise his ire. "And what have you got on me this time?"

"Evidence of trouble," says the voice with a melting Welsh lilt. "I've been doing some digging, Mr. Colt, as you know I do, and I've found reason to believe—"

"Bullshit."

"Do you want me to share what I know? I'd be willing if you'd oblige me with an interview. Or just a sound bite would do."

"You're a piece of work," says Rafael, shaking his head. "Is it really your prerogative to keep trashing my family until you succeed in destroying our foundation and everything it has done? Do you know how many children receive a decent education because of us? Or how many injured servicemen have been given proper rehabilitation because of our donations?"

"I notice you're not denying it."

"I know nothing about any scandal," he snarls. "You got us on alcohol addiction. You got us on embezzling uncles. And you did a fine job dragging my supposedly 'sociopathic' father through the gutter. But you won't get us anymore. You know that."

"Take your time, Mr. Colt. Give it some thought. If you decide you'd like to chat, you know where I am."

The phone goes dead. Rafael sits back, scrapes his fingers through his hair, down his face, drags them over his cheeks in long, desperate strokes. More headlines, more press intrusion. He dreads the fight. It hurt him so much when they went after Janey—not just the legal battles or the cost of the injunctions, but the sheer vindictiveness, their desire to tear her apart, one human to another—to see her in only one dimension, as another screwed-up rich kid. All because they believe it's "in the public interest." For what? Because the family has money, which they give to those who need it? *It's not in the public interest*, he thinks, *to strip a young woman—an addict, no less—of her dignity.* She never chose the life or the mess she was born into. Nor did he for that matter. Just let him do what he's intended to do. Let him be a good man, out of the shadow of his father and his grandfather before him.

Let him be good.

"This might cheer you up," says Mimi, handing him a folder.

After two years at Rafael's side, she knows to be thorough, which is why her list of potential holiday destinations spans every corner of the globe, every kind of getaway, and every kind of activity. She does, however, omit to mention that she has instructed the travel agent to come up with ideas for singletons who need to mingle, willingly or otherwise. Rafael sifts through the brochures.

"Safari in Zambia?" suggests Mimi.

"Too dusty."

"Trekking in Nepal?"

"Too cold."

"Kayaking in the Yucatan?"

Rafael eyes her suspiciously. "That sounds like a group activity."

"It is a group activity."

"No group activities."

"Atlas Mountains hideaway?"

He feels his eyes roll back in their sockets.

"The Maldives?"

"Crammed with honeymooning couples? No thank you."

When Rafael isn't looking, Mimi swears at him under her breath. Rafael, meanwhile, takes his attention to the window, where he spots a young woman outside, pacing from one side of the building to the other, as though she is considering but not quite finding the courage to enter. He squints, looks closer, feels his spirits bud. Those flame-red waves are unmistakable—as is that marble white skin, never been near a sunray in its life. He surges forward, presses his forehead to the glass and smiles.

"Francesca," he whispers, willing her to enter the building.

It is a full fifteen minutes until reception calls to say he has a visitor. Either his staff is busy or lazy, or she has taken as much time to approach the receptionist as she has to approach the entrance. Mimi dives for the phone, but Rafael grabs it from her and agrees to accept the guest.

"If you no longer want me to filter the time wasters," Mimi snarls, "I'll go back to my studies. Do you know you have a meeting with HR in two minutes? You don't have time for unscheduled visitors."

"HR can wait," says Rafael. "I pay them. Go plan your honeymoon or something."

A minute later, Francesca Delaney is brought to his door, wearing a '40s shirtwaist dress with cap sleeves and a matching belt, perfectly flattering her delicate frame. He looks at her from his desk, holds his poise, gives nothing away, not even a hint of surprise or curiosity that she has turned up here.

"Nice desk," she says, nervously filling the silence. She hates offices, their visionless sterility, their primary colors and rough seat covers.

Rafael leans back in his chair, keeps her waiting.

"My turn to apologize," she says hurriedly, "for running away. And I, um, wondered if maybe…you fancied…lunch? If you have time."

Rafael looks at his watch, then back at her, lingering over his response, holding her in tiny torture. He knows the answer, of course, but doesn't want to give it up too easily—just in case. He fiddles with a pen cup, flicks the corner of a stack of Post-it Notes, then finally addresses her.

"That sounds like an excellent idea," he says. "Let's do it."

Fran exhales. Torture over.

With Mimi glaring after them, the pair head for the elevator, easing their way with a gentle discussion about where to go, which leads to an agreement that sunny weather requires al fresco, making a picnic the only appropriate option.

⚬────⚬

The sun in their eyes and the breeze in their hair, they walk alongside Regent's Canal until they come to a row of small shops in a side street—a bakery, a delicatessen, and a tiny café with bistro tables on the cobbled roadside.

"For all our picnic needs," says Rafael.

He greets the deli owner like she's an old friend and selects a menagerie of cheeses, olives, cherries, nectarines, rye bread, and wine.

A thrill tingles through Fran's limbs. Mick was right. The risk is worth taking. Suddenly she is rediscovering how lovely it feels to be around someone who attracts her. Even simple tasks, like buying picnic food, become an exotic adventure.

Picnic in hand, they make their way to Rafael's silver Jaguar, which is parked on the next road.

"Now for the important question," he says, opening Fran's door for her. "Where to?"

"Green space," Fran suggests, since it seems quite apparent that Rafael has no intention of returning to his office, that the proposed lunch hour will become a lunch afternoon, possibly an evening, possibly beyond.

"My thoughts exactly," says Rafael.

With an unfamiliar pep in his soul, he ignites the engine and makes a line for the green lung of Epping Forest, where the air is fresh and the sky, bright blue. All those nights alone in bed, heart pounding, palms sweating, terrified that he has lost himself in a world that is meaningless, they are waning. She is here.

⁓⟡⁓

"So how exactly does one discover vintage wedding dresses are their thing?"

Fran lowers her eyelids, thinks carefully—how to explain without having to explain?

"I've always loved clothes. I started small, with a stall selling homemade fascinators, then I guess I got carried away."

"Just the one shop?"

"Oh yes. There's no plan to expand. The secret to my success is the personal care and attention I give each dress. Perhaps the best way to educate you about what I do is to show you." She pauses, dares herself. "Would—would you care to be my plus one? I have two more weddings coming up, of brides that I dressed."

"Two?"

"The summer months are manic. In July, I get more wedding invites than most people get in a lifetime. My brides like to include me, out of politeness or to show their gratitude. I always feel obliged to attend and sometimes I even enjoy myself, but still…" She pauses, takes a breath.

"Sounds like hell to me," says Rafael.

Fran sighs. "I love seeing my dresses in action. I just hate going to these occasions alone. It's the ceremonies—they make me feel so… Well, perhaps if I had a plus one, if you were with me…"

Rafael winces. "I don't know, Fran. As I think you've gathered, I'm not really a wedding kind of person. If you want my honest opinion, I think marriage is a sham, the domain of the deluded."

"Harsh."

"Is it? The number of people I know who are kidding themselves that they've found their ultimate meant-to-be soul mate, when in reality all they've got is someone to distract them from the acres of boredom and loneliness that is human existence… But who knows? Maybe I've got it all wrong."

"Come with me and find out," says Fran, a teasing glint in her eye.

As they pass the turn near Dryad's Hall, her senses prickle. "Will you show me the house?" she says. "I'd really love to see it again, especially the garden."

"I will," says Rafael. "As long as…" He pauses. "As long as there's no wedding dress talk."

Fran smiles. "I promise. At least, I'll do my best."

Rafael swings the car through the gates, up the willow-clad drive. They park at the front, then carry the picnic to the back of the house, over the terrace, and across the lawn, down to the lake and the beautiful ornamental gardens. The sun lays its golden brilliance upon the grass. In the distance, birdsong echoes from the treetops, while nearby, the dragonflies command the water and the bees control the scented bushes of roses and jasmine. In perfect peace, Rafael and Fran drink, eat, and talk. After a second glass of wine, they take a walk.

"This was her vision," says Rafael, as they meander through the narrow cobble pathways, admiring clumps of bamboo, miniature pines, cherry trees, and maples. "She spent years creating it. She wanted something beautiful in her life."

They come to a stop at a wooden bridge overlooking the lake, where fat, pink water lilies float like islands. Fran leans over the balustrade, feels the cool of the water.

"It's lovely."

"I come here when I can," he says, "whenever I need solace or to feel close to her. One of the first things I said to you—"

"She loved gardening."

"You remember?"

"Of course."

"When I was little, I used to imagine this bridge was magical, that if I walked into the middle and whispered my worries across the water, then they'd float away."

"Did it work?"

Rafael laughs ruefully. "It did not."

"And what did you used to worry about?"

"What my mother would say if she could." He looks down, throws a leaf into the water, watches it ripple and spin. "She never spoke, you see. She had… The doctors called it 'elective mutism.' They said she was able to speak but chose not to." He looks up thoughtfully, exposing the sadness behind his eyes. "I never knew the sound of her voice. She had her ways of communicating though. We understood each other. I was told she was perfectly normal before she got married. Her silence began, I gather, not long after the wedding. One morning, the words were gone. My father was patient at first, had her treated at all the best clinics and hospitals, but when nothing made a difference, his tolerance caved and she became an embarrassment to him. That's how she ended up here, in the woods, in Dryad's Hall, tucked away from society, while he carried on with his busy life in the city and at Hammonds."

"Hammonds?"

"Our family's main house up in Norfolk, a huge Palladian mansion in the countryside. It was sold a decade ago, after he died."

"I'm sorry."

"Oh, we weren't close. In some ways his death was a relief, certainly for my mother. He wasn't...the kindest to her at times. We clashed a lot in his final years. We had very different opinions about what to do with the foundation. His wish was to wrap it up, preserve the remaining Colt fortune. I wanted it to expand. The whole point of money is not the money itself but the opportunities it creates, right? The proceeds from Hammonds allowed us to kick-start our school building project. Although I'm sure my father would be turning over in his grave if he knew, especially now that his beloved family seat has been turned into a health spa and conference venue."

Rafael picks up another leaf, turns it over and over in the light, then releases it into the water, where it flips and twists and catches up with the first.

"You accused me of being cold," he says. "I fear life has made me that way. On the surface, the Colt family had everything, but emotionally—where it mattered—we were practically beggars."

Fran's compassion surges. She isn't put off by this candid disclosure, only grateful that he has found the wisdom to look within and the courage to share it. Whether he can do anything about it, maybe that's up to her.

"If you were one of my brides—"

"I'll never be a bride, Fran."

"Hypothetically speaking. If you were one of mine, I'd find you a dress that teaches you to face your past and let go. The war brides were good for that. Or something scratched out of the Great Depression. A dress that proves, regardless of a person's origins, they can learn to rise out of their circumstances and live and love well."

Rafael smiles. "Oh, Fran, they were generous with the sprinkles when they made you."

He offers her a strawberry and wonders quite how he has come to be sitting here in the sunshine, bearing his soul to a vintage wedding dress expert.

"What will you do with the house?"

"My plan was to sell it, but"—he sighs—"letting go is harder than I thought."

"Unfinished business."

"Exactly. Janey and I spent a lot of time here when we were growing up. We'd spend hours in the woods, building dens, playing games and make-believe. We could be children here, with our mother. Everywhere else, we were on show."

"You know I saw her."

Rafael stills.

"When I came here that night, when you wouldn't let me explain, I felt I saw her—not a ghost, just a sense of her, through the dress."

"We said no dress talk."

"*Please*," says Fran. "Just listen a moment. Hear me out. You said it yourself, she stopped talking after her wedding day. The thing is, I saw film footage from the ceremony. She had a bandage on her hand. You can't tell me that was a fashion accessory, not after I watched her—*felt* her—punch a mirror."

Rafael looks down, avoids Fran's gaze, uncomfortable with the conversation.

"She was in pain, Raf. Like I've never known. I felt it. Through the dress. Through her. She didn't want it. She didn't want the marriage. She was scared."

Rafael just stares at the water, at his own face disfigured in the reflection. He grips the balustrade and inhales deeply, as though the tug of his lungs will pull the pain back inside him again.

"I come from a long line of bad men, Fran," he says, unable to look at her. "It's always in the back of my mind that their cruel narcissism might well be indelible. You need to be careful. I can't promise I won't fuck up. Wedded bliss? All I've ever been shown is how to poison it."

Fran shuts her eyes. "But you're on the bridge," she says softly, masking her own tremulous fear. "They're just worries. Throw them into the water."

"If it were only that simple," says Rafael, taking her in his arms.

"But hey, this conversation is getting far too serious for such a lovely day." He kisses her softly, strokes her cheek.

The sensation sends sparks of pleasure through her skin. She feels unreal, suspended in a bubble of elation, as though she is bouncing along in a fine, fresh sky. Does he feel it like she does, flowering inside, gradually unfolding, that willingness to put aside barriers and doubts, to be vulnerable, be real, walk to the edge? Suddenly it occurs to her how unpracticed she is at all of this. She knows the rules. She has spent enough time with brides, read enough romantic fiction, but with her own heart...she is a novice.

*How did this happen? And he doesn't even like weddings!*

"Come on," he says. "Let me show you the orchard and the wisteria and the field where we used to keep goats."

"You kept goats?"

"And a horse. And seven rabbits. And then there were all the badgers that came at night...and the hedgehogs and the squirrels... although, technically, they were wild. Perk of living in a forest."

"You don't strike me as an animal person."

"Ah, Fran, trust me, I'm full of surprises."

"Well, that's good, because I love surprises. Nice ones, anyhow."

They fall in line together and wander through the summer haze, the sweet green grass at their feet, the gnats circling in the sunlight above them. They are both oblivious to time, lost in their uneasy euphoria, the prospect of all that they have to find out about each other rippling outward like an endless sheet of silk.

Lunch turns into evening, which then turns into an untethered, billowing weekend, in which London and everything it has to offer becomes their playground. They drive through the city, walk in Green Park, row on the Serpentine, admire samurai suites and Islamic silks at the Victoria and Albert Museum, ancient animal bones at the Natural History Museum, and strange, silent canvasses at the Tate. They rent bikes and cycle east, where they buy fresh flowers, eat pastries, and drink rhubarb gin on a rooftop in Hackney. They talk about everything, from politics to pop music, but they both stay away from the topic of the Alessandra Colt wedding dress—for fear of spoiling the magic.

The decadence ends at Rafael's Thameside apartment, where they finish the evening with glasses of rich, red merlot on the roof terrace. The apricot sky and the twinkling lights of London—a tiny theater set with cranes, power lines, and high-rises—creates a glittering canvas behind them.

"Are you happy?" says Rafael, the evening sun catching his eyes.

"Are you kidding?" says Fran. "This has been the loveliest—not to mention longest—lunch date I've ever had."

Rafael sighs, pulls Fran toward him. The way she flutters around him in floral chiffon, like a rare butterfly, he wants to snatch her from the air, trap her in the cup of his hand, and hold on to her forever, because just one moment with her has the power to eradicate the burden of a lifetime. No woman—apart from Mimi and sometimes Janey—has crossed this threshold before. Normally on the weekends, he goes to the gym, cooks, reads, surfs Netflix, or falls asleep early—but here she is, smoldering on his roof terrace with her compendium of vintage regalia, her tumbling hair and constant curiosity. She is an invader, and yet, she is a salve, the antidote to everything that is wrong with his world.

Never mind the merlot. He pushes it aside, leans in, and kisses her, feels her heart pound against his ribs, feels her curving into his arms. As his hands trace the skin of her neck, she gasps with pleasure and smiles with her eyes closed.

She wants him so much, but he too is an invader. No man, not for a decade, has come this close to her. She dares not lose herself in the fire, getting too close, too fast. Heart thumping, she pulls away, calms her breath.

He understands—she needs time. The moonlight leads them to the bedroom, where they fall onto the sheets, find the perfect spoon, entwine their limbs, and sleep in deepest peace, their bodies pressed tight together.

Seven o'clock Monday morning brings a reality check as the indomitable Mimi lets herself in and parks breakfast—protein smoothies, wheatgrass shots, and pastrami bagels—on the white kitchen island, then begins making coffee. It is strange to Fran that the mundane act of preparing breakfast should be the responsibility of someone else, someone like Mimi, an employee/substitute wife. Still muddled from sleep, Fran acknowledges her with a smiley yawn and wonders what she has to say about her and Rafael's paired emergence from his bedroom.

Mimi just scowls, suggesting she has little regard for messy bed hair and sleepovers. She hands Rafael a mug, reels off his list of meetings and appointments, then slices his bagel into halves.

"Is she going to feed you now?" whispers Fran.

Rafael doesn't get the joke or at least doesn't smile. "I have to get into the office by nine," he says, "but please, Fran, stay as long as you like. Make yourself comfortable."

"But not too comfortable," says Mimi, eyeing her.

Fran is glad when the two of them leave, all suited for business, and she is finally able to exhale and absorb the charmed folly of the situation, not to mention the heavenly blast of white that seems to be all around her. The impressive stats of Rafael's penthouse apartment—two hundred square meters overlooking the Thames— cannot compensate for its bachelor sterility. Every wall, ceiling, furnishing and fitting is white. Even the floors are white. As Fran walks through it, she is dazzled, feels unreal, as though she is having an out-of-body experience.

She eats Rafael's leftover bagel and showers in the one thing that isn't white, the en suite bathroom—its bronze-flecked stone tiles creating a cocoon-like coziness. The shower is so high-tech, with a computer screen instead of a trusty tap, it takes ten minutes to work out what to do. The water cascades like a rainstorm. She has never had a wash like it.

*Rafael. Rafael. Mr. Rafael Colt.* As the water drenches her, she rolls his name around in her head, then dares herself to test it for fit: *Mrs. Francesca Colt.* Her insides quiver at the thought—that butterfly sweetheart gladness. It feels wonderful…and so, so dangerous.

After showering and dressing, in the white silence, Fran doesn't know what to do with herself. She flops on the sofa, tries the massive TV, discovers it is set on rolling news. If she had a TV at home, particularly one the size of a cinema screen, she wouldn't watch wall-to-wall reality. Too depressing. Fantasy is better.

Agitated by the sight of politicians arguing, she switches it off and wanders around the apartment. She sees piles of papers relating to Rafael's work, leaflets about gyms; books about philosophy, sports, and architecture; but nothing familial. Nothing to link him to Alessandra and Lyle or his beloved Dryad's Hall. No keepsakes, no photographs, no personal items. Almost as though he has come from the air.

Restless, she goes through to the bedrooms, strokes her fingers along the satin finish of the walls, jumps on the immaculate guest beds, plumps the cushions, throws them, then plumps them again. The walk-in wardrobe calls to her. *What of his clothes?* Most of the rods are empty. The ones that are occupied contain a somber display of gray and black shirts and high-quality suits, all dry-cleaned and pressed—very impressive, not very fun.

And then, on a sideboard by the bed, she spies a scrap of paper, scrawled with the words: *Janey new phone: 07591 3788678.* Fran picks it up, thinks for a moment, turning it over and over in her hand. She then grabs her phone, notes down the number, and leaves.

"What's with you?" says Mick as Fran enters the shop, gripping a double-shot espresso, the pallor of her skin giving away the decadence of her weekend. "Too good for Walthamstow now?"

She is grateful for the sight of him, a face from her old life pulling her back to the comfort of the familiar.

"I was waiting for the call—*come and hang out, Mick, I'm bored*—but it looks like you got a sweeter offer."

"Sweet for now," says Fran.

"Don't tell me...you've joined a Colt?"

"Ha, very funny."

"So...?"

"Oh, Mick," Fran sighs, her eyes shining with bliss. "We had the most incredible weekend."

"Yes!" says Mick. "At last!"

Fran grins, fluffs the tulle skirt of the '50s ballerina dress, straightens the strings of pearls and flower garlands, rearranges the drapes of wedding lace that decorate the mirrors. She cannot hold her happiness in. "Honestly, against my better judgment, it just feels so right. In some peculiar way, we're perfect for each other. I know you wouldn't put us together, but maybe that's the point. Love isn't obvious. It emerges in places you'd least expect it to. I wonder if the dress—"

Fran winces, catches sight of the Alessandra Colt dress in the corner, its secrets still locked inside the folds of its silk. Is she a fool? Is she naive to think that Rafael's soul, behind his aloof cynicism, is a good match for hers—a romance-obsessed wedding dress enthusiast? No one, she reasons, in simple surprise, has come close to the boundary of her heart in a decade. *And now here is Rafael.* And it is happening so fast, so intensely, without her even being sure of who he is.

She has seen several sides of him now: charming, intelligent, humble, loyal, generous, confident…and cold…and full of rage. Who is he really? The excitement of him clouds with thoughts of Alessandra, the unflattering best man remarks, and Rafael's own proclamation: *I come from a long line of bad men.*

Meanwhile, from behind the shapely form of the ivory 1930s backless, satin, bias-cut number, the waterfall train of which he has just reattached, Mick is watching, anxiously observing the shadow that is gathering behind his friend's optimism.

"Three more customers have asked about it, you know," he says. "One of them wanted to buy it there and then, offered me five grand. I had to promise her you'd be in touch as soon as you're ready to find a match for it, but honestly, if we don't off-load it soon—"

"We're not selling it yet," she says.

Mick eyes her cautiously. "Never covet," he warns.

"I know, I know," she sighs. "But I can't pass it on until…until I know I can *trust* it."

"Trust? That's a big word, Fran."

Fran shrugs.

"I'm happy for you, girl," he says quietly, "but pace yourself, won't you? It wasn't that long ago that we were bitching about what a rude, grumpy arsehole Rafael is. You know how protective I am of you—the sister I never had. I just want to be sure you're sound, that's all."

Fran smiles, tries to hide the discomfort his cautionary tone gives her. She values Mick's opinion more than anyone's. He has known her since the days she first started selling homemade fascinators in Camden Market and was there at the beginning of the Whispering

Dress. He has helped her find magnificent vintage wedding paraphernalia in the unlikeliest of places, managed to charm her most
nervous customers, and indulged every whim of her whisperer's
research—visits to old churches, tea with grandchildren, sifting
through mountains of census records, wedding certificates, and
faded love letters. Above all, however, he has been an ally during her
bleakest hours.

That aching hollowness returns to her suddenly. All those years
she lived as a living ghost, a body with no feelings, desperate to believe
that the magic of true love was still out there somewhere, whispering
from the shadows. She shuts her eyes, momentarily returns to the
cold of the bathroom floor, where night after night, she lay sobbing.
In the grip of such sorrow, her senses prickled to life, put out the
alert: *Stay safe. Stay guarded.*

The dress looms in front of her like a marital specter.

"Who are you?" she whispers, willing it to reply.

Maybe all Rafael needs is the right person in his life, a person
who knows how to use the past for good, who can help him open
his eyes, face his story, and learn to accept, learn to let go. Bolstered
by this thought, Fran picks out the threads of a loose loop of beads.
One of the hummingbirds needs attention—its wing has come away
from the silk of the train.

She smiles again, tells herself to be brave, take a chance. "Look at
this embroidery!" she exclaims. "Exquisite! Every bit of it! Honestly,
Mick, the train alone must have been weeks of work, months even.
Everything hand stitched, every detail perfect. I only hope Alessandra
appreciated how lucky she was."

"Come on," Mick urges. "Let's at least get this big-arse gown photographed and online before you become an obsessive."

"Okay, okay. But I'm not selling it…not until I know for sure."

Once the last bead has been repaired, they hold it high, brush it down, and shape it around a tailor's dummy. It looks radiant and Fran cannot help but feel proud of its rejuvenation. She places it in front of an old cast-iron mantelpiece that Mick salvaged from a scrapper's yard, then stages the surroundings with her velvet chaise longue, a violin, a cut-glass decanter, and an assortment of shells and lace samples. She is, after all, selling a dream, a whimsical fantasy of history. There is nothing more dispiriting in the world of bridal wear than a joyless online sales photo. All those unremarkable gowns dangling glibly from wire coat hangers, sometimes with dry-cleaning film still wrapped around them, against a backdrop of a hallway or someone's dreary bedroom. A whispering dress needs an entire stage set.

Fran and Mick take a series of photos, adjust the light, play with filters, add a few more knickknacks, then take more and more photos until Fran is finally happy she has captured the true essence of the extravagance of the Alessandra Colt dress.

She uploads the photos to her website and adds a brief description:

*Captivating, rare House of Garrett-Alexia 1950s silk and lace wedding gown. One of a kind. Richly embellished hummingbird/lily detail. Four-meter train. Near perfect condition.*

"There," she says, with an air of reluctant pride. "It's done. Let's see what interest we get."

But in her heart, although she doesn't admit this to Mick, she hopes there is none.

"Thanks for meeting me," says Fran, a little nervous as she approaches the table.

The venue, a coffee shop in a slightly dilapidated Georgian town house opposite Hampstead Heath, was Janey's choice. Janey sits by a window, staring at nothing, her latte going cold. She turns, gives Fran a vague smile, then looks back to the window, to the street and the world beyond. The bruise from her fall is still visible, a faded purple-yellow bloom down the side of her face, but otherwise, she seems brighter. There is color in her cheeks, and her hair, still a nest of dreadlocks, has been twisted with wildflowers and piled into a bun.

Fran wonders how to begin. "I helped take you to the hospital with your brother a few weeks ago, when you hit your head. I wanted to check that you were okay, and, well, if you don't mind, ask a few questions about your mother."

Janey looks blank.

Fran wonders, despite explaining herself over the phone, if she even remembers. She feels foolish suddenly, embarrassed by the absurd depths her wedding dress obsession lures her to, all in the name of "fieldwork." She privately berates herself, makes to leave just as Janey looks up.

"Oh yes!" she exclaims, addressing Fran directly, eyes springing wide. "I remember! You were at the house, weren't you? I chatted with you in the drive. You were climbing out of a dumpster for some random reason…and then Rafael came along… That was a fight, huh? Same old, same old."

"Something like that," says Fran, guessing Janey has drawn a blank on the stair incident. *How odd*, she thinks, *to lose chunks of your life like that. How sad.* "You look well," she says encouragingly.

Janey sighs. "Do I? I feel like shit. Here, you haven't got any tobacco on you, have you?"

"I don't smoke, sorry."

Janey rubs her arms. "I'm literally roasting for a nicotine fix."

"Would you—would you like to go for a walk?" says Fran. "It's beautiful out."

"Sure. Um…who exactly are you by the way?"

Fran stiffens, caught in the flare of her morality. "I'm an acquaintance of your brother's. My name is Francesca, but call me Fran."

"You're not press, are you? I'm under strict instructions not to talk to journalists. Not after last time. Raf'll kill me."

"I'm definitely not press. I sell vintage wedding dresses, as it goes."

Janey perks up. "*Oh?* Are you and Raf…?"

"Not quite!" says Fran, blushing, brushing away the inference. "We've spent some time together, but in all honesty, I barely know him. The main reason I'm here, I suppose, is because he passed on a wedding dress that belonged to your mother. My plan is to sell it to a worthy bride, but I need to know more about it."

Janey pauses. Her gaze shifts upward. "That old thing? I didn't know it was still around."

"We found it during the clearance, tucked away in a wardrobe… almost as though someone wanted it forgotten."

"Wouldn't surprise me. She was a peculiar breed, my mother."

"Oh?"

"I mean, take one guess why I'm such a fuckup. Although I'm still not sure what it's got to do with you."

"Can we walk? I'll explain."

Janey glances at the wall clock. "I've got an appointment in twenty minutes," she says cannily. "If you buy me a packet of smokes, that twenty minutes is yours."

"Deal."

As they walk in the sun, over the heath, Janey shivers, her thin limbs addled by the cold and chemicals.

"I was wondering…I know your family had some difficulties, that your mother, Alessandra, didn't talk."

"Wow. Privy to the Colt Family vault? Raf must like you."

"It came up, that's all. He didn't say much on the matter. In fact, he got quite cagey. If I'm honest, it felt like he was holding something back. There's a sadness in him." She looks at Janey, sees it suddenly. "And in you. The Colt Foundation is so well regarded. Your parents had a wholesome public image, and yet you and Rafael paint a very different picture of behind the scenes."

Janey shrinks, unnerved by the observance. "So we're a fucked-up rich family pretending to be marvelous? What's new?"

"What do you mean, 'pretending'?"

"The precious Colt name, it cannot be sullied. Which is why bad apples like me get erased from the public eye."

"Oh, surely it's not like that. Rafael just wants you sober. He worries for you."

"Says his girlfriend of two weeks."

"I'm not… We're not…" Fran hesitates, scared to declare her connection to Raf. To her relief, Janey talks over her.

"I thought we were here to talk about my mother, not me. I get enough psychobabble from good Saint Rafael—"

"Fine. I'm happy to stick with your mother, but just so you know, for what it's worth, I'm not convinced your brother is that much of a saint."

Janey smiles, seduced by this co-conspiracy, but now Fran feels uncomfortable. She never had siblings. She always longed for them, for that particular familial closeness that couldn't be rivaled by friends or lovers. But this, this is closeness gone awry.

"So tell me," Janey says. "Are you and Raf an item? He never lets me meet his girlfriends. Not that he ever keeps them long enough for me to meet."

Fran blinks, unsure what to say—the wish to know and yet not know. "Has he ever had a long-term relationship?" she ventures.

"Are you kidding? The eternal bachelor? Raf's idea of romance is a one-night stand, which is why it's rather impressive that you're still hanging around him. You must mean something. Usually he doesn't let anyone past the defenses, apart from his witch of an assistant and his cleaner."

Fran frowns although is quietly grateful that someone else has seen the cow in Mimi. "You make him sound like an arsehole."

Janey shrugs, lights a cigarette. "Look, you seem like a nice girl," she says through a mouthful of smoke. "But I'm warning you, Rafael worries about no one but himself. He's an island, hard to reach. My hunch is he resents being the chosen one."

"The chosen one?"

"Surely you've heard the phrase *heir and a spare*? Well, you're looking at the spare right now." She yawns, stretches. "Plus, I look like my mum, which probably didn't help my plight. No doubt I just reminded my father of his dumb wife and that put him off, but there you go."

Fran slows, faces the sun and the expanse of heathland ahead. "So, about the wedding dress," she says, keen to move on from the discomfort of Rafael's faults. "I've seen footage from her wedding day—"

"*Her* wedding day?"

"Your mother's."

"Are you sure you don't mean my *grand*mother's? The dress was originally made for her back in the '50s...1953? 1954 maybe? As a Colt family ambassador, I'm supposed to know this stuff, except, technically, I'm not allowed to be an ambassador anymore, because of all of the, you know...glug-glug, snort-snort!"

But Fran is distracted, her thoughts elsewhere. Two owners, grandmother and mother? Perhaps this explains the alterations in the waist. It also allows for the conflict of eras. Garrett-Alexia was defunct by the time of Alessandra and Lyle's wedding in 1978 but was at its peak in the early 1950s.

"What was her name, your grandmother?"

"Janice, my namesake."

"Was she...like you?"

"A drunk, you mean?"

"No, I mean chatty, friendly."

"Hardly. I'd say waspish at best. We were all terrified of her."

"But she got a heck of a wedding dress."

"She loved attention and extravagance. And, yes, if you must know, she liked a drink. The rumor, on the inside, is that *she* was the reason my grandfather set up a charitable foundation, so he could stop her from blowing his entire fortune on gambling and parties."

Fran nods slowly. Usually the challenge of slotting the pieces of a wedding dress puzzle together is the most thrilling part of her work, but this, this feels daunting.

"The footage was definitely from your mother's wedding," she continues. "But she wore the same dress."

"I expect she didn't have a choice in the matter. Old Janice trying to live out her past glories via her poor, put-upon daughter-in-law. Janice was a control freak. They all were."

"I noticed your mother had a bandage on her hand. I think she might have hurt it the night before the wedding."

Janey shrugs. "So?"

"Did your parents…did they have a difficult marriage?"

"Well, generally things *are* difficult when you're in the Colt family. Are you sure you're not press?"

"I promise. I'm only asking because the dress is worth a lot of money, thousands possibly."

"Is it, now?"

"Yes. And I hope to restore it and give it a new life with another bride, but in my line of work, I can't pass it on unless I know its true provenance, the energy it's inherited."

"Inherited?" says Janey. "If that dress has inherited anything from *my* family, I'd say it's better off locked away."

Fran stills.

"Oh, look at that…we're two minutes over. Well, thanks for the smokes. I better go, otherwise I'll miss my appointment. Maybe see you around."

She walks away, but a few steps in, turns back to Fran, gives another of those strange, unreadable smiles.

"All of us have our pasts, right?"

"Of course," says Fran, unsure whether she is being teased or consoled.

# chapter 5

CEDARS IS EVERYTHING A GEORGIAN COUNTRY MANSION SHOULD be—harmonious lines of stone stucco fascia and large, well-proportioned windows, capped with a parapet roof, all neatly positioned within an elegant landscaped park. *They knew*, thinks Fran, *those old-day aristocrats, fresh from their Grand Tours and hand-written pages of romantic poetry, how to extol the natural virtues of their surroundings.* The grounds have suffered a multitude of insults including car parking, a gym complex, and the scourge of too much low-maintenance ground cover—purple slate chippings, bark mulch, and pea gravel—but the lawns and tree-lined vistas retain the essence of sweeping eighteenth-century garden design. Up the hill behind the house, she spies a mock ancient temple and, to the side, a lake with an island. She would like, very much, to step inside the silk slippers of the past, to see girls in empire-waist day dresses and men in boots and breeches, on their way to a Regency ball, but instead, she is greeted by a parade of glitter-covered human statues.

The estate itself has been harried into the modern era with a glass extension and multicolored LED downlights that bathe the aged sandstone walls in magenta, turquoise, and neon yellow. A full bar has been fitted in the former ballroom; a bowling alley, game room, and cinema in the cellars; a basketball court in the drawing room; and the upstairs chambers have been turned into spa suites of various sizes.

The theatrics build to a crescendo at the entrance gates, where waiters in clip-on bow ties hand out pink champagne against a backdrop of illuminated fountain water. The bride, Rachel Joseph née Pointer, and her groom, Elijah, proceed up the drive applauded by their guests and flanked by two stout miniature ponies wearing glittery bridles and fake unicorn horns. Rachel and Elijah both smile continuously, but neither look comfortable.

"What *were* we thinking?" says Rachel, nudging her new husband.

"Don't look at me," he says. "This was all your idea."

"I think," she whispers, as a flock of white doves flutter overhead. "I think I might have gotten a bit carried away. I told the planners to go all-out, but…did I really agree to these funny little horses?"

Elijah shakes his head and smiles. "Good thing I love you, Mrs. Joseph."

"I love you too, Elijah. But I tell you what. When we renew our vows in ten years' time, let's hire a room in a pub, drink some cider, and eat pies."

"That," says Elijah, squeezing his bride around the waist, "sounds like a great idea. You look lovely by the way. Not the kind of dress I thought you'd go for, but…it's charming."

"It's vintage," says Rachel. "Chosen especially for me."

They kiss, too love-bombed to resent the crazed pomposity of their day. The guests cheer, over three hundred of them, mostly adults, all in for a night to remember. Thankfully the weather gods have smiled and Rachel has been granted her wish of sunshine.

"This is a wedding venue on steroids," whispers Rafael as he and Fran find a peaceful corner of the knot garden to sip their drinks and watch the procession.

"It takes all sorts," says Fran. "You wouldn't believe some of the places I've been—barns, backyards, beaches, pub back rooms, forest glades, muddy fields. These days, anything goes."

"I didn't know there were so many ways to use crushed velvet and zebrawood veneer. And if I see another drop crystal chandelier, I think I might need a migraine tablet."

Fran smiles, nervous of his sarcasm.

"In fact, the only thing that doesn't scream bling is...the dress."

"Thank you," says Fran, gazing at Rachel as she parades up the drive, the blousy Victorian gown fluttering in the breeze, its cut so pretty and honest. "That's the point. I matched her with a dress that provides the antidote to her fixation on...excess. To be honest, she resisted when she first saw it, but as soon as she tried it on, its energy enveloped her, brought her back to the heart of what really matters in life."

"Which is?"

"As if you don't know."

Rafael shrugs. Somewhere in the distance, a string quartet starts rehearsing Puccini. The music drifts toward them, wraps them in its tremulous, soaring joy.

"Love," says Fran as though it is obvious. "True love. The dress that Rachel is wearing came from a girl who married for nothing but."

"How romantic," says Rafael drily.

"Isn't it?" says Fran, hopeful she can raise Rafael's opinion of betrothal. "There are many reasons why couples decide to tie the knot, but from my experience, the marriages that last and work have love at their core."

"I would have thought that was obvious."

"You'd be surprised how confused people get. Some brides fall into the trap of thinking they should marry because it's 'the next step' or because everyone around them is doing it and they don't want to get left behind. Some do it because they believe it's a mark of success or that it might prove a point to an ex. Others hope a marriage will mean they're provided for. Or that a sealed deal will give them more control over their partner's behavior. Some simply don't want to let their partner down. And some, some are forced."

"When you put it like that…"

"Whispering dresses have a lot of work to do."

The sun arcs over them. As the party expands—photographs on the lawn, a sweets cart and Pimm's, the string quartet playing rock ballads—Fran and Rafael huddle closer. Within so much spectacle, their number one interest is each other.

"My mother," says Fran, smoothing the skirts of her blush-pink organza dress—one of her favorite wedding guest efforts, originally worn to the first ball of the season by a debutante in 1954—"used to say that time is like a limitless sheet of silk, spread across the universe, always happening at once and together. The past doesn't stop existing just because we're no longer in it. I believe my dresses carry their pasts within in them, like archives of life, and that they pass this energy on to whomever wears them next."

Rafael smiles. "Cute idea, but you're crazy."

"Well, it's better than being dull. And I make brides happy." Her eyes brighten. "My job is to encourage good, healthy love."

Rafael stiffens, adjusts the collar of his shirt. How did he get here? How did he agree to attend not one but two weddings in the company of this otherworldly woman with her shop full of wedding sprinkles and absurd ideas about love and time travel?

"The energy has to be right of course," Fran persists. "There are challenges involved. I get particularly fretful about brides who try to marry under pressure, grabbing the hand of the nearest, next, or nicest available suitor because their family expects them to, or their friends, or their body clock, or their god. There are very few dresses that can ignite a love that simply isn't meant to exist in the first place...yet still, the modern world is brimming with ill-conceived proposals."

She stares at Rafael now, his thoughtful eyes, his air rarefied, then sips the last of her champagne, musters her courage. "What would you say if I told you I've become rather fond of your mother's old wedding dress?"

"I'd say it will be a blessing when that damn thing is gone from my life."

"Along with every other trace of your family," she whispers without quite intending to.

"What do you mean by that?"

"I mean, it feels like you're, I don't know, blocked...that there's a wall between you and your past."

"Is there, now?"

"Just an observation."

Rafael shakes his head. "You're one of a kind, that's for sure."

A commotion on the lawn draws their attention. A group of men in gray-and-blue suits step aside as the women rush into the middle, studding the grass with their heels.

"She's going to throw the bouquet," Fran exclaims.

"Stand back," Rafael suggests.

"Believe me, I always do. Just because I sell wedding dresses, doesn't mean..."

The guests fall silent as Rachel takes her position at the head of the crowd and, picturesque in her cotton dress, waves her elaborate bouquet aloft. The women, a gaggle of floral prints and faun-colored bodycon, raise their arms. Fran ducks farther inside the cave of hedgerows.

"Three, two, one..."

Despite the vigor of Rachel's throw, the weight of the bouquet sends it hurtling to the side. It skims a sea of eager fingertips, is nearly grabbed by a tall woman in cerise, then batted out of hand, onward toward the knot garden, where it crashes over the hedge and lands at Rafael's feet. He and Fran look at each other.

"Oh," says Fran.

"Oh dear," says Rafael.

He picks the bouquet up, stares at it, then offers it to her.

"I think, by rights," he says quietly, "this should be yours, but—"

Five women with clawlike manicures come diving and cackling through the hedges.

"Mine!"

"No, it's mine!"

Peppered by a peculiar mix of fear and amusement, Fran throws it back to them.

"Let's get out of here," she says. "We have another wedding to attend remember?"

"As if I could forget."

Across London, on the fringes of Streatham, left to her own devices, Melissa West has taken her discovery of bold color to a new level. The community hall is an explosion of orange, green, and blue, with scarlet ribbons on every chair, to match her dress. Fran stands in the middle of this kaleidoscopic vision and grins. Who could deny her work has been done, as Melissa glides from guest to guest, brimming with confidence, telling them all about her wonderful dress and the slightly incongruous tropical theme she has last minute alighted upon? Meanwhile, the cousins and sisters scowl beneath a trio of fake palm trees and make a point of not catching Fran's eye. They are, however, keenly interested in the tall handsome man at her side, who looks wealthy and slick and a little bit familiar, like a celebrity, but surely not, not on the arm of that weird, silly woman.

There is a hog roast, a buffet of finger food, a photo booth, a slightly pervy magician, a fake ivy archway, a white chocolate fountain, fairy lights, and a light-up disco floor. The onslaught of wedding pizzazz—hit with everything Melissa and Rob can throw at it—is also overrun by children; a dizzying contrast to the Rachel Joseph née Pointer affair, in which under-sixteens, aside from a few carefully vetted bridesmaids, were notably absent. This one is a free-for-all. Everywhere Fran and Rafael look, they are there—by the buffet, chasing tangled strings of bunting; on the porch, throwing leftover confetti; and on the dance floor, teenage boys anguishing in three-piece suits while girls in taffeta minidresses make teasing moves to wind them up, the game of love in its infancy.

This time, Fran and Rafael use the chocolate fountain as their refuge. They hover behind the veil of sweetness, their view of the festivities obscured by an enormous inflatable flamingo. Fran dips a strawberry, then a marshmallow, then a chunk of waffle.

Rafael politely declines the offer of a skewer and, instead, makes an inspection of the cheese board. "Edam? I haven't eaten that since I was at school."

Fran cannot tell whether he is being polite or sarcastic. She prods him with the point of her cocktail umbrella.

"Be honest," she says. "Do you hate it?"

"I wouldn't go that far. It's just…"

A waitress comes by to refill their tumblers of "special cocktail."

Rafael offers his cup to Fran to say cheers. "Thank you," he says, "for introducing me to the extraordinary world of provincial weddings."

After the buffet, the dancing begins. They watch the revelers shimmy in and out of the light. Melissa and her new husband are in the center of it all, waving their arms, swaying and singing. The husband, Fran notices, is drunker than he should be. He staggers more than walks and has spillages down his semi-unbuttoned shirt. A shame, thinks Fran, given how gorgeous and well turned out his new wife is.

Eventually Melissa twirls over, the marabou trim of her stole fluttering like baby hair.

"You look like you're enjoying your day," says Fran smiling. "I'm so pleased for you, Melissa."

"It's all in the dress, you know," Melissa whispers tipsily. "I'm never taking it off. Is this your plus one? Hello, sir. Don't you two make a lovely pair? Any wedding bells on the horizon yet?"

"Oh, no," gasps Fran.

"Maybe one day," says Rafael, to her surprise—and his.

Fran blinks at him.

He just shrugs, the disco lights tracking in front of his eyes.

"No hurry though, hey?" says Melissa, saving the moment with her witless excitement. "I guess you spend too much time dealing with other people's big days? Puts you off. Like my Rob. He earns his living building houses, but will he put up a set of shelves for me on the weekend? Not a chance. I still love him though."

As Melissa spins away, Fran hugs her own waist.

"So that was bride number two?" says Rafael. "And what was her whispering dress requirement? Don't tell me…needs toning down?"

"The opposite actually," says Fran. "But you saying that makes me realize my success. Melissa was actually quite insecure when she first came to see me and now look at her."

"A red wedding disco diva with feathers."

"Exactly," says Fran, the zeal bursting out of her, filling the space between her and Rafael.

She smiles, remembering a story she'd heard from one of Meryl Percy's old friends of how Mr. Percy would walk to the end of their street every night to make sure Meryl got back safely, never mind the fact that she'd spent all day in a car factory handling dangerous engine parts. She hopes, in his way, Rob will do the same for Melissa. And perhaps Rafael might do the same for her.

The car enters the weave of Walthamstow streets. The non-wedding-day world is cognizant again, the close-packed coffee shops and bright boutiques all competing for attention through the traffic-clogged roads. Rafael pulls up outside the Whispering Dress. Fran is excited to see Mick has begun work on a new window display—art deco magnificence, an explosion of sunbursts, zigzags, and cocktail shakers to show off the fabulous '30s fishtail with its flawless ivory satin, narrow sleeves, and floor-sweeping hem. It was designed by an Anglo-American designer who liked to drape tall women, but despite its cute story—a pilot and an heiress who fell in love on a transatlantic flight—she knows it will be a devil to match. Unless she can find an unusually tall woman in need of a shot of old-school glamour.

"Here," says Rafael, opening the car door for Fran, "your spiritual home." He hesitates, not quite ready to separate or burst the Fran bubble. "I'll see you in."

As they approach, however, they see that the front door is ajar, even though the shop should be closed. Rafael makes space for Fran to pass, but they both stop short when they notice gouges on the doorframe, as though the lock has been forced open.

Dread forms in the pit of Fran's stomach. The door swings wide. Her eyes survey the scene. "Oh...oh no!" She drops her keys and runs inside, falls to her knees. "My shop!" she cries.

Rafael follows behind, blinks at the mess. The Whispering Dress, Fran's vintage wedding wonderland, is now a disfigured muddle, furniture upturned, china smashed, pins and buttons and sequins everywhere, and white upon white, her wedding gowns pulled off their mannequins, thrown around like worthless rags. A shaft of anger slices through him. When she'd first showed her shop to him, he'd been dismissive, put off by such matrimonial excess, but now—now that he is tuning in to the nuances of her quirks, discovering what they mean—this...*this* is not just an attack on the Whispering Dress, but on her, his love, who she is, what she does. Who has dared to do this? He lowers to comfort her but knows there is little he can say.

Her mind is jumbled, wretched. Her beautiful dresses, her incredible historic dresses—all the veils, the tiaras, the flower garlands, her mother's wedding lace. Her research, the newspaper cuttings, love letters, photographs—and the wall of dead grooms, beacon of hope when the manners of modern man elude her, all torn and scattered across the floor. She stares in despair at the ragged mess.

But there is something missing.

As the realization drains through her, she looks up, eyes wide with alarm.

"The dress!" she gasps, cupping her mouth with her hand. "Oh god, the dress...Alessandra's dress...it's gone!"

A sickening thought begins to grizzle in her stomach, bourgeoning dismay that she may have brought this trouble upon herself, after displaying such a valuable dress for all to see across her website. Rafael sighs, rubs her shoulders, contemplates the empty sewing table where the dress once lay.

"I never thought I'd say this," he says, "but I want it back. At least I want *you* to have it back."

"Francesca?" Rishi from the chicken shop appears at the door. "Oh, Francesca, are you okay?" Mouth open, he hands Fran a box of chicken. "I came to bring you your favorite hickory wings, thought you might be hungry, but…what on earth's happened?"

"There's been a break-in," says Rafael, eyeing Rishi warily.

Fran sniffs, wipes her cheeks, nods between them. "Rafael meet Rishi. Rishi meet Rafael. Did you see anything?"

Rishi shrugs. He loves Fran, loves seeing what she wears each day. The dainty, old-fashioned cuts of her dresses, the peculiar footwear, the fanciful bags—they are the antidote to all those gray tracksuit bottoms and football shirts, uniform of the bloke that he has to endure over the road among the fryers. "Sorry, Fran. I was in the kitchen all day. We were short staffed. The guys would have said if they'd seen any trouble."

He thinks for a moment. "Come to think of it, they did mention someone. Earlier today, they mentioned a young woman hanging about. I just assumed it was one of your ladies, but the thing is, they kept going on about her, ridiculing her, because she had this…crazy hair"—he gestures big curls around his head—"like dreadlocks, with flowers in them."

Rafael pales, shuts his eyes, rocks back on his heels. "Oh, Fran," he says, the exasperation raining down on him. "I'm so sorry. I know exactly where we'll find the dress. You better come with me."

They jump into Rafael's Jaguar and speed toward the West Way. Rafael drives like he's entitled, faster and pushier than anyone else on the road.

"She must have found out I gave it to you," he says, hands tense around the wheel. "Then got wind that it's worth something and looked up your address. I tell you, she's something else."

Fran bristles, remembering the conversation with Janey on the heath. She'd made it clear that the dress was valuable but hadn't sensed any interest on Janey's part. Then again, maybe it is never wise to rely on the surface reactions of Colt family members.

"Perhaps—perhaps she hopes to wear it herself?" Fran replies sadly. "I mean, it is kind of hers by rights, given it was worn by her grandmother and mother."

Rafael scoffs. "Janey doesn't care about the dress, Fran. She'll sell it, take whatever amount she can get for it, then spend the money getting wasted. She used to steal from me all the time—watches, books, laptops. Once I came home to find she'd stripped my kitchen of small appliances. I'd go to pay for things and then somehow, out of nowhere, my wallet would be empty. When I put a stop to it, she started shoplifting. She's been up in court three times."

"But why does she need to steal? Surely she has money?"

"I went to the family lawyer, got him to freeze her allowance. It was the only way. She was drinking it dry. I always take care of her, give her what she needs, and I'll reinstate her own money when she's ready, but my requirement is that she sorts herself out…which seems less and less likely these days."

"Where are we going?"

"To her flat. She'll be there, partying with her favorite troupe of dropouts and bottom-feeders I expect."

They crawl into the mesh of Hampstead's residential streets, among the grand redbrick mansion blocks.

Once parked, Rafael squeezes Fran's hand. "You have every right to be angry with her," he says, "but just so you know, I love her dearly and I believe she has a good heart underneath it all."

"I know," says Fran.

The heavy wooden door of Janey's flat is ajar. The interior is dim, but through the corridor, they hear dance music and laughter. A party is in full swing. Rafael pushes his way through the crowds in the living room, approaches a skinny man in a leather jacket. "Where's Jane?" he demands.

The man grunts, looks away.

"You know me," says Rafael fiercely. "We've spoken before." He gives the man a nudge, bordering on a shove. The sight is unsettling.

Fran has never known, let alone cared about, someone like Rafael before, someone who has the ability to flip from quiet defender of decency to commanding menace in so short a time frame. She watches, a little wary and a little endeared.

"Tell me where she is."

"She's in the kitchen, mate. Settle down, yeah?"

Rafael pushes on, Fran behind him. They find Janey sitting on her kitchen counter, swinging her legs, sharing a bottle of vodka with some "friends." She is wearing the wedding dress over the top of her jeans and sweater, casually flicking cigarette ash on the skirt. Fran stares in horror. After everything the dress has been through and is answerable for, that it should end up here, worn in jest at a seedy house party, flaunted like a scrap from a playroom costume box.

Rafael turns the music off.

The silence spurs Janey to look up. When she sees the new arrivals, her expression turns to fury. "Who invited *you*?"

"You're despicable, Jane!" says Rafael, snatching the vodka out of her hand. "Take the damn dress off!" He then turns to the guests. "Go home, everyone. The party's over."

They dither, exchange awkward looks.

"Now!" shouts Rafael, scaring them toward the door.

Janey hops down from the counter, yanks the dress off, and dumps it on the floor.

Fran runs to the mound of silk and lace, scoops it into her arms. There are spills of drink down the front, and the train is gray and gritty where it has been dragged through dirt, but it is back in her grasp at least, and still in one piece.

Meanwhile Rafael marches Janey to the bathroom. "Take a cold shower," he demands. "Get yourself sharp, then you and I need to have a talk." When he returns, suddenly, spontaneously, as though he cannot help himself, he pulls Fran toward him, hugs her tight. A sunray beams through the window and bathes them in light, while the dress, pressed between their warm skin, binds them with its mysterious energy, the atoms of history fizzing and crackling through its fibers.

"I'm sorry," he says, stepping away. "So sorry about all this."

"It's fine," says Fran, flustered, blushing.

Janey emerges minutes later, wet and bedraggled, lips blue, a tatty robe wrapped round her. "What are you trying to do to me?" she sniffs, sad eyed.

But Rafael has no tolerance for her tricks. He has been here before. She is playing for sympathy, the please-don't-moan-at-me-I'm-fragile look. At least she is calmer now, more willing to reason, instead of plowing on with her own deluded rhetoric. He orders her to drink a strong coffee.

"Was it really necessary for you to mess up Fran's shop?" he demands. "She's done nothing to you."

"Wasn't me."

"Don't play innocent, Janey. You've already admitted it. You wanted the wedding dress, I get it, but you didn't need to trash Fran's livelihood in the process. She's spent years building her business, collecting those dresses. They mean everything to her."

"It's my dress!" Janey rails. "*My* fucking wedding dress! You took it and gave it away to that...*fairy woman*. Well, I want it now."

"No," says Rafael. "I gave it to Francesca. That's final. Besides, it's the least I can do now that you've destroyed her shop. Honestly, Janey, what were you *thinking*? The damage you caused...it's criminal. You could go down for this, you realize? Breaking and entering? Damage of property? Theft?"

"So?"

"So…don't you know what that would do to you? To us? To the foundation?"

"Oh, yeah, boo-hoo, the poor foundation."

Rafael groans, screws his fists into two tight balls. "I despair."

"It's *my* dress," she persists, now sulky and sullen. "And I want it."

"What? So you can pawn it and waste the cash on discount vodka? If I thought for a second that you genuinely cared about it, I'd give it to you without question." He narrows his eyes, forces her to look at him. "But I know you don't care, Janey, because if I know you at all, I know you feel the same way about it as I do. It's nothing more than a specter, an abomination from our past."

Janey scowls, pushes her bottom lip out.

Meanwhile Fran catches Rafael's eye, surprised—and a little pleased—to hear him talk so protectively about the Whispering Dress. They take each other's hands.

"Who exactly *is* she anyway?" says Janey, riled by the tender interaction between them. "She's not one of us. She's not family."

Rafael sighs. "Like you ever cared about family. I'll have to pay for the damages, of course. I don't want you to lose money, Fran."

"And what about *my* money?" says Janey.

"Oh, grow up. I've told you a million times, you'll get all the money you want once I can be certain you won't use it to do yourself over with a mammoth cocktail of toxins."

"Whatever."

"Jane, this has to stop." Rafael's eyelids lower, dragged down by the burden. "I can't…I can't *do* this anymore."

"So don't," she snarls, standing up at the island. "Leave me alone.

Get on with your own life. The world loves you, Rafael. The public loves you. Even *she* loves you. The prissy fairy dressmaker loves you."

Rafael twitches. *Love* is not a word he is used to.

"I might be drunk half the time, Raf, but when I'm sober, I'm sharp as a tack. I can see it all. She's in love with you, and you're in love with her."

At this, Janey crumples, buries her sodden dreadlocks in her hands, and sobs, tears running into a stream of snot.

But they are different tears, thinks Rafael, to the ones she usually squeezes out on cue. These are raw, unprocessed, honest even. Could it be that Fran—tiny, kind Fran—is a threat to her? Is she frightened that Fran might take her place as his number one priority?

"Oh, Janey." He pummels his head in despair. "If you only knew what matters in life, what truly matters, then you'd let go of all this game-playing bullshit. You deserve to be happy. I deserve to be happy. Without jealousy, without bitterness, without shame."

"You can't leave me, Raf. You can't forget about me."

"I'm not leaving you, Janey. I'd never do that. But if you really want to know…*yes*." His eyes brighten. "I am falling in love with Fran."

Fran's mouth drops open, and a million tiny butterflies flood into her heart. Those words. It has been so, so long since someone has said those words to her. She stares at him. Her heart wants to burst. But her amazement is quickly eclipsed by Janey's spite.

"Oh yes, that's right," she says, laughing cruelly, "along with all the others you fell in love with. What were their names? Bella? Rosie? Megan? Victoria? Angelique? Oh, Angelique—remember her? The professional skier? You really fell in love with Angelique, the one you proposed to on top of a mountain. Didn't work out though, did it? When she discovered you were sleeping with a bunch of barmaids and threw the ring back in your face."

Rafael straightens, his entire body tensing.

"I was barely twenty years old," he spits. "Trying to make the wrong girl commit to me. I made a mistake…big deal."

"So let me ask you this, Raf: Why is it okay for you to make a mistake but not me? Why am I always the fuckup?"

Rafael has no answer for her.

Janey straightens, widens her eyes as though coming to a place of clarity. "Oh, Raf, it's not my fault. I don't want to fuck up all the time. I want to be better, but it's them. It's *their* fault. They're the ones. They ruined us."

She doesn't need to explain. He knows whom she means.

"Why couldn't we have been born into a normal family? With nice, normal parents with a normal marriage, parents who loved each other, who were kind to each other. Look at us. What have we done with our lives? I'm a loser and you're a workaholic who's frigid about relationships. They never showed us the right way to live—or to love. There was no warmth, no stability, no loyalty. All the crap we've hidden from, Raf, it nudges at the door, no matter how deeply we bury it. And it won't disappear simply because we don't want to deal with it. It'll lie in wait. We're fucked."

Her eyes flood with tears, the guilt of decades, the anguish of a lifetime, hitting her like lightning. She falls into his arms and they hug—for the first time since childhood—and a feeling passes between them, stronger than love, stronger than hate, the bond of blood. "I'm sorry," she whispers.

"Me too," says Rafael.

"I mean it this time," says Janey.

And she does, he thinks, as a haze of long-wanted relief and tenderness descends upon them both.

Fran, meanwhile, slips quietly away. She has heard enough.

Years of collecting and caring run deep. Fran stares around the Whispering Dress—her work, her life, her security blanket, her *everything*. The tulle of the '50s ballerina dress has been torn in three places. A gown that has graced the aisle of a cathedral, dazzled three hundred guests, made a minister blush, then survived nearly seventy years in a suitcase, traveling from England to India to Jakarta to France, tremulous with a lifetime of hope and warmth, now wrecked in an instant.

The 1938 ivory satin fishtail, due to be the jewel of the art deco window display, never mind that on the eve of World War II, its eye-catching cut stopped traffic as the bride and groom left the church—a last burst of glamour before the darkness descended. So much power, so much to say, and now it lies in a crumpled heap, with a footprint on its skirt. *Poor thing.*

Fran gathers it in her arms, cuddles the satin to her cheek. She will fix it, she determines, and love it a little more, so that its story can continue, so that one day it can mean something to another deserving bride.

She gathers all the scraps of antique fabric and lace. She rebuilds mounds of beads and sequins, rehangs flower garlands and tiaras, piles her sewing table with cotton reels and pins, then retrieves the scatter of newspaper clipping and letters, and the photos, her dead grooms.

"I'm sorry," says Fran, dripping silent tears onto their sepia faces—Anthony Clay and James Andrew Percy and all the good men who have watched over her from the wall, her great hopes, her protectors. They never lie, never cheat, never cause her doubt or pain or confusion—with them, she had the safe way to cherish, admiration at a distance, only paper and daydreams, no real hearts involved. She patches them up, tries to rearrange their portraits as neatly as she can. With a twinge of self-pity, she goes to the art nouveau wardrobe in the corner. How ironic that the only gown that hasn't been mortally damaged is the one she would most like to get away from, the one that hurts most.

Slowly, she opens the door. There it is, her own ex-wedding dress. It has been years since she's looked at it, but tonight, the melancholy grips her—all her happy passion, her delight in other people's wedding joy, that sees her bounce from one day to another, suddenly it is funneled into a narrow vial of despair.

Anguished and crying, she tugs the dress from its hanger, takes it over to the mirror, rips the eyelets apart, and steps inside its viselike bodice. It still fits, but the fabric is scratchy and stiff. The seams are cheap, hastily machined in some anonymous mass-production sewing room—a dress from a factory, hardly romantic, no heart in those stitches. She remembers the chain store where she bought it, the obsequious smile of the sales assistant who assured her, even though it was synthetic, that it would move like the genuine organza she'd admired, that strapless gowns were the most sophisticated of all when, in reality, they were the most common and most encouraged because of their basic form and ease to fit and alter.

She knew so little back then but was blinded by the buzz of becoming a bride. She didn't know the pain it would bring her or how she would come to regret the moment she ever said yes. She runs her hands down the creased skirt. Suddenly it feels like the pain will never leave her, that it will always be there, whispering from the shadows. In anger, she throws her fist at the mirror. The glass cracks and a red ribbon of blood trickles down her wrist. Aghast, she collapses in a heap, broken and pitiful.

Sometime later, serene after a long cry, Fran picks herself up, bandages her hand, and starts to work cleaning and repairing the Alessandra Colt dress. Usually she finds sewing alone in the moonlight the most soothing of any activity, but now she feels frantic. It is written across the furrow of her brow, in the tightness of her lungs. The pressure keeps squeezing. She wants the dress more than any she's ever encountered, and yet she fears it too. She shakes the bodice, sponges the beer stains, brushes off the grit, then notices another spatter of marks on the skirt—very faint, unobvious to the unknowing eye, the damage of a substance hastily applied. A crime to a dress so valuable, but when you're in a hurry, under stress, trying to get to a wedding on time? It could be rubbing alcohol or even a

little diluted ammonia—trusted remedies for the removal of stains…
stains like blood.

"Tell me your secrets," she whispers, running the silk through
her wounded fingers, hunting, searching. "I have to understand you.
I have to know what it is that has made Raf so disregarding of love,
so afraid to commit. Otherwise, we'll never make it, will we? I know
there's an amazing man in there, a man I trust with my heart, but
unless he's honest with me, honest with himself…"

She looks in the mirror, then down at the dress. A sense of
anticipation flutters through her body, the tantalizing pep of a dress
whisperer's challenge. Whether it is good for her or not, she will
follow it. She looks over at her dead grooms, not the same now that
they've been trashed and trampled on.

"Maybe it's time," she whispers. "Time to move on from you,
take a chance on a modern man."

Her reverie is suddenly broken by the ring of her phone. She
reaches for the handset but doesn't recognize the number. "Hello?"

"Is this the Whispering Dress?"

"Er, yes."

"To whom am I speaking?"

"My name is Francesca Delaney. I own the Whispering Dress.
Are you…are you looking for a wedding gown?"

"I could be, but this is not business. It is something of a…per-
sonal interest. I'm a designer and fashion collector. My partner and I
have a large compendium of fine and historic evening wear. It is our
passion. And we believe you have a dress, Ms. Delaney, that is rather
extraordinary to us, designed by Garrett-Alexia."

Fran sits up. "But I only recently put it online."

"Indeed. I hope I'm your first inquiry. It was forwarded to me by one of my eagle-eyed scouts. It is a fine dress, no?"

"It's remarkable."

"Introductions maybe. My name is Fabian Alexia."

Fran gasps. "Fabian Alexia? As in…?"

"The House of Garrett-Alexia. Gilles Alexia was my father."

Fran laughs, incredulous. Her head fills with questions, so much to ask, so much to say.

"You know something of fashion history, Ms. Delaney?"

"Of course."

"Bravo. Then we should talk. I live in Paris. I have to be in Milan next week, then Los Angeles, but maybe I can fly to London after that. I would like very much to see the dress. It has a lot of history for my family. Just out of curiosity, how did you come to own it?"

"I—I acquired it in a house clearance."

"A house clearance? You mean to tell me that no one wanted that incredible piece of couture?"

"I found it at the bride's family estate, which was being cleared for sale. I believe there were two brides actually, Janice and Alessandra Colt. Both wore the dress and both are now dead. And it seems the next generation of Colts have little interest in family wedding gowns."

"Then they have no idea. My goodness, Ms. Delaney, I have known of the dress's potential existence for many years, but the established wisdom is that it was lost, destroyed even. And now you have found it. We must meet. In a few weeks perhaps?"

"How about sooner?" says Fran.

"I'm afraid I'm tied up with business. I have my own fashion label in Paris. We have a shop near the Champs-Élysées, the same building where the House of Garrett-Alexia was begun by my father and his colleague all those decades ago. We still have their old sewing machines in our lobby. I like a sense of history, don't you?"

"Oh yes, I do."

"If you would be so kind as to keep the dress aside, I will get to it as soon as I can."

Fran's eyes widen. "My intention is to find a bride for it, but if you'd like it for your collection—"

"I'm not saying I want to buy it, Ms. Delaney."

"Oh."

"I have a curiosity of another kind," Fabian Alexia explains. "How do you say…a score to settle?"

"Oh, right."

"I want to know what the dress can tell me."

"You and me both," says Fran.

"I must go now, but I hope we can talk again. Until next time. It's been a pleasure, Ms. Delaney, and delightful to know that you share my sympathy for beautiful old things. *Ciao*."

Rafael kisses Janey goodbye, urges her to stay on track, and promises he'll return over the weekend. He then gets back in his car and drives aimlessly for an hour, eventually arriving at Dryad's Hall. The house looks ghostly with its lifeless windows and rustling overgrowth. As he unlocks the front door, he sighs. Soon the estate will be sold forever, to be bulldozed no doubt, turned into luxury gated apartments. The house has little value to anyone other than him. The land is the asset.

He misses her now, remembers the sight of her alone in the kitchen, rolling pastry on cold marble, twisting it into plaits, sprinkling the surface with olives, pine nuts, and rosemary—a favorite recipe, good Neapolitan food. The family didn't like her going in the kitchen, even though it was the one thing, other than her garden and her children, that gave her pleasure. The Italian. His father always referred to her as "the Italian," in a derisory way, treating her Mediterranean heritage as a misplaced mistake. The way he marginalized her, left her out, cast his attention everywhere else. The way he spoke about her, over her, around her, but never *to* her, as though, in choosing a silence, she had somehow denounced her right to exist. How she didn't rise up and punch him, he'll never know, but perhaps, by then, she'd been broken, her will snapped in pieces. Suddenly he regrets he wasn't there for her more, to look after her, protect her. But it was never his choice to go to boarding school or spend every summer jetting abroad, spending two weeks touring the "poor countries" and the rest on a yacht in Monaco. He would have liked to be here with Alessandra, living quietly in the glades of the forest. Her silence never bothered him. What seemed strange to other people was normal in his world. *Words*, he thinks, *are not the only way to talk.*

He knew what was in her heart, probably far better than her own husband ever did. How she'd hoped for so much more, catching the eye of an eligible young man, having him chase her, court her, trap her. A shy girl from Southern Italy with dark almond eyes, pummeled and pressed and pushed into uncommon shape by Colt family dysfunction. If she'd known when she'd accepted the marriage proposal that, along with her name, she was giving away her freedom, would she have said yes?

He thinks of the wedding photo that used to hang above the stairs—that bandage on her hand, such an ugly accessory for a wedding day. Fran doesn't understand. She sees the dress's beauty, all its sparkly surface opulence, but she doesn't know what it represents, what it *really* represents. She sees something in it that he simply can't, something hopeful. And maybe that's the difference. When he saw her that day, when he caught her trying it on, the radiance in her, it was…overwhelming.

"A date?" says Fran, yawning from sleep, her brain not quite alert.

It is early in the morning, not the romantic time to call, unless of course he has been up all night thinking about her, twisting in the sheets, too restless with want to wait for a civilized hour. Fran stares across the sky, to the city in the distance, the sun dazzling bright between sheets of darkening gray, like a poster for a sci-fi movie.

"Only if you'd like to," says Rafael. "Maybe tonight?"

"Like a grown-up date?"

"We can call it that."

She smiles, the frisson of flirtation waking her up. A raindrop lands on the window and slithers down the glass. They both look up as the rain sweeps over the city. It comes hard and fast, the kind of rain that soothes and revives and leaves everything bright. Down in the streets of Walthamstow, the market traders wrap themselves in tarpaulins and the early-bird commuters pump open umbrellas. Out on the Thames, in front of Rafael's penthouse, the river dances with ripples and the dog walkers take cover under trees.

"Where are you?" says Fran.

"Watching the river."

"Wave."

"Wave?"

"I might be able to see you. If I stand on tiptoes I can see the London Eye from here, just about."

"You're daft."

"At least that's better than some of your other appraisals of me."

"Which I didn't necessarily mean…"

"I think you did, but you're forgiven…and probably not wrong."

"How self-reflective of you," says Rafael. "Francesca Delaney, are you about to tell me you've suddenly realized you spend half your life in a fantasy land?"

"No."

"Either way, could you possibly put aside your bride-boosting schedule and allow me to take you out this weekend?"

"I have wedding dresses to repair."

Can they wait? Should they wait? Is a date—an official date—the first she's been on in years, with the only real-life man that she's liked in a decade, more important than other people's wedding dresses? She wavers, the devil of exaltation on one shoulder, the angel of duty on the other.

"I'd really like to take you out, Fran. It's the least I can do, after everything Janey did."

Fran frowns.

"So, dinner?" he suggests. "Or maybe lunch? Or both? Where would you like to go? Name a place. It doesn't have to be local or London even. We can travel. I have a few restaurants in the country that I prefer, but the choice is yours."

"Anywhere?"

"Anywhere."

A thought creeps across Fran's mind. "How about Paris?"

# chapter 6

SHE LOOKS BEAUTIFUL IN EMERALD SATIN, STROLLING ALONG THE Left Bank, her dress fluttering in the breeze. They walk and talk and laugh, and all the while Rafael cannot help but keep glancing at her, to see that she is really there. Does she always set her hair and paint her lips, or is it just for his benefit? Some muted, mysterious part hopes it's for him, although he guesses, given her proclivity for sartorial drama, it's her natural way. She seems awed by Paris, but of course she would be. The city of love, crowded with history, is everything she treasures. From avenue to boulevard, the old swamp groans with the weight of its Gothic cathedrals, Renaissance domes, neoclassical theaters, Napoleonic military monuments, and flamboyant palaces of the belle epoque, but its true charm is much subtler than its grandiose catalogue of architectural styles. At its core, Paris is a city for walking and eating and watching, for taking the time to feel pleasure for pleasure's sake. This, thinks Rafael, is the pace of holiday he needs, and Fran, with her habit of living from moment to moment, seems like the perfect companion. Once again, with her as his muse, he has dared to step outside of confinement, to shed the order of his daily existence, and it feels like a brilliant liberation.

Fran cannot believe she is here in Paris with a man, a living man. Her mood soaring, strolling along the sunlit riverbank, the water in the Seine sparkling, the *bateaux-mouches* cruising up and down, she chooses to reject all doubt for the day. When she suggested Paris, she hadn't expected such an easy, delighted yes. She had assumed Rafael would defer to his assistant or make some excuse about his hectic work schedule, but instead he gave her a thirty-minute warning to get dressed and find her passport. Champagne at Kings Cross, Eurostar first class, and now they are here, looking for lunch.

"I know a place in Saint-Germain," he says, eager to please her.

They take the metro, which is hot and noisy and full of buskers, and alight in a perfect Parisian square, plump with clichés— canopied cafés with iron seating and marble bistro tables spilling onto the cobbles, a mounted bronze statue in the center, a domed newsstand, and a dozen elegant people watchers. More Paris than Paris. They take a table outside at Les Deux Magots and eat fat, garlicky chicken and perfect *frites*, washed down with goblets of cold French larger.

She has the address of Fabian Alexia's shop in her pocket. It wasn't hard to find. Before leaving, she typed his name into her laptop and learned he runs a small, discreet fashion label for the mature woman. If she can only meet the man who cares as much about the dress as she does, instinct tells her she will unlock its ghosts. But time, in a city where clocks come second to unplanned journeys of decadence, is not on her side, and the pressure of it thrums in the back of her thoughts, becoming ever more bothersome as the second hand ticks.

"If you check your phone one more time," says Rafael, "I'll make the assumption that I'm boring you."

"No, no," Fran hastens to tell him. "I'm just thinking about all we want to do here. There's so much."

"Well, I thought we could get macarons at Ladurée. They do these incredible little pistachio ones, with centers that ooze. Then maybe have a browse through the Galeries Lafayette. Or the Marais district. Or there's always Montmartre if you want to be mobbed by other tourists."

"Sounds lovely. All of it."

*She is definitely twitchy*, he thinks, *more distracted than normal.* Is she nervous? Is this too much? It isn't his intention to show off. He senses she'd see right through any attempt to impress her with Colt money or Colt status, but he wants to give her Paris in her hands, because he wants to make her happy.

"We could walk some more," he suggests. "Through the Jardin du Luxembourg or along the river? Or see some art. Name a gallery, Fran. Just don't say you want to see the Eiffel Tower."

Fran fidgets. She knows what she wants to do but is scared to expose it, for fear he will take offense and then all the momentum that has gathered between them will collapse.

"We have all day, all night. Just tell me what you'd like to do."

*Understand a dress*, thinks Fran, breathless with the burden. A bus passes by, direction Champs-Élysées. She takes it as a sign.

"I'd like to see the most famous street in the world," she says, unnerved by her ability to lie with conviction.

The sheer graciousness of the wide avenue, cutting a straight groove from where they stand in Place de la Concorde, to the Arc du Triomphe, is enough to make Fran gasp with astonishment.

Rafael is quick to explain that its history is not all glorious. "This used to be called Revolution Square. It's where Marie Antoinette and Louis XVI were executed during the French Revolution. Not a good time to be born into money."

"You'd have been done for then."

"I like to think I'd have been with the revolutionists," he says, a glint in his eye. "I want respect for the things I do and how I act, not for what I was given."

Fran smiles to herself. "You are every inch worthy of any dead groom."

"What?"

"Never mind," she giggles, tipping forward and kissing him on the cheek.

They walk hand in hand down the wide, tree-lined pavement, past the designer boutiques and flagship stores. When they come to the turning of the Rue de Berri, Fran veers, tugs Rafael with her. The air is quieter here, away from the main drag. Tall stone buildings flank either side. Voices sing across the road, from the high shuttered windows and wrought-iron balustrades. After a few meters, they come to the shop front that bears the name *Fabian Alexia*. Mannequins wearing crinkled, mustard-colored smocks over gray felt palazzo trousers stare vacantly from the windows.

"You want to go shopping?" says Rafael, perplexed.

"I want to go to this shop," says Fran, holding her breath and smiling. "It belongs to the son of Gilles Alexia, of the House of Garrett-Alexia, the designers who made your mother's—originally your grandmother's—wedding dress."

Rafael freezes midmotion, drops Fran's hand from his. A chill sweeps over him, destroying all sense of joy. Why? Why is she ruining it?

"Does your wedding dress obsession know no boundaries?" he snarls. "I thought I made it clear. I don't want anything more do with that dress. I thought you'd taken the hint, but this...*this*... You planned this, didn't you? You knew all along you wanted to come here. You led me here. How could you?" He barges past her, leaving her crushed, ashamed of herself for triggering such a reaction.

"I'm sorry," she says, pleading, addressing the empty space where he was standing. "I only wanted to..."

Rafael stops, breathes, tries to compose himself, his fists in tight balls at his sides. He hates it when anger consumes him, but internally, he feels besieged, the slicing invasion of his mother and her anguished nighttime howls—the only impassioned sounds she ever made—terrorizing the moment. He opens his mouth to explain, but no words come, trapped by the emotional whiplash of all the dysfunction he's worked so hard to bury.

"Please," he says, jaw tightening, throwing the words over his shoulder as he continues to walk, "take the dress, enjoy it, sell it, burn it, turn it into curtains. Do what you like, Fran, but don't bring me to some random shop in the middle of Paris like a fucking ambush and expect me to play along with your absurdist fantasy that wedding dresses talk to you."

"I'm sorry, Raf, really sorry. I didn't mean to hit a raw nerve. I just thought it would be an opportunity to—"

"Raw nerve? Oh, Fran, you have no idea."

She goes to him, heels pressing into the paving slab beneath her, body tall, desperate to be brave. "I went to see Janey," she confesses.

"What?"

"That's how she knew I had the dress. I met her in Hampstead."

"Stop dragging her into this. You've seen how fragile she is."

"I know. I wasn't trying to cause her any upset. I just wanted some background that you weren't willing to give. I never thought I'd get so caught up in the story…or in you." Her eyes fill with tears. She doesn't want to ruin it. Despite everything, she wants to be close to him. She wants his love.

"Janey admitted your family life wasn't a happy one," she whispers. "She made it clear she blames her upbringing for her drinking problems."

Rafael shudders.

"There's no need to hide from it," says Fran. "I get it. We all have our complicated pasts. God knows I've got mine. One way or another, we've either screwed up or been screwed up. That's life. But maybe it does us no good to keep running away?"

Rafael sighs, the worst of his anger now drifting to the sky, somehow severed by Fran's patient words. She speaks wisely for one so daft. She speaks like a person who has counseled a thousand bridal parties. He would like not to run away, he thinks, he just doesn't know how.

"I know you have your reasons to hate the dress," Fran continues.

"But for me, coming here, it feels like an opportunity." She pauses, looks down at her feet. "Mick and I advertised the dress online. I had a call from Fabian Alexia not long after. I practically collapsed when I realized who he was. Back in the '50s, Garrett-Alexia, it was fashion royalty. Fabian was very keen to talk more about the dress, but then he said something about having a score to settle. He said he lives in Paris, and when you told me you'd take me anywhere, I just...dived in."

"You do a lot of that."

"Yup."

"Sometimes, Fran, it pays to hold back, be a bit more measured, think before acting."

"I know."

She glances at her watch, gives Rafael a small, hopeful smile. They both look up at the shop front, eyes widening as they trace the grand stonework and the baroque carvings above the arched windows, achingly elegant.

"Amazing to think this is the very place, sixty years ago, where the dress was made," says Fran. "Now that we're here, couldn't we just have a peek inside?"

"You're insufferable."

"Which is," says Fran smartly, "interchangeable with 'driven.'"

The door chimes. As they enter, the tall windows spread a river of light across the marble floor. The scent in the air is jasmine, delivered from a reed diffuser that sits on the reception desk alongside a carafe of iced water made from fine cut crystal. The sales assistant, effort-lessly chic, dressed in a simple black shirt and pencil trousers, nods a greeting.

"Bonjour."

"Bonjour…um…we'd like to…*nous voulez*…if at all possible… *parlez avec* Monsieur Fabian Alexia?" Fran stutters through her effort, until Rafael takes over in fluid French.

The sales assistant responds with fast, lilting vowels, leaving Fran clueless but hopeful that progress is happening. The receptionist then turns to a leather-bound diary, scans the dates and days.

Fran presses her hands to the desk and leans forward. "*C'est très important*," she says. "It's about a wedding dress. Tell him we talked on the phone."

The assistant backs away.

Rafael placates her with his charm, delivers another string of flowering French that is lost on Fran, due to all those days and weeks of school she missed because her mother thought she'd get a better education in the company of various touring theater troupes than in a dull, artless classroom. Thankfully, whatever Rafael says works, because the receptionist picks up the phone, makes a call, and bids them to wait.

While Rafael chats on, Fran takes a turn of shop. She spies the old sewing machines from the Garrett-Alexia heyday mounted in glass boxes at the back of the room. She presses up to them, draws their history into her veins. As tools of design, they are impeccably elegant, their shapely black bodies and floral gilded inlay testifying that beauty can and should be everywhere.

"What did you stitch?" she whispers, her imagination unfolding, rejoicing in the air of the past.

She turns and gazes around the rest of the room, removes all the sleek chrome rails, the designer lighting, the high-tech air-conditioning, and the electric shutters. She covers the white walls with wainscoting, decorates them with framed fashion prints from *Vogue* and *Harper's Bazaar*, lays a plush carpet across the marble floor and leans rolls of fabric, sourced from the finest ateliers in Paris, against a streamlined countertop, upon which she conjures a box of feathers. Tiny filaments quiver all around her, the finest plumes from the best male birds, destined for capes, trims, fans, and boas. *There should always be feathers*, she thinks, *feathers for fun, feathers for love— look what they did for Melissa West.*

She gives the back half of the shop a pair of noisy sewing machines, worked by two women with finger-wave hairstyles, but this clattering mirage doesn't hold her attention for long. She is only interested in one thing: the imminent union of bride and dress. Gasp-inducing aisle walks have their place, as do admiring glances from sweetly nervous grooms, but the moment, the one moment that truly ignites wedding-day fire has to be the bride's first encounter with her gown: the icon of matrimony, all conjugal hopes formed at once within those swathes of fine fabric, for better or for worse. The brass bell above the shop door tinkles. She stills, holds her breath.

"Here she is!" says Gilles Alexia, who in Fran's vision is much like Errol Flynn. "Our bride du jour…Janice. Come here, darling, let's get you out of that coat—"

Janice is flawless, bright skinned, red lipped, dressed in a

crimson sheath dress with matching jacket and pillbox hat, acces-
sorized with pearls and a pair of dainty wrist-length gloves. She is a
goddess, tall and shapely, with an impossible wasp waist. Her initial
demeanor is commanding, but her expression softens when she spies
the feathers on the countertop. She is here for joy. The moment has
come. The dress is in front of her, hidden beneath a cotton sheet.
Fran moves closer, teasing the vision toward clarity. She wants to
see everything—the crease of Janice's eyes, the flush in her cheeks,
the twitch of her mouth—every nuance will tell her something new
about the emotional ascent of the Colt family wedding dress.

"Ready?" says Gilles, fingers poised at the sheet.

"Of course."

The sheet drops. The dress meets its owner. The silk skirt is so
full, it rises like a white mountain, but its drama is perfectly coun-
terpoised by the sweetheart neckline and delicate lace overlay. The
pearls and bugle beads shimmer in the sunlight, imbuing the bodice
with otherworldly brilliance.

A smile blooms across Janice's face. She steps forward, shuts her
eyes, and touches the silk, takes in the spread of the train. The dress,
the wedding, the marriage—it is all ahead of her.

Fran holds her breath, squeezes her eyes shut, then opens them
again. More—she needs more.

She looks to Rafael, who is still distracted, practicing his French
with Fabian's sales assistant, then dives back into her '50s reverie.
Entranced, she conjures the scene of the first fitting. Janice, aided by
half a dozen French sewing girls, stands in the center, in front of a
floor-length mirror. The dress fits her perfectly, but then of course,

Garrett-Alexia are famed for their brilliance in fitting the hourglass form. The sewing girls chatter among themselves, proud of their weeks of pinning, threading, stitching, and pulling. So much optimism, so much delight. A dress of hope and promise. *How*, thinks Fran, *did it go so bad? How did its energy become so torturous?*

Janice turns to Gilles Alexia, the dress designer of choice, and smiles with her eyes.

"It's breathtaking, Gio. You're a genius. There isn't another gown in the world I'd rather wear. You've given me everything I asked for. I'll be Sammy's queen. And when all those critical eyes are on me as I walk up the aisle, staring me up and down, no one will be able to doubt it. In this dress, I'm worthy of every second of his attention."

"Samuel Colt is a lucky man," says Gilles, taking her hand and squeezing it.

Janice looks down at the train. "Are they hummingbirds?" she asks.

"They are."

"Why hummingbirds?"

Gilles pauses, exhales slowly. "A symbol of infinity," he says. "I suppose one hopes they might…enchant the marriage."

Janice's face sours. "And you still have reason to believe my marriage needs enchanting, Gio? What have you heard now?"

Gilles leans forward, whispers something into her ear, and a furrow of rage shadows her eyes.

The vision shatters.

*No!*

Desperate to know what was said, what was whispered, Fran

stares into the space ahead of her, tries to reclaim her daydream, but too late. Just the glossy white walls and the hum of the air-conditioning. She looks to Rafael, but he is oblivious, lost in French small talk.

Surely Janice Colt didn't doubt her husband mere days before the wedding? And for what reason? Bad behavior? Infidelity?

Fran's head starts to thump. She tries to rub the pain away, does her best to remember what Janey had said about her grandmother, that Janice was a social climber, an attention seeker drawn to extravagance. She'd painted a picture in which Janice was the problem—the reason why Samuel Colt had started his foundation, to prevent her from "blowing his entire fortune on gambling and parties"—but now Fran can't help wonder if there is more to Janice's story.

In 1954, the public would not have been ready for romantic indiscretions. The sexual freedoms of the '60s and '70s were still in the ether. Extramarital relations would have been scandalous, better suppressed, concealed from public knowledge. Which didn't mean they didn't happen. *Oh, Janice…*

"Fran? Are you with us?"

"Uh, yes." Fran blinks.

"You're in luck," says Rafael. "Fabian Alexia is able to meet with us."

"Oh."

Moments later, Fabian Alexia bursts through the door, with silver hair slicked back, a deep tan, and razor-sharp cheekbones. His eyes are keen despite his advancing age, and he observes Fran and Rafael with a mix of delight and conceit.

"You came all the way to see me?"

"Sort of," says Fran.

"We happened to be passing," says Rafael for Fran's benefit.

"I was so intrigued to find out what you know about the dress," says Fran, still startled by what she's just seen. "I couldn't wait."

"Is it here?" says Fabian, suddenly tense.

"No. It won't travel with ease. It's enormous."

"Thank goodness," says Fabian. "I must say I'm not quite ready to face it yet. Anyway"—he ushers them forward—"you are here. And that is a start. Shall we convene in my office upstairs?"

A wrought-iron spiral staircase leads them to a narrow corridor, which then gives way to a vast double-height hall with glittering views of the city.

"Some office," whispers Fran.

The walls are adorned with art of all kinds, from enormous eighteenth-century pastoral oils to nudes to portraits to modernist gray oblongs. A brief glance tells Fran she is in the company of more than one Picasso, a Munch, a Klimt, and a selection of Turner watercolors. There are sculptures of bare-buttocked Grecian boys and cast bronze horses. And among the art, there are gatherings of exquisitely dressed mannequins. They stand alone and in groups, almost as though they are visitors in a gallery, there to peruse the masterpieces, unaware that they are, in fact, masterpieces themselves. The finest-clothed mannequins have the honor of standing on plinths or behind glass cases. Fabian smiles, takes delight in his guests' awe.

Fran is less certain. She tugs Rafael's arm, digs her heel into his toe. "We need to talk," she whispers.

"Not now," he whispers back, smiling to cover himself. "Did no one ever teach you that whispering is rude?"

"But I've seen something, something disturbing—"

"What? Where?"

"I—I had a vision of your grandmother."

Rafael sighs, grits his teeth. "Not now, Fran, please," he growls. "You brought me here. Let's just show some polite interest, then leave."

Fabian approaches. "Welcome to my vault," he says, sweeping them into the center of the room. "If you're lovers of art, then I have plenty to show you. If it's fashion that interests you, I have collection pieces from the world's top designers, past and present—some classic, some rare, some historic. Do you know Lanvin?" He points to a stunning black satin evening gown. "This one was worn by a well-known opera diva."

Fran stares, mesmerized.

"I have been collecting for many years, but I take a particular interest in the Garrett-Alexia label, for obvious reasons." He leads Fran to a cluster of '50s ball gowns, each as elaborate and elegant as the next, three of them in jewel-colored satins with drapes and gathers and large cascading bows, one in black with a long tulle mermaid skirt, and two more in ice blue, both tiered with lace, bearing the same nature-themed embellishments as the wedding dress.

"I—I've never seen so many of their dresses together in one place," says Fran, entranced. "They can't have made that many... before... Oh, the shapes are so beautiful, I could cry."

Fabian smiles. "You have taste."

"I've built my life around vintage dresses. This is…heaven."

"Please," says Fabian. "Take your time. Enjoy my gowns."

He pours sparkling water into crystal goblets and hands one to Rafael.

Rafael notes that the goblet is monogrammed in gold leaf: *F. A.* He gives Fran a smile, but she doesn't notice. She is too busy circuiting the room, drinking in the color and texture.

She finds it hard to believe that Fabian does not want the Alessandra Colt wedding dress. Clearly he isn't short of money, and it would be such a rare and defining asset to his already remarkable Garrett-Alexia collection, perhaps one of the best in the world.

Over the years, Fran has learned to tune in to the thought patterns of vintage fanatics and fashion collectors. Their appetites are more than just surface. The desire to gather and possess runs deep into the core. They get territorial, competitive, obsessive even. There is much prestige involved, a lot of feather fluffing. But in her own heart, she is clear: Clothes are clothes. They don't need idolizing. They need handling, wearing. That's where they get their energy from.

"You told me you don't want the wedding dress," she says. "But it would be such a boon."

"You, sir," says Fabian, sidestepping Fran's inquiry, addressing only Rafael, casting his gaze down the length of his trousers. "I sense you have an eye for men's tailoring. Are you a fashion connoisseur too?"

Rafael laughs. "Arguably no."

"Well, you know the right trouser cut for you at least." Fabian prowls around him like a stalking cat. "And your name?"

"Rafael," he says, wondering whether to offer the Colt appellation, or whether such an utterance will tip the man's ego over the edge.

"A fine French name, but you're not."

"My family liked to think of themselves as old English, but I believe there was some more exotic blending down the line. And my mother was Italian…so I guess that makes me a mix."

"Your surname?"

Rafael pauses, holds his nerve. He knows Fabian's curiosity in him is more than just flattery. "Colt."

Fabian stills, takes a moment to gather his thoughts. The ornate clock above the mantel chimes three. Outside, the traffic along the Champs-Élysées gets rowdy.

"And so you are," he says eventually. "Well, we *are* in hallowed company. I think, therefore, we should drink more than water. This requires a proper toast." He presses a buzzer and instructs a maid to bring a bottle of champagne and three flutes. He then invites them out to an elegant balcony with views across the Parisian rooftops. "So," he says, utterly poised as Fran and Rafael take their seats, tense with anticipation.

They both know, in their ways, that there is unspoken history between the Colts and the Alexias and that, perhaps, it is about to unravel.

"We have much to talk about," says Fabian, turning to Rafael. "What exactly do you know about the dress and its origins?"

"That your father designed it for my grandmother, Janice."

"That is the fact. Did you also know they were close friends?"

Fran flinches but realizes this is not her conversation. *Hold back—be a bit more measured.* She sits on her hands, resists the urge to jump in with her questions. Rafael, she notices, is sweating a little, his usual cool demeanor showing cracks.

"It is not my intention to offend you, Monsieur Colt, but I heard she was a vile woman."

Rafael shrugs. "She had that capacity, yes. No offense taken."

"I am only sad that my father, Gilles, wasted his life and his brilliance on someone like that. Had she been a sweet, warmhearted creature, like our Francesca here, I would have understood."

Fran blushes.

"But it was not so. She allowed him to get caught up in her mess, and it cost him dearly. He was just twenty-two when he created your grandmother's dress. Did you know that?"

Fran and Rafael both shake their heads.

"His designing partner, Monsieur Garrett, was in awe of his natural talent. Together they could have been up there with the likes of Lanvin or Lacroix or Dior. Instead, it all fell apart…before it barely began."

Rafael hardens, waits for the blow.

Fran sits up. It is coming, she senses, the undoing of a long-held legend. She leans forward, listens intently, hanging on every word that slips from Fabian's lips.

"Falsity is a deeply destructive force," he says, pouring the champagne. "Living with a truth when no one else knows it—or cares to know it—is a terrible way to frustrate the nerves. It gnaws through the day, through the night. I have a hunch, Monsieur Colt, that you know the same story I know, but let's see, shall we…who destroyed my father's career?"

"It was his partner, Mr. Garrett," rushes Fran, unable to help herself. "The infamous undoing of a '50s fashion house, how an intense rivalry provoked the premature end of one of the greatest design duos of the era…supposedly."

"There we are. That's your version, Francesca, but I'm mostly interested in your friend's."

Rafael frowns. He hates the feeling that he has been lured into a corner. He takes a slow, purposeful breath, bunches his shoulders, looks Fabian in the eye, but says nothing.

"Very well. Francesca, you know the public story but not the real story. The world was told that my father had his hands maimed by a pair of hired thugs at the behest of his partner, Monsieur Benjamin Garrett—apparently the result of some petty argument over a dress design. It was quite a scandal at the time. The headlines spread as far as New York, where my father's dresses had been much admired. Now it is just the padding of history, of interest only to you and I, but still…there is no price that can be placed on the truth, and between us alone, I think we can now take the trouble to, shall we say, raise the stakes."

Rafael holds his nerve. He knows what is coming.

"Your grandfather Samuel didn't like the gossip about him," says Fabian. "In fashion, we are well connected with what is going on in the lives of our clients and their worlds. Gilles overheard plenty about Samuel and his associations with other women and everything he heard he shared with Janice. I suppose for a man of your grandfather's status, it can't have been easy to discover his new bride had knowledge of his infidelities and, worse, was freely confiding about them—with her dressmaker no less. I believe your grandfather's reputation as an upstanding Englishman was deeply important to him—more important, in fact, than another man's future. Your grandfather, Monsieur Colt, he was responsible for Gilles's injuries. When he learned of Janice and Gilles's confidences, and the risk it posed to his reputation, he arranged for the thugs to break each of Gilles's fingers. To warn him off. And it certainly worked. Gilles cut ties with Janice and never designed again. No more dresses. No more Garrett-Alexia. So," he says, drawing breath, "this wedding dress we're all so fascinated by, its power surpassed mere weddings. It brought down a fashion house."

Fran sits motionless, unsure what to do with the pink champagne fizzing in her glass. She looks to Rafael, to see his reaction, but his expression is cold. He doesn't speak, doesn't rise up, doesn't try to deny it.

"I was told all of this by my mother," says Fabian. "Wait." He slips away for a moment, then returns with two letters, hands them to Fran. "I have kept these ever since she passed," he explains. "She wanted me to understand what really happened to her brilliant husband. I think she hoped I might right the wrong. She was quite a bitter woman, but I suppose she had reason to be. She'd seen their prospects, their glittering future snatched away. They lived in poverty after Garrett-Alexia collapsed."

Fran takes one of the letters, its old paper scented with age. She opens it and reads.

*18th March 1958*

*My dear Gio,*

*Please tell me the dress is ready. I am so thrilled at the thought of it, although, as per our previous conversation, I fear Sammy is not being true again. He goes out at the most inexplicable hours and guess what? I found a set of feminine gloves (not mine) in his drawer, which is rather upsetting, if not surprising. But I do wish to be married and secured in society, so despite your kind advice, I have decided I will continue to put up with the nonsense and can only hope that a dress of such beauty, as you are creating for me, will be enough to turn his head my way, or at the very least, distract the society cats from their bait. Dear Gio, am I a fool? I hope not. Anyway, thank you for your loyal friendship and for being the very best couturier in the world. I shall be the envy of London thanks to your genius. Until May.*

*Forever,*

*J*

*22nd December 1961*

*My dear Gio,*

*Please let me know that you are well. I write and write, and you never reply. I miss our chats. I have no real friend in the world*

*now that you shun my letters. Sammy is an awful pig, you know.*
*I had hoped that once we were married, he would change, but*
*lesson learned. He has no interest in me whatsoever, yet I am*
*routinely forced to play along and do the tedious doting-wife*
*act when it suits him. I hate it, and I'm never allowed any fun.*
*Dear Gio, save me like you used to. It's all so cruel and unfair.*
*I do wish you would find the courage to design again. I hear*
*that your hands are healing well. One day I will need a trous-*
*seau for my daughter-in-law. That's right. I now have a baby*
*son—one good thing in my life. He was born last week and I*
*have named him Lyle. He is a Colt through and through, poor*
*mite. I miss you terribly and, as ever, am sorry, very sorry for*
*any inconvenience you may have suffered.*

*Forever,*

*J*

Fran folds the letters and passes them to Rafael. Her soul feels cold. No wonder the dress has such conflicting whispers. Designed with hope, made with passion, only to be reduced to a wasteful, dispiriting cloak of deceit within a sham of true love.

"It takes a special level of narcissism, no?" says Fabian. "I get the feeling Janice looked upon my father as her pet, there for her own amusement, someone to whine to, someone to dress her up in pretty fabrics and prime her for society. She talks of the 'incon-venience' in many other letters, as though it is mere trivia to her."

He sighs, shakes his head. "If Gilles had only stuck with dresses, just made dresses like he was born to and not played into her vanity. I suspect your grandfather gave quite a few bribes to the authorities to make sure the truth of his barbaric act was buried. The papers of course blamed Benjamin Garrett, who also died in poverty. Who are we though, we Garretts? We Alexias? Mere fashion men. But you Colts, you're philanthropists. In name at least."

"Do you want something from me?" says Rafael coldly. "Is that what this is about?"

"No," says Fabian, raising his champagne glass.

"Are you planning to take this to the press?"

"I don't deal with the press, my friend, unless it is about fashion week. I only want you to understand. I don't hold you responsible. It happened sixty years ago, long before you were even an idea. But, like I said, falsity is damaging. I no longer want to live my life smoldering in anger about the lies of history. I have watched the growth of your foundation with interest, and it seems that you, at least, have gone on to do great things in your family's name—a true giver, in spite of, or perhaps *because* of, your ancestry. As for me, I've built my own empire. If it had simply been handed to me, maybe I would not feel so satisfied. To learn that the wedding dress is still around, however… this reopens the wound. I wonder if seeing it might somehow be healing, but I don't know. For now, at least, I will shake your hand if I may and leave the ghosts in the dust." He holds his hand out to Rafael.

Fran watches in silence, unsure what Rafael will do. A moment passes, then seconds. *Please*, she wills him. *Take this chance, smooth the jagged edges, face the truth that hurts, and let it go.*

He remains stony, hard-faced, his lower jaw grinding into his top, but then she notices a single, silent tear trickling down his cheek. He accepts Fabian's hand. The shake turns into an embrace and the air all around them fills with peace.

They escape to the green relief of the Jardin des Tuileries, where the wide gravel promenades are bathed in evening light and the lawns are lush with grass. Every turn seems to be crowned with a fountain or statue, while under the shade of aging elms, friends mingle at outdoor cafés, sipping citron presses and tiny cups of Pernod.

Rafael pulls Fran toward him in a low-slung embrace and they amble toward the octagonal pond.

"I feel a hundred pounds lighter," he says, checking his hands and feet as if to work out where all the weight came off. "Fabian Alexia had incredible dignity, don't you think?" Suddenly he breaks away, runs toward the pond, and flings his body into the water, laughs like he's a child again.

Fran watches, isn't quite sure what to make of it. This is certainly a side of him she hasn't seen before, but he is happy, and this makes her happy. He runs back to her, grinning, almost feverish.

"Don't you see? This changes so much, Fran. I don't have to feel *guilty* anymore. I don't have to be beholden to the vile fuckups of my deceased relatives. I've made peace with the one person I needed to. The rest of the world can go to hell."

Fran smiles. "I'm so glad for you," she says, "but I have one question…did you know?"

"The story—one of many—has dogged our family for years, all

hush-hush of course. I never heard it directly, only in whispers. One of those Colt family things…everyone knew, but pretended they didn't." With Fran at his side, the numbness he has carried in his heart starts to lift. His thoughts uncurl, and the more they uncurl, the more they urge to be released.

"All your daydreams about dead grooms and the good old days, Fran, when people were so polite and respectful and charming, maybe now you see it wasn't so rosy. Arguably Lyle and Samuel were two of the most illustrious dead grooms you could ever imagine. Their philanthropy meant they were revered, untouchable. But behind closed doors, you know what? They used their vanity and their power to control everyone around them, and they had no respect whatsoever for the sanctity of their marriage vows."

He bows his head, tries to calm his racing mind. "Have you any idea what it's like to watch your own mother waste away in isolation? It was no wonder she lost the power to speak. She was tormented. He treated her like a stupid, worthless fool. They all did—my father, my grandfather, even Janice, when she wasn't drunk out of her head, shouting at staff, throwing chairs in the lake. As for your wedding dress—*their* wedding dress—it's nothing but vile to me. Why do you think I wanted nothing to do with it? It wasn't an icon. It was a prison sentence."

He has never before said so much to anyone. He feels raw, exposed, vulnerable. The sense of it shocks him.

Fran cups her hand over his, lets him talk.

"You know, I could never understand why my father, a man who gave so much to society, could have nothing for his wife," he says.

"She was like an outcast to him. Occasionally he'd pull me aside and tell me to keep an eye on her, but that was the most care he ever showed. His priorities were always elsewhere, like Samuel."

"In the genes," says Fran quietly.

"My father traveled a lot—'a girl in every port,' as the saying goes."

"Why did he stay married to her?"

"Guilt, I imagine. And to keep up appearances."

Fran lowers her eyelids. *Poor Alessandra. Did she sense it,* she wonders, *that evening, trying on the dress? Did she fear it coming, the heartache, the betrayal, her life and freedoms squeezing down to nothing? Is that why she punched the mirror?* "I have to wonder why she went through with the wedding. She could have backed out, ditched him at the altar. I mean, it's a pretty low blow, but under the circumstances, I would understand." She feels his hand tense beneath hers.

"He gave her no choice," he says grimly. "She was pregnant."

"Oh." Fran ponders the altered hem of the dress, its expanded waistline.

"My grandparents didn't want the scandal of an illegitimate child," Rafael explains. "They were still frantically trying to cover their own indiscretions."

"Lots of brides find themselves accidently pregnant on their wedding day," says Fran reassuringly. "It happens."

"No, Fran. This wasn't an accident."

His eyes glaze with tears. "They met at some weekend jolly in the country. Her father was an Italian shipping magnate. She was only nineteen, shy and naive, fresh from finishing school. Her English was shaky. I imagine he charmed her, like he charmed everyone. He charmed her…and then he forced himself on her."

Fran gasps.

"I, Rafael Colt, am the product of a rape. There you go. How's that for a headline?" He looks up at the sky, blinks away tears, then looks back at Fran. "So now you know."

"Oh, Raf," says Fran. "I'm sorry. No wonder you were so skeptical about marriage, so afraid to let anyone in."

"'Were'?" says Rafael quizzically.

"It's not set in stone. People can change."

"Maybe," he says, sighing.

He pulls Fran toward him. She sinks into his arms and they remain that way, silent and still, unnerved and elated, the sun setting around them. Unaware of the synchrony of their minds, they both dare to start thinking about the possibilities, a future together—a future that suddenly seems uncannily obvious now that they have shared this truth, chased it into the open, raw and unedited. When they finally return to the moment, it is as if both their worlds have changed.

"I meant what I said to Janey, you know," Rafael whispers, "that I'm falling in love with you. It's real. Ever since I saw you."

"Saw me?"

"Never mind. Don't talk, just kiss."

Fran obliges, her stomach fluttering, captivated, in his arms. He has faced his demons and is ready to love. She feels it. Aches for it. Dare she say it too? She shuts her eyes, braces herself.

"I—I think I'm falling in love with you too." The words rush out of her, make her feel exhilarated, alive—and exposed.

Beneath the shade of a nearby willow tree, they lie down together, arms entwined, faces close, the boughs cloaking them in their leafy dome. The air is warm and sweet, vibrant with the sounds of crickets and song thrushes. *Nature*, thinks Fran, *is the only thing that matters more than love.* Just them and the earth. It is perfect.

He holds her gaze, leans toward her, kisses her slow.

The breath leaves her body, circles up to the treetops. She feels light and suspended, caught in the bliss of the kiss she has wanted all her life, the Prince Charming kiss.

He shakes out her neat pin rolls, sets free that glossy mane of auburn waves.

She loves his scent—musk and spice—and the shape of his shoulders, the way his arms surround her. Her heart beats hard as he runs his hands through the folds of her dress, finds a passageway to the skin beneath.

The emerald satin of her dress ripples and settles, gathers between her legs. She feels his hand against the inside of her thigh and a volt of pleasure shoots through her soul, ignites the desire she had all but forgotten. She wants it to hasten, but then also, to take forever. Each touch, each kiss fuels the fervor. They are mere meters from one of the busiest streets in Paris, but no one would know, hidden inside their own secret sphere, the willow fronds forming a gracious veil all around them.

Oblivious to the world, they strip to their skin, consumed by the urge to feel more keenly the realness of each other. It has been long, *so long*, since either of them has felt such honest, sensuous physical connection. He traces a finger down her neck, draws teasing circles on her breasts. Her whole body arcs, and she takes his erection in her hands, kisses him deep, then kneels to straddle him, and takes him inside her. He throws his head back, shuts his eyes, and sighs. They make love in perfect synchrony, the breeze unsettling their willowy veil, then rest in each other's arms, silent and still, both paying respect to the peculiar fortune that has somehow, through the tracks of their distant and different lives, brought them together, brought them to this moment—as though it were meant to be.

They spend the night in the Hôtel de Crillon, an eighteenth-century mansion where Queen Marie Antoinette once took piano lessons, now an homage to luxury travel design. Inside a sumptuous bedroom with a vast Carrara marble bathroom, they talk little, sleep little, kiss lots. Their passing dreams are peppered with scenes of the days' intimacy, while their tired minds process the shift in them. Stunned that the tendrils of romance could burrow so deeply, flower so tantalizingly, Rafael turns over in the sheets. Fran, never believing she could do it again—give herself away so completely to another— murmurs with restless astonishment. Two locked-out souls on their way back to the most primal emotion in the universe.

In the morning, the shuttered sunlight lures them into the day. When Rafael goes to the bathroom, Fran, unable to contain herself, takes the chance to bounce up and down on the canopied bed, to indulge its plush layers of feather and silk. She has never seen an interior of such splendor before, never stayed in a hotel that has more staff than guests. Spellbound by the lavishness, she doesn't notice that Rafael sees her through the door.

The sight of her untamed playfulness brings him to confront the many other women he has known in his life—the disastrous infatuations of his youth, the one he proposed to then betrayed, the one who betrayed him, the one who wouldn't leave him alone, plus all those liberated types from Seekers, whose faces blend into one, with their boozy, no-strings one-night stands and clumpy mascara. Of the women he seriously dated, only two were "approved" by his father, who'd never been shy about expressing his marital expectations for Rafael, or making it plain that the prospect had to be proper, preferably blue-blooded. But they were so dull, those women, so preoccupied with their wish to be seen in the right way, in the right place, with the right person. So unnatural. Fran is altogether different. She is potent.

He pushes the door open, and Fran, blushing and giggling, shovels herself back under the covers, pretends she's been lying there all along.

"We could stay another night," he offers. "I have a few meetings on Monday, but I'll call Mimi, get her to postpone."

"Don't," says Fran, shutting her eyes.

"Don't what?"

"Don't talk about reality. Don't remind me." All she wants to do is revel in spontaneous decadence. She sighs, hears the *ticktock* in her head that tells her she has brides and dresses that need her attention. "I have to get back," she says. "I have wedding dresses to match, love to improve."

"And you really believe that?" says Rafael, leaping back onto the bed. "That your dresses have such power?"

"But you saw for yourself, at the weddings. Melissa, Rachel, Kate—they were…enhanced."

Rafael shakes his head. "It was you that 'enhanced' them, Fran, with your good advice. You may be bonkers, but you're not without sagacity. You said the right things, gave them the pep talk they each needed to hear, and somewhere deep down, it had an effect on them."

"Oh no," says Fran. "I was simply nice to them. The dresses did the work."

"And you think this work will have a lasting effect?"

"Obviously."

"In that case," he says, smiling, "I challenge you, Francesca Delaney: in six months, go back to your brides, go back to Melissa and Kate, and see where they're at. If they're still happy," he says, a glint in his eye, "then I'll marry you."

She stares at him, mouth open.

"Well, given your gift for engendering marital harmony, I'd be mad not to," he says.

"And if they're not happy?"

"Then we're all doomed."

# chapter 7

Days turn into weeks, weeks into months. Apart from their working hours, Fran and Rafael are barely apart. They don't think about it; they simply follow the instinct that tells them to connect—dinners in Rafael's favorite restaurants, evening swims at Hampstead Ponds, movies in tatty old cinemas, lots of sex, and lots of walks.

Mimi has few positives to say about Rafael's amorous inclinations, despite her own wedding day looming. She finds him vague, distracted, and irritatingly pleasant mannered. Fran meanwhile is not such a dedicated wedding-dress seller suddenly, but a love-struck dreamer. Mick scratches his head in frustration, finds himself unable to galvanize her into action. He can sell a dress when required but doesn't have her knack. He struggles to match a rayon '70s maxi with an angry teacher from Cardiff. He does his best with an embroidered white organdy number from 1959, but his bride of choice, a second-time-lucky divorcée from Bristol, keeps missing appointments. And he has no luck finding a tall, serious bride for the 1938 ivory fishtail. Even the Alessandra Colt dress lies dormant, lurking in the corner of the shop, as Fran pays no attention to the inquiries about it.

One evening, as they lie in each other's arms, overlooking the lights of London, Rafael sits up. "I've been thinking," he says. "It's time."

"Time for what?"

"Time to be official."

Fran arches an eyebrow. "As in…?"

"I have an engagement coming up, a London dinner. It's a big, stuffy affair that happens annually. I don't care for it particularly, but it's one of the highest profile social events in the capital, and it's important for the foundation. I'll be making a speech. I've been going for years on my own, which hasn't helped the speculation around my ability to maintain honest heterosexual relationships. One minute they shortlist me for bachelor of the year; the next they link me to a string of gay nightclubs, then the next, I read about how I've supposedly slept with three female prostitutes in one night. Which I've never done by the way, nor am I gay, nor do I care to be a high-status bachelor, but such is the way."

"I wouldn't care if you were any of those things."

"You're sweet, but I'd rather you did care."

"Oh really?"

"Yes, really."

"So if I care, what does that mean?"

"It means we should go public, make it official. We are a couple."

Fran smiles. "Rather than an indecent womanizer from a corrupt family and a deluded wedding dress fanatic getting up to naughty things under willow trees?"

Rafael laughs—then turns serious. "You have to understand, Fran, official in my world isn't a minor matter. I've had to give this some thought. Don't take it the wrong way, but you're a bit…maverick. You're not the type of girl they'll expect to see on my arm. I mean, if my grandparents or my father were still alive, they'd have paid you off weeks ago, had you removed to some remote corner of the globe, and shoved some well-connected debutante horror in front of me, insisted I produce a ring."

"You mean I'm too common for you?"

"I mean they were too old-fashioned. But they're long dead, Fran. And I couldn't give a toss. Their marriages were built around status, money, and maintaining appearances, but they were…toxic. Love didn't come into it. The point is," says Rafael, cheeks flushed, "will you be my official girlfriend?"

"I'll think about it," says Fran, teasing, coquettish, while inside she is bursting.

"One thing," says Rafael. "Please behave yourself. Or at least try to."

"Yes, sir."

"The press will be there. If there's any nonsense—"

"Impeccable behavior. Scout's honor."

"And you'll need a dress—"

"The best part!" says Fran, jumping up. "What kind of dress?"

"Something fabulous, but it can't be too revealing. No loud prints. No giant safety pins. We don't want dear old Lord and Lady Eyebright choking on their lobster bisque."

"Trust me," says Fran, "if there's one thing I'm capable of, it's coming up with the right frock for the occasion."

~⁂~

Regent Street is lined with paparazzi. Suited men and women in ball gowns flow along the red carpet toward the entrance to the Hotel Café Royal. The fame-hungry stop to pose or give a comment, the important give a nod or a very serious wave, but everybody fans themselves because the air is so close, dense with heat and the promise of a storm.

Rafael's car pulls up. Fran stares out of the window at the grand stone facade of the hotel. She stifles a giggle—no nonsense, best behavior. She is determined to do him proud, to make the best of their moment of official-ness. She has chosen a 1940s long gown and sequined bolero dinner jacket—elegant, sophisticated, with a hint of sexiness.

"Will it do?" she says.

"It's perfect," says Rafael. "Here, I have a gift for you." He hands her a box.

She looks at him.

"Open it."

Inside is an antique diamond bracelet. Fran gasps. She has never been given diamonds before. He has chosen well, a graceful Edwardian filigree bangle, special more for its age than its value.

"I believe," he says, taking her wrist and slipping it on, "it's over a hundred years old. Who knows? Maybe it once belonged to a suffragette."

Fran smiles, kisses him a thank-you.

"Shall we?" He offers his arm.

She threads her jeweled wrist through the crux of his elbow, and they step out of the car. The city is alive. The evening traffic rushes beside them as they stride toward the red carpet. The neon lights of Piccadilly glow bright against the gathering clouds.

"Stick with me," whispers Rafael. "As we get closer, they'll start calling my name. Don't panic about the flashbulbs. They're a little intimidating at first, but you'll get used to it." He squeezes her arm. "Ready?"

"Ready," says Fran, exhaling.

They step forward. The cameras snap and flash. The frenzy of light is so dazzling Fran is momentarily blinded. She hangs off Rafael, pulls him close, draws from his confidence. She thinks of Alessandra, immersed by the crowds on her wedding day, Lyle on her arm, the glory of her dress belying her shyness.

"Mr. Colt!"

"Over here, Mr. Colt!"

"Congratulations, Mr. Colt! This is going to be a big night for you. Can you give us a few words about the foundation's future plans?"

"Mr. Colt! Would you be so kind, with your partner, to pose for a moment. We'd love a few pictures."

"Is this your new girlfriend? Give us a smile!"

As they enter the doorway, Fran turns and smiles, happy to let the cameras catch her joy, but Rafael is impatient.

He grips her arm, a little firmer than necessary, leads her away. He wants to be inside the building, away from the all-seeing eyes of the cameras. They enter the lobby, its historic opulence now refreshed with modern design, the warmly lit surfaces of marble and mirror dominated by a dazzling glass chandelier. An usher greets them with champagne.

Fran gazes around her, entranced by the thought of the hotel's many famous patrons, of Virginia Woolf, Oscar Wilde, and David Bowie, whispering through the wrought-iron balustrades and the gilded ceilings.

Ahead, they see Mimi. She is wearing head-to-toe black, a column dress with no embellishment, poorly fitted. With her height and figure, thinks Fran, she could—*should*—be more daring.

"Good evening, Mimi," says Rafael. "Obviously you've met Fran already, but before the evening gets underway, I just want to let you know that we've decided to make our relationship official, so if the press start asking questions"—he looks at Fran, smiles—"we're together."

"As you wish, Mr. Colt," says Mimi, begrudgingly acknowledging Fran with a nod. "Here is your speech. I've highlighted the key points." She hands him a tablet.

He looks to Fran again. "I think I might need a minute to go through this. Will you excuse me? Perhaps you two could get a drink or something?"

Mimi scowls.

"You'll look after Fran won't you, Mimi? Maybe show her the ballroom. Did I tell you, Fran, it's where my parents had their wedding reception?"

He walks away, leaving Mimi and Fran in prickly silence, neither of them wishing to engage with the other. Around them, the new arrivals—men in tuxedos, women in ball gowns—gather and chat.

Fran studies the paintings on the ceiling.

Mimi looks at the wall clock.

Eventually, at the same time, they declare their positions.

"We don't have to be friends," says Fran, just as Mimi asks if Fran would be able to find her own way to the ballroom.

"I'm sure of it," says Fran, sweeping her dress as she turns away.

*How does he stand her?* she thinks, as she glides down the corridor with irritated bluster—but her ire is soon mellowed by the sight of the ballroom, with its explosion of Louis XVI grandeur, fluted Corinthian pillars, and gilded mirror frames. Everywhere Fran looks, the light bounces, twinkles, and shines.

"So," she whispers, casting her eyes to the elaborate ceiling, her thoughts flashing to the Alessandra Colt dress—the only dress that could upstage a venue like this. "Here is where it happened. Here is where Lyle and Alessandra danced and drank...and celebrated."

She stalls on the word, turns to look in the mirror, and feels it creeping over her—that sorrowful anguish she'd felt at Dryad's Hall, Alessandra's inner pain. She imagines the two of them, newlyweds, preparing for their first dance—Lyle, with his dark, deerlike eyes and coat-hanger shoulders, immaculate in a tailcoat and bow tie, luring Alessandra over with the curl of a finger. But all the while, his eyes roam the room, looking for the admiration of others, delighting in the power he perceives he has over any woman he desires. He grips Alessandra's wrist, pulls her close, forces her tiny, nervous hands to his waist. They start to move, then he orders her to kiss him... A kiss for what? Not for true love, of that Fran is certain. His mannerisms—the finger curl, the domineering grin, the self-satisfied glint in his eye—they are not the body language of affection. They are gestures of a power play.

Fran stills.

Is she kidding herself that Rafael will break the mold? Maybe the signs are there: telling her what to wear, how to be behave, when to be official.

*Once we're married, I'll change him.* She thinks of these words, said so often in the Whispering Dress, and recalls the number of times she and Mick have caught each other's eye, quietly shaken their heads in dismay. Perhaps he is merely concealing his dark side, suppressing the twisted dysfunction he was raised in. When it seeps out, no doubt it will get the better of him. In her mind's eye, she sees the dance get faster. Alessandra cannot keep up, the weight of the wedding dress is too heavy, the train too long, but Lyle forces her. They swirl and turn, until they are little more than a macabre blur of ivory silk and heartless laughter. Suddenly it feels like the air in the room is thinning, restricting her, suffocating her. She feels dizzy, staggers backward, then a hand tugs her arm.

"Fran…Fran, let's go. They're calling us in."

"Yes," she says absently. "Yes, of course." She feels vulnerable, defenseless, a hundred knots of secret anxiety twisting in her stomach. "I just need some air first," she says.

Before Rafael can argue, she hastens through the crowds, out of the main entrance, to the front steps, where the lights of Piccadilly and the traffic and the paparazzi are still active.

"Fran, what's going on? We have to go back in." He sees the camera lenses shift his way. "Come on," he insists, but Fran is distracted.

"The past is everywhere," she says, staring into the headlights of the oncoming cars. "I—I think the dress is trying to tell me something."

Rafael sighs, frowns, checks his watch. "Fran, we haven't got time for this," he says. "Get yourself together. Come *on*."

He bows his head in frustration. He doesn't mean to be so cutting, but she infuriates him. This is not the time.

But Fran doesn't hear his plea. Her attention is elsewhere. For a moment, she doesn't believe it, cannot bear to believe it…

She hasn't seen his face in years, but a second glance confirms it is him, definitely him. She'll never forget those devilish green eyes, that crown of curly hair. Besides, his name—in enormous font, across the side of a number 88 bus—declares it: Miles Ferguson. Her legs and arms flood with adrenaline as the sting of the pain she'd tried so hard to escape—the rejection, the sorrow, the humiliation—takes hold.

Rafael, meanwhile, perplexed that she has stumbled into this disturbed trance, whispers to her, tries to take her hand and lead her inside. She shakes him away, stares wordlessly at what she can only understand as a sign.

In the background of her daily distractions, she'd always known Miles's star was rising. She'd deliberately stayed away from media gossip, from television and film reviews, but when someone makes a blockbuster movie that's so successful it sees their face splashed across a poster on a double-decker bus on the other side of the world, well, it can no longer be avoided. His face, his horrible, great big, devious face, bigger than life, bigger than bearable, is right there in front of her, declaring victory.

As the shock sets in, a cloud bursts overhead. The first fat rain-drops hit the ground.

"Come *on*," pleads Rafael. "They'll be waiting for me."

Fran sniffs, holds her hands to her head. What to say? Where to start? All that soul-crushing, heart-slaying, awful, hideous hurt that has made her feel she can never trust her heart with another person again—could he even begin to understand? Her thoughts are pulling in too many directions. The fear has gripped her again and she just wants it gone. Her mind floods, swills with panic. Tear-stricken and shaking, she breaks away from him, hitches her skirt, and bolts from the scene, leaving a cacophony of chatter and flashbulbs.

They were nineteen. The play was William Shakespeare's *As You Like It*. He had a minor role, but it afforded him a few good lines, which he performed with gusto. Fran could tell he was destined for great-ness. Miles Ferguson. When she saw his name in the program, she read it over and over again. Everyone in the company loved him. His eyebrows seemed to dance when he talked. His hair was a shock of brassy curls, which flopped and bounced with every eloquent, witty, exaggerated expression. He was foppish and charismatic and young enough to get away with it. Backstage, he was often the topic of excit-able gossip, mainly from the chorus, who all vied for his attention, but it was Fran who caught his eye—little Fran with her costumes.

The feeling was mutual. When charged with fitting his doublet, she had to bite her lip to stop from smiling as she worked her hands around his taut chest. Little did she know that he was smiling too, because he'd watched her during rehearsals, sitting in the back row, stitching, always stitching, the dead spit of her mother, who was forever in the costume department, into everyone's business.

They stayed back late to hang out with the lighting crew, who always had beers in the theater after the show. One night, he made one of the technicians mic him up, then asked Fran out over the loudspeaker. She blushed and said yes, but only if he promised never to embarrass her again. He took her to a boring exhibition at the British Museum, which they both pretended to be fascinated by. They had miniature bottles of wine and salad platters at the Café in the Crypt in Trafalgar Square, which felt very sophisticated indeed, especially when their diet consisted of Pizza Hut and instant noodles. They kissed on the steps of the National Gallery, the whole of London at their feet. In less than a week, they were deeply in love. Within a month, they had moved into a room in his brother's flat in Camden, where the windows rattled whenever trains went by. The brother was also an actor, mostly toothpaste ads and voice-overs. He had different girlfriends every week. *Must be his minty fresh breath*, they used to joke.

When they had no money, they spent hours lying in bed, kissing and screwing and telling each other stories. When they were flush, they'd buy pizza and tobacco and sit all night at the top of Primrose Hill, talking about what would happen when Miles had his big break, which was coming, he assured her. And she believed him. After all, he was Miles. He was everything. She spread her little life beneath him and let him lead. She loved him so much, so intensely, it was all she could do. There was nothing else she needed nor, indeed, wanted.

Stoked by the know-it-all will of her early twenties, she refused to pay attention to her mother's words of caution. Because her mother, although keen to offer counsel, was hardly an expert in successful relationships. The best of her wisdom seemed to be: be careful, actors are tricky. Fran had grown up with the backdrop of her mother's fleeting, tangled love affairs—a different actor-boyfriend in every play she'd worked on. She always seemed to favor the arrogant ones. So really, it wasn't her place to cast aspersions on Miles, whose flirtatious habits were all part of his theatrical personality and, therefore, forgivable.

For three years, they were glued—or so Fran thought—to each other and to the nocturnal mayhem of theater life: late nights, mad weekends, performance highs, and after-show comedowns. They'd sleep through the morning, wake around midday, spend their afternoons in town, lazing on the lawn in Hyde Park or mooching in the cafés of various museums and galleries, being very arty and serious. At night, when Miles was at the theater, Fran would stay home, play house, sit alone in the living room mending and sewing, happy in her cocoon, waiting for her actor.

He wasn't the best at looking after himself. She called him the man-child. Left to his own devices, he would fall into unhealthy ways, drink too much, sleep too little, eat nothing but freezer food for weeks on end. She held him together though. She cooked him vegetables—from a freezer bag, but they had vitamins at least. She talked him up whenever he seemed mired in self-doubt. She adjusted his costumes, made sure he always looked immaculate onstage. She helped him learn his lines for performances and auditions, and encouraged him be his best self.

When a scout from the States contacted his agent to suggest he'd be perfect for the "Englishman" role in an upcoming soap pilot, Fran was thrilled—and a touch nervous that everything would change. How could a big break feel as frightening as it did exciting? Her fears were allayed, however, when, out of the blue, up on the crest of Primrose Hill, he pulled out a ring and proposed. It was his pledge, he told her, that no matter what happened in his career, she would always be his number one priority, that he couldn't imagine life without her. She fell into a fit of delight, so sure, so romantically defined.

She knew there and then, as the city unwound for the night, that she would make her own dress. The next day, woozy from the two and a half bottles of cheap champagne that they'd swigged, she set to work researching and planning and sketching. It couldn't be any old wedding dress. It had to be the dress that exemplified their moment at the altar. She pawed over archives of bustles and petticoats and peplums and veils. She spent more time thinking about the dress than anything else. The cake, the flowers, the vows were all quick decisions. The dress was monumental.

But when Miles came to her in a fluster, saying he'd been offered the soap pilot in the U.S. and would therefore have to spend the whole summer in the States, the wedding plans flew into the wind.

"We could always bring it forward," he suggested, pained by the sight of Fran's disappointment, desperate to please. "But that would only give us a few weeks to get everything sorted."

Perhaps she should have pulled back then. Perhaps she should have listened to her instincts and questioned the prudence of squeezing a wedding into a gap that simply wasn't big enough, but the matrimonial dream had been set in motion. Her heart was on fire, and in the depths of it, there was a burgeoning fear that she might, without sealing the bond, lose him to success. And so Fran's elaborate vision for a self-created dress never came together. Instead, she made a hasty purchase in her local bridal shop and the big day spun forward.

Ted Bowls was to give her away. Her father was supposedly a well-known opera tenor, not to be troubled, though probably, thought Fran, more likely to be Ted Bowls, the technician from the Wyndham's who looked out for her like a father. The day was beautiful, warm but not hot, with no clouds and a high sun. Her mother helped her get ready. She'll never forget that final moment in the mirror, the dress encasing her like a silver flower, turning her into The Bride.

The drive to the church was thrilling. The service was to be held in a little Norman chapel in Miles's home village on the Oxfordshire borders. He and Fran weren't fussy about the nuts and bolts of religion, but his parents had insisted. Tradition. Fran liked that, the idea of a family with traditions, rather than the wonderful but unstable reality of touring theater and cooking her own dinners since she was eight.

An idyllic village wedding, the path to the church door scattered with daisies. When they reached the churchyard gate, asway with the purple-and-blue-floral bunting she'd wanted, Miles's father rushed out, his face twisted with panic.

"I'm sorry, Francesca," he gasped. "I don't know what's gotten into him. It's…despicable. We've tried to talk him around, but I'm afraid he's resolute."

"What?"

"He's gone. I'm so sorry, my dear. It's off. He's called off the wedding."

"How? He can't—" In that instant, all she'd lived for since she was nineteen, her first and only love, crumbled.

He had a lot to say. There were letters, phone calls, and messages about how sorry he was, what an arse he was, how he shouldn't have led her on, about the fear that had gripped him as he'd stood at the altar, that it wasn't her—*oh please*—that it was him. His life, he'd realized, had a different path. He'd had a call two days before the wedding, from an agent in America who was so excited about the upcoming pilot, loved his "English gent" charisma and wanted to offer him representation. Apparently, he'd felt torn—so torn that he'd booked himself a flight to LA for the day after the wedding. And when challenged, had admitted he didn't love her anymore, or at least not enough to include her in his bigger and better fortunes.

She chose to hate him. Not so much for the fact that he had picked his career over her, but because he had taken her to the point of absolute degradation. Nothing, she learned, is crueler than a public breakdown of love, in front of all your family, your friends, your frenemies—the holes blown up inside you, on show for all to see.

She hid for a month, spent most of her days and nights—since she rarely slept—despairing about what she would do, now that her life map had been swiped out from underneath her. It was her mother who encouraged her to make fascinators—as she'd made such beautiful ones for her not-to-be bridesmaids—if nothing else than to occupy her time, given that the prospect of returning to work in the theater made her feel physically sick.

Little by little, Fran dug in and found her nerve. She took her fascinators to Camden, where she met Mick, who, twenty years her senior, gay, and benignly avuncular, offered uncomplicated friendship and a patient ear. He introduced her to the vintage clothing sellers in the stables, and there among the stalls of suede jackets, patterned shirts, feather boas, and retro cocktail dresses, she got her zest back. A chance encounter with a box of unwanted wedding gowns—the stallholder gave them to her for free, since they were too "novelty" for him to shift quickly—led to an obsession that would take over her life.

In the worst hours of her despair, with the doomed wedding still a fresh wound, she made twisted sense out of her decision to rush and buy a soulless, last-minute, mass-produced dress, rather than hold out and take the time and care to create her own heartfelt design. Could this have saved the wedding? Her moment of undoing, a curse on the nuptials? Good weddings, she concluded, needed good energy. And what energy could be better than the authority of been-there-done-it experience?

The Whispering Dress was born. Wedding dresses of history would guide the way for modern brides, and she would lead the crusade. For all that Miles Ferguson had taken from her, he wouldn't take away her belief in true love. If anything, her zeal for it expanded, her fulfillment now bound in the magic of enabling others to find themselves through her dresses and, in so doing, open the door to wedded bliss.

But not for her.

Her own heart had closed.

The pain of it ticks as she walks over the Thames, crossing at London Bridge. She has walked all night, barefoot, in the rain. Her elegant dress and bolero, now sodden, look ghoulish in the dawn. Each step along the bridge takes her back to the steps she never took up the aisle.

Rafael calls repeatedly, but she doesn't answer. She knows she owes him an explanation, but she is scared, sickened at the thought of bringing the past back to the surface.

The sunrise splinters over the steeple of Marylebone. She sits on a bench and watches a pair of pigeons scrap over a half-eaten burger bun. The church bells sound out the glory of Sunday morning. She recalls the nervousness of Alessandra as she walked out with Lyle. If she'd only listened to her anguish and not worn the family dress, not gone through with that extravagant, showy wedding, maybe she would have lived a happier life. Fran thinks of Rafael, the first, the *only*, person who has gotten past her defenses. He cares for her, of that she is certain, but it feels too dangerous. The gap between them, where their personalities clash and their pasts interfere, can it pull together? Can it be love, safe and true? She closes her eyes and aches.

He opens his door. The sight of him is bruising. She breathes hard, waits for the invitation to enter.

"Oh, Fran. Thank goodness."

At the sight her tear-stained cheeks and dirty, cut-up feet, he ushers her inside, leads her to the terrace, where she immediately curls up in the rattan armchair, lets the warmth of the morning sun bury her. He brings her coffee and toast, but her body has no desire for physical nourishment, so they sit together, share the silence, watch the boats on the river. The streets are quiet, save for the odd early jogger and the nannies in cashmere pushing their rich infant charges.

"I've failed, haven't I?" she says finally. "My opportunity to make us official…"

"Yes," says Rafael solemnly. "I rather suppose you have."

This isn't the answer she wants, but she understands it's the answer she deserves. She hangs her head.

"It was just a dinner, Fran—listen to some speeches, take a drink, make some small talk. I appreciate I built it up into a thing of importance, the 'officialness,' but really, it wasn't that big of a deal. I hate to think what the papers will make of your panicked flight. They all think I did something horrible to you, you realize. They'll be crowing about it, working up some new way to portray me as a posh degenerate rogue. But you knew that. I warned you. And still you made a fool of me."

"I'm sorry," says Fran.

"I've been up all night," he continues. "I've been searching the streets, calling you constantly. Didn't it occur to you that I'd be worried? And what exactly is your explanation anyway? One minute we were insanely happy, then suddenly you were tearing away from me into the storm. I thought you'd seen something awful, a car crash or a mugging, but…it was nonsensical. You just ran. Then I had a bank of photographers on my case, asking if you were all right. I didn't know what to tell them."

Fran sniffs, holds her head in her hands. The thought of Miles's matured face now ugly with vanity, his name stated in bold, like the world should be made to sit up and care. Is it not enough that he left her high and dry at the altar? Should she really, ten years later, have to have his movie-star success rubbed in her face? She wonders if he thinks of her ever, whether he regrets the callous act. She doubts it. But bitterness is ugly. It corrodes. She has to forget—just forget, block it out, shut it down.

"I got spooked," she says, bailing from the detail, reinforcing the wall.

"Spooked by what?"

"My past."

"Exactly what from your past?"

"Oh, never mind. It doesn't matter. Just…I don't want to talk about it."

"That's not good enough," he says. "Everyone has a past. We learn to live with it, then we let it go. You taught me that. If you can be so quick to dole out advice to others, then you can damn well take it yourself."

If she would only face herself, face him, tell him what's truly on her mind.

"The whole night was a mess," says Rafael, frustrated by her secrecy. "If you'd just answered my call, let me know you were okay.

I just wanted to know you were okay, Fran. I nearly missed my own speech because I was looking for you."

"Because it's all about you, right?"

"Oh, for god's sake, Fran." He's riled now. "Don't be so petulant. There are millions of people in this country who rely on the support of the foundation. I have to take care of things. I can't just run away. It's easy for you with all your fluffy whispering dress bullshit, but I have responsibilities. The foundation comes first. Always."

"Whispering dress bullshit? If that's what you truly think, Rafael, then clearly you don't accept me for who I am."

Without a word, she gets up from the chair, goes inside, and starts shoveling her things into bags. She should never have let him in, never given away the only fragment of her heart that remained.

"What are you doing?"

"I'm leaving," she says. "I don't belong here. I need to go." Part of her hopes he will snatch the bags from her hands, beg her to stay, work it out, put things right, but he does nothing.

"Yes," he says coldly. "Yes, I guess that's for the best."

"I must say," says Mick, "I was never entirely sure it was that healthy in the first place. Such a whirlwind for you, Fran, after years of, you know…dearth. You practically got through your first meeting, first date, first kiss, first foreign trip, first taste of spending every waking minute with each other within in a matter of weeks. The only thing missing is the wedding dress."

"Except it isn't missing, is it?" says Fran solemnly. "It's the dress that brought us together."

All the while, the Alessandra Colt dress sits in the corner. It blocks the sewing table and gets in the way when Mick wants to snooze on the chaise longue. He despairs at how Fran just sits there, staring at it so solemnly, as though she's in mourning.

"Sell it," he says. "Give it away. Wear it. Dance in it. I don't mind, Fran, but just stop moping about it."

She cries anew, so Mick fixes her a double whiskey, which, he assures her, is how he solved the pain of his second breakup.

As Fran stares into the drink, she pales. *There is no point looking for an escape*, she thinks, *when there is no way out.* In frustration, she shoves the whiskey across the table. It won't help.

Mick sighs, rubs her shoulders.

She resigns herself to selling it to the next bride who wants it, never mind its significance or legacy, never mind the risk. It is best to get rid of the dress and all the drama trapped within it, put the whole affair behind her—and then curl up alone, safe within her world, bury herself deeper and deeper into the love-misted sanctuary she has so artfully created. It is all she needs.

Later that day, Fran adds a link to her website, then posts images wherever she can think of—bridal forums, buy-and-swap sites, vintage clothing hubs. There isn't time to be discerning. She just needs that sale.

An hour later, the call comes in.

"Oh, hiya, is this the Whispering Dress? I'm interested in a wedding dress you posted for sale, some '50s designer thing? Is it still available?"

Fran stiffens.

"It is."

"Then I need it," says the voice. "I'm desperate. Had our first date last month, got engaged last week." Squeals of excitement. "Whirlwind romance, right? We want to do it straightaway, no hanging around, so I'm on a mission. I need a knockout dress like no one else will have." The woman talks quickly, in husky tones, barely breathing between words. "Just so you know, it'll be a high-profile event. I'm Karina by the way. Karina Thomas."

"Um—"

"I'm in the media. I've done a load of reality shows, but most people know me from Instagram. Your dress popped up on my feed, and I just knew straightaway…bang on. I showed it to Jez, and he said, 'Babe, make it happen.' So what do you say?"

"Uh…"

"Can I come to your shop and try it on?"

Fran hesitates.

"Pretty please?"

"Yes. Yes, of course. How about this evening? Around six o'clock? Come to my shop in Walthamstow. It's near the tube."

"Sweet."

That afternoon, Fran prepares the Alessandra Colt dress. Despite all it has been through, with a bit of careful preening, she makes it look almost as fine as it did the day Alessandra stepped out of the church at Marylebone with her nervous smile and hidden pain.

The way it fills the room, almost human in its energy, its personality bigger than all of Fran's other dresses put together, it has certainly tested her. She hopes Karina will take it, not just for the money, but for Fran's sanity. Even so, it is strange and sad to think this is the last she might see of it. She brushes her hand down the lace, caresses one of the hummingbirds, closes her eyes…

But there is no time to wallow in self-pity. Karina is on her way.

At twenty past five, Fran spots a lurking car, one of those big American-style Hummers, way too flashy for her neighborhood. A tall, curvaceous, big-haired woman climbs out, leans into the driver's window, says something, then totters toward the front door. Lip filler, cheek filler, white veneers, tiny nose, perfect forehead, shelf-like false eyelashes, fake tan—Karina is definitely not the type of bride Fran imagined for the dress.

She goes to the door, greets Karina with the best smile she can muster. Up close, Karina is startling. Her prodigious, magazine-grade features burst from her face with terrifying splendor. Her body is unfeasible, aided, no doubt, by a surgeon's scalpel.

"I'm Karina," says Karina, absorbed by her crystal-encrusted phone. "And you've still got this dress?"

She waves the photo that Fran had posted. When Fran nods, Karina smothers her with an excitable hug. Up close, Karina smells of vanilla frosting. Her skin is warm and oily. As they enter, she continues to chat, apologizing for the urgency, for her hectic schedule, and the trail of paparazzi that are desperate to get the scoop on her engagement. Fran suspects she is telling her this not really to apologize but to make it known: she is a person of fame.

"We've only been together a few weeks, so the papers are loving it. We met on the set of *Celebrity Love Snap*. Did you watch it?"

Fran shrugs. "Sorry. I don't have a TV."

"No TV? What do you do all day? Anyway, it's Jez, obviously. Jez Butler."

Fran shrugs again.

"Blimey, you are out of touch! He does fitness videos online. He's got loads of followers…but not as many as me, hah! I tell you, though, he's the kind of guy I always thought I'd marry. So buff. Honestly, he's got proper ripped abs, and his biceps are like this." She traces an oversized circle around her arm. "We're perfect together."

*Are you?* thinks Fran. *You with your lip fillers, him with his proper ripped abs. A really sound basis for a marriage.* "Perfect together"—a phrase she's heard too many times, usually from the mouths of those who are clamoring to convince themselves, let alone others, that their love is a plush, pink, heart-shaped cushion when, in fact, it's a rag…

She stops, shivers as though she has walked through a ghost, shocked by her own thoughts. What has happened to her? When did she grow so cynical? When did her views on weddings and love—so purposefully rose-fresh and optimistic—take such a nose-dive? She moves aside, allows Karina to see the full glory of the Whispering Dress.

Karina, however, is already back on her phone. She holds up a finger, then yaps into it while maintaining a stream of dialogue with Fran.

"It's him," she says. "It's Jez. He's with my driver outside. They've managed to park. He's badgering me to come in. Can he come in?"

"Actually, I generally don't have grooms in here. No sight of the dress before the wedding day and all."

Karina laughs. "Oh, c'mon. You'll love him. He's lush. Funny story…the other day we did this photo shoot at this really cool rooftop—*All right, Jez, hang on!*—this rooftop bar in Brentwood, and it had a pool and all the barmen were topless, except they had these little fake bow ties and one of them fell in the—"

"He can't come in," Fran interrupts, the tips of her fingers pressing together, a tiny subconscious shout of dismay. "It's a superstitious thing."

"A what?"

"For luck. No grooms."

"Oh, okay, whatevs," says Karina, plowing her glistening mouth into her phone again. "No, Jez, this is a girls-only thing. Wait there. Love you. Kiss kiss."

Then she thrusts her entire body through the shop, flinging her arms up as she feasts on the spectacle of the Alessandra Colt dress.

"*So cute!*" she declares.

Fran winces, while Karina, without invitation, starts shoving through the folded piles of silks, chiffon, and sheers, scooping the dishes of carefully restored, century-old beads as though they're candies. She stops at the dress, flicks her hair, pouts, and takes a selfie.

"Do you think it will fit around my implants? I had them done to a G last year." She prods her chest. "And I've got this," she adds, pulling down the sleeve of her stretchy yellow jumpsuit, revealing a full back and shoulder tattoo, a menagerie of roses, skulls, and nymphs in chains. "Cool, isn't it? My new direction. I'm trying to get an edge. My manager says bling is dead, so I'm going more hipster. So this dress is perfect. It's old, right?"

"Yes."

"And it's a big princess dress. Because obviously I want to be princess for the day."

Of course she does. Everyone does. The biggest cliché of them all.

"A vintage princess. That sounds so fucking cool. I'm thinking of, like, Jessica Rabbit. She's vintage, right?"

"In a way."

"Look." Karina moves close, intensifies her gaze. "I'll be honest with you. I've got a massive magazine deal hanging on this wedding. The right dress could make me—and you—a lot of money. You get me? There'll be photo shoots, interviews, loads of press coverage."

Fran nods, wonders whether she should be pleased. After decades of relying on word of mouth, finally here is a golden opportunity to get some proper attention. Yet somehow her soul is shriveling. She is losing herself. All her life, she has worked for love. And they've felt it, her brides, the curious transformation the minute they don their Francesca Delaney vintage, bespoke wedding gown. It isn't something that can be rushed. It has to be handled with care. It cannot be faked. It cannot be forced. Yet here she is, pushing a cursed dress onto a fake bride who is clearly more interested in followers and magazine deals than in creating a sound marriage.

Suddenly, the door flies open. Before Fran can react, her sanctuary is invaded by a tall, dark-haired gentleman, whose swagger is as insolent as his low-crotched tracksuit bottoms and designer T-shirt.

Karina throws out a cheerful "hiya babes" and starts furiously photographing. "What would you call this style of interior?" she says, working the phone around the room. "Gypsy chic? A sort of hippie-boho-Ibiza vibe? I like it. I think I could do up a restaurant like this. I've always wanted a restaurant."

Fran surveys the intruder, Karina's fiancé, Jez. He is everything she imagined he would be—not that she had much time to get a picture of him in her mind—with his square jaw; massive, muscly body; and statement clothing. A poseur.

"You're so impatient, babes," says Karina. "I told you, stay in the car." Then, she waggles her thumb in Fran's direction. "It's not me. It's her, the dress lady, she's funny about having blokes in here."

Jez turns to Fran, a cocky fix in his green eyes. "What, you think I might be a weirdo or something?"

"Not at all. I just..." She realizes she cannot be bothered to explain. In fact, she has no explanation—no rational-sounding one, at least. Just that...she doesn't want this. Any of it.

"Listen," says Jez, raising his hands, as if to reassure her that he's harmless. "I won't do anything. I won't touch anything. I won't even say anything. Just let me rest here, on this fancy chair." He pats the chaise longue. "The thing is, I need to approve this dress pronto. It'll be paying for some hefty bar bills, so it's got to look banging. Not hard for Karina though, is it? I mean, look at her." He admires his future bride up and down. "She rules every nightclub from Essex to Sussex. Social media loves us together. They've been bidding for aisle-side exclusives. I like your cave, by the way, all this old-fashioned shit."

Then he pulls her aside. "Okay," he concedes, with a whisper, "whatever you've heard about me, it's probably true. I'm a bit of an arsehole when it comes to commitment, but I *could* be loyal, with the right person. I just don't do possessiveness. I mean, what is it with you women? The moment you get it up in your heads that you're 'the one,' all the fun stops, and we get hysterics on the sofa at midnight, just because a text wasn't answered."

His phone pings to announce he has reached a million followers, and the delight of this eclipses everything. "Yes!" he says, punching the air. "C'mon!"

Sullen, Fran watches as he launches himself onto the chaise, leans back, and splays his knees with classic alpha arrogance. Once settled, he pulls a baseball cap from his pocket and covers his face, attempts to snooze. She hates the way his tracksuit bottoms sag and bunch. It is one thing to enter the Whispering Dress with the worst of modern manners, but another altogether to bring the worst of modern tailoring. Somehow she knows this betrothal isn't going to end well, regardless of the unsettling energy that surrounds the Alessandra Colt dress.

Fifteen thousand pounds. She knows it is worth so much more, but it gets them out of the shop. A quick fix, the cash in her hands. The trouble is, the sale is joyless. As the dress is driven away, she stands at the door and sighs, remembering the first wedding dress she ever matched, an adorable 1920s cocktail dress, knee-length, drop waist, shimmering with silvery beads, half of which were damaged or missing. Its poor state of repair didn't affect the magic though. It was the epitome of fun, the sartorial antidote for a bride who'd taken her vows so seriously she'd forgotten how to enjoy herself. *The wife-shaped woman*, Fran thinks. *Where is she now? Wedded bliss? Big house? Three kids? Hopefully she is living it up every now and again, despite her devotion to her family.*

Then there was the darling 1964 traditional gown. Fran thinks of it and smiles, remembering its fun, feminine style—raglan sleeves and a full-length A-line skirt with little bows around the neckline. It had been donated directly by the original bride, who had given up her partying lifestyle to care for her sick husband, whose sudden and grave cancer diagnosis had hit a mere month after the wedding day. Life, she'd said, handing over the dress, had its habit of throwing curveballs. She understood Fran's mission innately, had much to say about what marriage had taught her, not just about being a pair, but about being an individual within a pair, about patience and tolerance and the deep peace that can come from selflessness. She hoped the dress would make another bride feel as strong as she did, a dress of warmth and hope. A few months later, Fran found its perfect match: a spoiled, stroppy madam who did nothing but moan until the day of her dress fitting.

And of course, she couldn't forget the 1941 wartime austerity dress, hastily adapted from the original wearer's Sunday best—a grounding tonic for the bride whose main obsession in life was how much money her husband made. And the floral-print '70s maxi. And the 1984 ecru ball gown with the enormous chapel train. So many dresses, so many brides... *Where are they now?*

"Penny for them?" says a voice behind her.

"Mick."

"Chin up, girl," Mick sighs. "I don't know, Fran, that dress has a lot to answer for."

"That dress," says Fran, unsure whether she should be celebratory or sad, "is no longer our problem. I sold it half an hour ago."

"Oh," says Mick, a little dejected. "So that's that, then."

Three days later, while Mick is sweeping up the scraps from a rehemmed veil, Fran spies the folded pages of the day's half-read *Evening Standard* strewn across the countertop. She puts her sewing down.

"It's me," she says, eyes wide, astonished.

Mick peers over her shoulder, reads the headline: *Leading the Way with Vintage Wedding Dresses.*

Their eyes scan the half-page article. Fran's heart thumps fast, nervous as to what she might read about herself, but the piece is flattering.

"They're calling us a brand. The Whispering Dress is a brand… although I'm not entirely sure how I feel about that. I've never seen my work in that way, but oh, Mick…Karina was right. She said there'd be lots of interest."

"Relish it," says Mick coolly. "Most businesses never get this kind of exposure. You've done it."

Fran hugs the article to her chest, takes a breath, then reads again.

"It's very complimentary," she says, unable to contain her pride. "Listen to this: 'With one of the hottest weddings of the year on the horizon, speculation reigns over TV and media personality Karina T.'s choice of wedding dress. Our sources reveal that Karina is working with the London-based brand and vintage wedding dress experts the Whispering Dress.'"

Mick grins.

"Well, perhaps this is the first day of the rest of our lives. The Whispering Dress is about to go nuclear."

"Now you sound as deliriously optimistic as I used to be."

"Used to be?"

"It's been a long week," she says.

"I know you were fond of that monster dress, Fran, but that train was ridiculous, too much, too showy."

Fran stalls, suddenly overwhelmed. Her hype collides with the searing image of Alessandra, freshly married, standing beside her husband on the steps outside Marylebone church, that anxious smile, those sad, self-conscious eyes, the lace of her sleeve tugged over her bandaged hand. *The dress was a prison sentence.*

Just then her phone buzzes.

"Answer it, then," says Mick. "Could be another young bride who's seen the papers and is eager to jump on the latest wave of vintage cool. Go make your fortune."

"In a minute," says Fran, her insides churning.

"What's the matter?"

"Why do I feel like I've sold my soul?"

"Fran," he says, "it's just a dress."

She nods, smiles in agreement, but it isn't just a dress of course. It is more, so much more.

"So," barks Karina, her sentences coming through the phone faster than Fran can take in. "I've been in talks with my manager. We've had five of the top-selling magazines make six-figure bids. We've gone for an exclusive with *Good Life* as they're the best of the best. They already work with Jez and their online platform is global. Honestly, this is going to be massive. They think the vintage dress concept is a winner and guess what. They want to do a piece on you!"

"Me?"

"That's right. I told you, didn't I? I'll get you deals. Welcome to my world. Your whispering-vintage-bespoke whatever is about to get a serious attention fix. Consider yourself the hottest new bridal wear business in town. Rags to riches, babes, you watch."

Fran sets her gaze on the rippling satin of the 1930s fishtail. It shimmers in the sunlight. *Pinch me*, she thinks as an incredible lightness fills her body, makes her feel weightless, as though, without anchor, she might float up entirely, drift to the sky. Is this right? Is this really for her? She listens for Mick's worldly-wise tone.

"You deserve it, girl," he says. "You deserve it."

"The thrill of the chase is what keeps fans keen," says Karina. "Don't say anything to anyone about what the dress is made of or what color it is. Save it all for *Good Life*, because they've got the exclusive. They can have a few nuggets, just so they feel like they've got their money's worth. After all, their check is paying for half the wedding."

"Okay," says Fran, baffled by the game. "Nuggets."

"Don't worry. The *Good Life* girls are lovely. Complete pros.

They broke the story when I had that sex-tape thing with my ex—they were brilliant. I made nearly seventy grand from that one."

So this is the value of modern love? What happened to holding hands, kissing in the dark, opening doors, and giving up seats? Suddenly Fran feels sorry for poor Alessandra and Janice—if they only knew that their extraordinary wedding dress would be reduced to this.

⌒☙⌒

Press follows press. There is a full-page spread featuring silhouettes of gown shapes from different eras, called "Karina T.'s Guess the Gown Competition," endless hints and tips on how to wear vintage, and half a dozen articles about famous wedding dresses and the stories behind them—Grace Kelly; Wallis Simpson; Diana, Princess of Wales; Elizabeth Taylor. The nation has gone crazy for bridal wear of provenance.

Fran is inundated with messages from bloggers, vloggers, and Karina T. fans, all wanting to catch a hint of what the dress is about. It is enough to fill her days, but on Karina's instructions, she keeps the details quiet, offers nothing more than the odd hint or suggestion.

Two days later, Fran finds herself in the lustrous offices of *Good Life* magazine. Everyone in the building is excruciatingly young and fashionable. *Nuggets*, she thinks as the two women interviewing her lean forward for a handshake.

"My name's Ayesha, and this is Kath. We've been lifestyle reporters for *Good Life* for about six years. Best job in the world, isn't it, Kath?"

"Totally. Lovely to meet you, Francesca. We're really excited about this interview. We love Karina T. She'll make a stunning bride. We're doing a six-page foldout, looking at every aspect of the wedding, from the cake to the flowers to the guest list—and then there's the dress obviously. Who doesn't love a big old wedding meringue, hey? By the way, don't be intimidated by the tape recorder. Just pretend it's not there. So, Francesca, have you worked in the bridal industry long?"

Fran winces. She hates the word *industry*, but she loves this, the sharp-focused attention on the work she's so proud of.

"All my adult life," she says, trying not to gush. "I never went to fashion college or anything like that. I grew up in the theater. My mum made costumes for operas and touring plays. She taught me everything I know about dressmaking."

"Aw, sweet. And what got you into wedding dresses?"

"Um…"

"Are you a big softy? Do you love romance?"

"In a word, yes."

"Tell us a bit more about the dress. We understand it's antique. Vintage is so popular right now. When Karina T. told us about you— she's fab, isn't she?—we just knew we had to do a feature."

Fran smiles nervously. "I like old dresses, that's all. Dresses that are special."

"Okay…and what's so special about Karina's dress? We've heard it's beautiful, but…"

Fran presses her hands to her lap, leans forward, considers where to begin. This is all she has ever wanted, to be able to share the power and magic of history's bridal wear—and now she has a captive audience.

"The thing that struck me," she explains, retracing the moment she first set eyes on it, how she hadn't been able to resist trying it on—and then Rafael had seen her, their gazes had met across the dusty silence, and it had all begun...

Suddenly she hesitates, struggles to organize her thoughts.

"The—the first thing I noticed was that it was made by a fashion house from the 1950s called Garrett-Alexia." *Leave the emotion, stick to the facts.* "Not many people will know of the label these days, but anyone who can tell their Dior from their Balenciaga might recall the story."

"Oh, tell us more. We love a story, don't we, Kath?"

"We do."

"At the peak of success Gilles Alexia was supposedly attacked by his partner, Benjamin Garrett, during an argument. All that the pair had worked for fell apart and that was the end of the label, lost to history. In recent years, Garrett-Alexia evening dresses have become highly collectible, but their wedding dress, *this* wedding dress, the only one of its kind, has remained a forgotten mystery, until...until I found it in a house clearance."

"A house clearance?"

"Not just any old house. It was the estate of a...very old English family."

"Fascinating. Who?"

"Um..."

"Do tell. Your work is so intriguing."

"I—I don't think I'm at liberty to…"

"Oh, come on," says Ayesha with a chummy smile. "Off the record, just between you and us."

"Every detail helps," adds Kath. "Obviously we want to talk up your work as much as possible, so if we can get a really clear sense of the origins of the dress—"

They wait. Fran shuffles in her seat, worries about how much she should and shouldn't say. She wants, so much, to relish this opportunity, but the scrutiny makes her nervous.

"I think it was the Colts," she says quietly, hoping the name will mean little.

"The Colts? As in the charity family? The philanthropists? With the daughter who's always falling out of nightclubs and the snooty son?"

"Are you saying the dress originally belonged to a Colt bride?"

Ayesha and Kath exchange glances.

Fran purses her lips. *Stick to the dress, bring it back to the dress.* "The thing is," she says, fanning her reddening cheeks. "What I try to offer my brides is…not just dresses, but their wisdoms."

"And what wisdoms are you offering Karina T.?"

"I guess I'd like her to be more honest with herself."

"Honest? About wanting to marry Jez? Aw, they're made for each other, don't you think?"

"No…yes…I just… Honesty's always good, isn't it? Good for the soul. If you can face your truth, learn to be comfortable with who you are, where you came from, then I think that's a healthy basis for letting another person into your world."

"Not just a vintage wedding dress expert, are you?" says Ayesha. "You're kind of a marriage counselor too. Cute. So how will this fabulous wedding dress show Karina T. how to be honest? What can the Whispering Dress teach her that Vera Wang can't? I expect our readers will be curious."

Fran feels very hot suddenly. "Within the stitches of every item of old clothing," she says, "there's a story. And wedding dresses, I suppose, have the ultimate stories, because they mean so much to us. When a bride steps into such a dress, she absorbs something of its wisdoms. Honestly, I've watched it happen. It's...transformative."

"Right."

"I research all my gowns thoroughly, get to know their provenance inside and out. It makes all the difference."

"And what research did you have to do for Karina's dress?"

Fran pauses. "I—I traveled to Paris."

"How romantic!"

"It's where the dress was designed and made," Fran says carefully.

"By Garrett-Alexia, the fashion house you were telling us about? How did that play out, then? I thought you said they were doomed."

"They were, but I got to meet with Gilles Alexia's son. He runs his own label. He was...delighted to know that the wedding dress still exists."

"And will he get an invite to the big day, do you think?" says Ayesha, grinning.

"Oh no. Monsieur Alexia wouldn't want... His feelings toward the dress are...complicated."

Kath nods.

"I can see why you get so caught up in your work, Francesca. This wedding dress story just gets more and more curious."

"So do you think the Colts will get an invitation?" says Ayesha.

"I doubt it," snaps Fran.

"Ouu, sounds like bad blood?"

"There's no bad blood. It's just…Raf and I…"

"Raf? As in Rafael Colt?"

Fran stills, stiffens, winces. Emotion has gotten the better of her. She has said too much. "Er…" She's flustered. "Is that the time? I really ought to go now. I'm terribly sorry. Thank you for the opportunity."

"If we could just get a quick photo?"

"Yes. Yes, a photo. Where do you want me?"

Work continues. Rafael buries himself in its routines and rituals. Mimi is a constant. She hasn't much to say about his strange diversion into love with a vintage wedding-dress seller—a match so inappropriate it's laughable—or the fact that it has now, thankfully, waned, but she does everything she can to make sure he's busy, focused, distracted. There are meetings with donors, a tour of a special needs school, an interview with *GQ* magazine (some positive, well-controlled press for once), board meetings, going-away parties, and a selection panel for new bids. This is his realm, he thinks, where he thrives, where he does best. Yet, even so, he misses her impishness, her green eyes, her tumbling red hair. With every cell in his body, he regrets that he has not had the courage to speak to her in person, but he has been doing a little better recently. He fears rediscovering the bruise of her sudden, humiliating exit, just as he has started to think about letting go. They are not good for each other and that is that.

But still…

It pains him *so much*.

All through the day and night, his mind is peppered with thoughts of her. And then one morning, as the clouds gather over the green of Regent's Park, Mimi bursts into his office with a frenzied look on her face.

"I thought you'd cut ties with that woman," she snaps, thrusting a magazine in front of his face.

He looks down, sees a photo of Fran's face next to that ghastly looking reality TV star. Karina T.? The headline, in bold type, stark across two shiny pages, reads:

*Karina T.'s Wedding Dress Secrets Revealed!*

He reads on, Mimi leaning over him.

*As Karina T.'s star-studded big day approaches, here at Good Life HQ, we got the scoop from vintage dress expert Francesca Delaney about the eerie secrets behind Karina's choice of gown. According to Francesca, who loves researching the stories behind her vintage bridal attire, the unique dress, which will be revealed on the big day, once belonged to the illustrious Colt family. Our sources have hinted that the dress may also be linked to the original designer's demise in 1954. The dress, originally made for Mrs. Janice Colt, was then handed down a generation and worn by the late Alessandra Colt, who then*

*fell into decline after a period of mental instability. Francesca,*
*who has grown very close to the Colt family, personally reveals*
*that their struggles continue, with tragic youngest daughter,*
*Jane Carolyn Colt, heading back to rehab, and Rafael Colt,*
*once voted Britain's most eligible bachelor, now struggling with*
*sex addiction. Let's hope the dress brings more luck to Karina*
*and Jez!*

Rafael shudders, shuts his eyes. Sex addiction? That's a new one. Typically there is no mention of the foundation and all that it contributes to the upkeep of those that society has otherwise overlooked. He clenches his jaw, tension coiling in the pit of his stomach. How could she do this to him, to Janey, just as she's starting to make proper progress? The phones start ringing. He looks out of the window, sees a mob of photographers circling. He knows from bitter experience that if no better story comes along, they will wait there all day. He'll have to call Janey, send her extra security, instruct them to make sure she doesn't venture out unattended, not while she's so vulnerable.

Fran has no idea. Any regret about her sudden and unfinished exit from his life—those pangs of longing to have her back in his arms—is gone in that instant. He is done.

The moping has drained Mick's reserve of patience. It is obvious—to him at least—that Fran cannot shake this man. Despite getting rid of the monster dress, despite all the fun of her newfound fame and success, she is lost. She needs closure, resolution, or, best of all, restoration.

"Just call him," he says. "Don't be proud. If he likes you enough, he'll have you back before you can say 'wedding dress.' If he doesn't, well, at least you'll know he wasn't worth the trouble."

Trouble? She's the trouble. He did nothing wrong. She curses herself for her weakness, for her inability to express and share the pain she has masked for so long.

"Perhaps if you explain yourself," says Mick, "he'll be able to understand. I know what went you through, Fran, but he's got no idea. Sometimes we have to show ourselves, *really* show ourselves. That's where I failed with my Theo. You know what he said on the day he left me? He said, 'I would have liked you more, Mick, if you'd just shouted at me once in a while.' I thought I was doing the best thing, being Mr. Nice all the time, always placative, the one who walks away from the argument or softens the bad mood with a smile. But actually, what he wanted was a fight...not even that, Fran, he just wanted me to *share*, share myself, the person I am on the inside, which, I tell you, isn't always Mr. Nice. Show yourself to Rafael, Fran. If he loves you, truly loves you, he'll forgive. Who knows? Maybe he's missing you as much as you're missing him. But one of you is going to have to back down and make that call."

Fran fingers her phone, turns it over and over in her hands. She feels like a teenager again, aching with first-love blues. She wants to put it right, make it good, get back to where they were, rolling through the haze of bliss, but the fear is big. Rejection is costly.

Her phone buzzes. She blinks, nearly drops it.

"Oh my god! It's him. It's Rafael! Mick…it's Rafael! He's calling me."

"Telepathy," says Mick with a grin. "Must be a sign."

Fran's spirits soar. Mick is right—always right. "Raf?" she says, trembling at the thought of his voice.

There is silence, a quiet sigh.

"Raf? Are you there?"

"Yes."

Something is wrong. His voice sounds flat, as cold and emotionless as it was the day she first met him.

"I—I'm sorry about everything," she says, desperate to pull him back to her.

"So am I, Fran," he says. "Sorry I ever wasted my time on you. Sorry I ever fooled myself into thinking you were someone I could get close to, someone I could love, someone I could trust—"

"Wha—?"

"Bailing out of the Café Royal dinner was unhelpful, but what you've done to me now… You've got some gall, Fran."

Fran blinks, bewildered. What has she done? "I don't understand—"

"How much did they pay you?"

"Huh?"

"Whatever it was, I hope it was worth it. Oh, Fran, I was giddy about you. I was *transfixed*. I never let anyone get as close as you have. I allowed you in, and now…all you've done is betray me."

"What? Tell me. What have I done?"

"You sold us out, me and Janey. You did some tacky little interview with *Good Life* magazine and gave them everything they wanted. Now everyone is jumping on the story, and my phone hasn't stopped ringing. I wouldn't mind you doing interviews, Fran, snatching some positive promotion for your business, but surely you knew I'd never want the dress linked to me. Do you have any idea how much damage this could cause? Listen to this: 'Jaded family's dirty money: how a vintage wedding dress holds the key to corruption.' Or how about this gem: 'Rafael Colt, heir to the Colt fortune, linked to an age-old crime.' And then of course there's this one: 'Jane Carolyn Colt: My Drinking and Drug Shame.' She's beating it, Fran. She's doing the best she's done in years. *She doesn't need a fucking media storm.*"

Fran opens her mouth. She cannot find the words she wants or needs. His anger is raw and true, from the core, and she can't deny him it. She knows what it means to him.

"Don't ever come near me again," he says with the finality of death, then the line cuts out and she is left to her silence.

She shuts her eyes, senses Mick watching her. She doesn't want to hear his wisdom now. She just wants to reverse time and erase all her blunders, take back every overeager interview comment, cancel the dress sale to Karina, remove all traces of her self-inflicted ruin. She pictures those two gushing women with their leather jackets, big smiles, and wall of questions. So kind, so interested, they made her feel like a star, a shining, bright light that the world wanted to see. And she fell for it. What a fool. It washes over her, the feeling that she has come undone, and worst of all, she has done it to herself.

"I need it back."

"What?"

"The Alessandra Colt dress."

"From a bride whose wedding is…this afternoon? You can't, Fran! You of all people know how devastating that would be—"

"For what? For Karina's wallet? For her Instagram profile? She doesn't love Jez Butler. And he doesn't love her. It's a media sham, and I don't want to be part of it. I should never have been part of it, Mick. It's not what a wedding should be. That dress—for all the trouble it's caused me—it deserves better. I'll pay her back the money. I'll buy her ten dresses in any style she likes. I just need that one dress back. If I have any hope of proving to Rafael that I didn't sell him out intentionally, that I'm not a shallow, doting idiot who can't get my shit together, then I need to stop that dress from being exploited."

Mick shrugs, knows better than to argue. When Fran has a passion, she stops at nothing until it's satisfied. Besides she is already frantically searching through her gowns, looking for substitute offerings. What would Karina T. want? Need? How should she fix such an already heartless betrothal? The 1930s fishtail is too fabulous. The '50s tulle prom dress is too sweet. Then she spots it—the perfect alternative, languishing inside the art nouveau wardrobe.

# chapter 8

THE BENTLEY ROOMS ARE AWASH WITH GOLD: RIBBONS, BOWS, sashes, flowers, balloons, novelty sequins, and paper pom-poms. Head bowed, with an armful of dress, Fran races up the stone steps, Mick beside her. They brush past the doorman with such determination he can only assume they are part of the emergency cheering crowd, called on to soothe Karina T.'s crazed tantrum. The lobby, grand and old school, at odds with the explosion of gold frippery, is swarming with people of all types and purposes. Fran sees a huddle of casual-dressed paparazzi in the corner, their cameras slung over their shoulders. She bristles with anger.

"Blend in," she whispers, as they head for the stairs.

She has attended enough of these occasions to know that, at this stage in proceedings, people are too busy to care who's in and out of the door. Just as they reach the first floor, however, their shoulders are clamped by a burly security guard, hands like frying pans.

"Bride or groom?" he says, his deep voice booming.

"Bride."

"Let's see your ID then."

They scrabble in their pockets. Mick produces a pocket watch and a beard comb. Fran produces a Whispering Dress business card and a thimble.

"What about your lanyards?"

Fran shrugs. Lanyards? At a wedding? The thought depresses her.

"If you haven't got clearance, you're not going up. Strict orders."

"Please," says Fran, holding up the dress. "I'm the famous London-based vintage wedding dress expert. We have to get this to Karina urgently. She's waiting for it."

The security guard gives a belligerent sneer. "And I've got to do my job. You press will try anything, won't you?"

"We're not press. We're—"

The guard folds his arms. "Come back when you've got your lanyards."

Fran and Mick march out of the building. There is less than an hour to go. The parking lot is filling up. Guests are starting to arrive. Suddenly an almighty banshee cry comes from the upstairs bay, followed by a pair of hair straighteners, which fly from the open window and land in a baroque fountain.

"Well, at least we now know what room she's in," says Mick.

"Maybe we can climb up there," says Fran, pointing to a secluded, wisteria-clad porch. "It'll give us something of a ladder at least."

"Are you kidding? I'll never manage that."

"Got a better idea?"

Before he can argue, Fran jumps onto the trellis, tests it for strength, then begins to ascend.

"Why do I get the feeling you've done this sort of thing before?" says Mick, slinging the spare wedding dress over his shoulder.

"Hasn't everyone?"

"Oh, Fran," he sighs. "The things I do for you."

Eventually, after some heaving and hoisting, they find themselves in a never-ending corridor of yellow damask, gold sconces, mahogany doors, and maroon carpets. Members of the wedding party flit from one room to another, forcing Fran and Mick to press against the wall.

"Okay," says Mick. "I admit, this does have some excitement factor, but we're running out of time."

"This is it," says Fran, taking the dress and approaching the door of the executive suite.

"We can't just bundle in—"

Another burst of screaming erupts through the mahogany veneer. Karina's voice rings out: "It's not working! It's not right! Fix it, for fuck's sake!"

"At this point," says Fran, "I don't think anyone will care how we enter, let alone who we are." She pounds the door.

A weary-looking bridesmaid answers.

"Can we see Karina?"

The banshee wail again.

"I warn you, she's in a right mood."

"Let us help," says Mick assertively, pushing into the room.

Once inside, they see Karina in the dress, sitting on the end of the bed, mascara streaked down her cheeks, face twisted in rage.

"You?" she sniffs.

"Hi," says Fran, "I just wanted to check how you're getting on, because—"

"It's awful!" wails Karina. "Look!" She stands up.

To Fran's horror, the dress has been butchered. Half of the skirt and all four meters of the train have been sheared off, in a botched attempt to raise the hemline. Emotions of all kinds rush through Fran, none of them good. "Oh god no! What have you done?"

"I couldn't walk in it," whines Karina. "I got Max, my assistant, to cut it off. He said he'd do it neatly, but he's totally messed it up!"

"You don't say," says Mick, aghast.

"Now it looks like a scarecrow made it. They'll tear me apart in the glossies. I'll be ridiculed. This was supposed to be the making of me...and now it's fucked!"

Her friends gather around, pat her on the shoulder, dab her tears.

Fran feels slightly queasy. She glances sideways at Mick, then begins tearing the cover off the alternative dress.

"Lucky for you," she says, "I might just have the answer. I have this—" She offers her own old wedding dress.

Karina looks up.

"Now," says Fran calmly, confidently. "Relax. Let me fix your dress disaster. If you wear this delightful number"—she presses the dress to Karina—"I think you'll have a fabulous day. It's a beautiful cut for you, and I can do all the required alterations right here, right now, so it will fit like a glove. The cameras will love it, full princess overload."

"Where did it come from?"

"Oh, I've had it for a while. Never found the right bride for it. But you...you've got the exact attitude to pull it off."

Karina sighs. "Okay," she says, brightening slightly. "I suppose I could try it. I always look fierce in silver."

Collective relief fills the room as Karina yanks off the remains of the Alessandra Colt dress, freely exposing her enormous silicone breasts to the room. Her entourage gathers around and helps her wriggle into the alternative dress. It is two sizes too small, but this doesn't stop them squeezing and squishing, forcing buttons to fasten where they shouldn't. Normally Fran would balk at such stitch-straining dress abuse, but it is weirdly gratifying to see her nemesis gown being punished in this way.

"There," says Karina, gasping with joy—and the tightness of the corset, the flesh around her armpits spilling out. "I don't think it needs altering at all."

"It looks hot," says her makeup guy. "Much sexier than the other one."

"Totally. Thanks, babes," says Karina, like she'd never shed a tear.

Crisis over. Her entourage regroups to begin fixing her eyelashes and rearranging vast sections of fake hair. Fran and Mick, meanwhile, gather up the Colt dress and the remnants of its train and make a swift but discreet exit.

The press attack dies away. The lawyers secure an injunction to stop inflammatory comments about Jane Carolyn Colt and peace is restored. All Rafael is left with, however, is a lake of loneliness. The loneliness itself isn't the hard bit. He's used to it. He knows how to fill the void with work and Netflix and books. It's the not knowing when or if it will ever end. Especially since…since he has now had a glimpse of an alternative way to be.

Mimi struggles with his gloom. Bad business decisions are happening all around him, but he doesn't seem to care—or even notice. He is limp. He has lost all interest in running the foundation, and she is tired of picking up the loose ends. She wants some time off for her forthcoming nuptials—she hasn't had a chance to plan or find a dress—but every time she mentions it, Rafael gets grouchy.

"Does Anton really make you happy?" he demands, hunting for chinks.

"Happy enough," says Mimi. "I find his conversation a little tiresome, but he works a lot, so I don't think it will be a problem."

"Do you love him?" he asks.

Mimi shrugs. "We get on. That's enough."

"Really? That's it?"

"I need a visa and I want a child. I'll love my child, of that I'm certain, but I have no interest in flowers and chocolates and flying cupids. I simply want a stable home and reliable genes for my offspring."

"Okay, noted: never turn to Mimi for advice regarding matters of the heart, or she'll cut you down with her emotionless scythe."

"You can think I'm harsh if you like, but really, I'm only calling it how it is. Love is a bit of frippery designed to distract people from the dullness of their day-to-day lives. It's a shiny coating and, let's face it, shiny coatings are for shallow people."

But he isn't shallow, he thinks. And yet he has felt it sparking, crackling, burning through his heart.

"The moment I saw her," he says, staring vacantly, "standing there in that damn wedding dress. We caught sight of each other and…I knew it then, right there and then, that I'd fall in love with her."

He breaks down, sobs into his hands. With a grimace, Mimi strokes the tip of his elbow, hopeful that human contact might stop the outpour.

That night, as Rafael paces his empty flat, he finds a scrap of Fran's lace on the floor. His big white box suddenly feels so sterile without her. He pours a glass of wine, places the lace in front of him, drinks alone. He thinks of Paris, of how they lost themselves in the city of light and felt like they never wanted to return to normal life. No good though, no good can come from ruminating.

The calls stop. No one seems interested in whispering dresses now that Karina T.'s hotly anticipated legacy gown has disappeared from sight. Karina even talks publicly, with strong emotion, about how she was let down by her supposed dress "expert," that the gown she ended up wearing was nothing like the gown she'd always dreamed of. This has triggered a queue of online rants from sympathetic brides who've also been let down by their dressmakers. Hems cut too short. Extortionate alteration costs. Straps falling off. Plus all manner of stains, rips, snags, and botched fastenings. The *Evening Standard* runs a feature: "Wedding Dress Disasters of the Rich and Famous."

Yet days later, all trace of the dress-swap fiasco is eclipsed by the gossip from the honeymoon. The internet is awash with photographs of Karina in a white bikini, posing with an unnamed millionaire.

There is also some footage of her and Jez arguing in their Maldives hotel, throwing mojitos at each other: "Explosive celebrity bust-up, honeymoon cut short." The rumor is out there, that they have already had the marriage annulled and are now in talks about a new TV reality show: *Karina and Jez: Happily Ever After?*

The dress has been cut so crudely, with no care or thought for the lie of the weave or the delicate embroidery. *Fabric is like skin*, thinks Fran. *Once it is cut, it scars forever.* She repairs the damage as carefully as she can, a surgeon to a patient, and all the while, her tears drip into the seams—tears for the demise of marriages based on love, tears for all the brides over the years that she believes—*truly believes*—she has helped; tears for Alessandra, pushed into a marriage she wasn't ready for; tears for Janice, who'd deluded herself that a big, white wedding would be the solution to her fiancé's philandering; tears for loneliness; tears for herself.

But if nothing else, she still has the Whispering Dress, her whimsical fantasy of history, where brides are saved and soothed by the silvery threads of time-earned wisdom. The magic is real, *surely?* Even if she has no Rafael, she still has that—the gift of love that she has given to so many others. She will always have that.

She remembers he challenged her:

*I defy you, Francesca, in six months, go back to your brides, back to Melissa and Rachel, and see where they're at. If they're still happy…then I'll marry you.*

But if not?

There is no *not*. New tears form, but these are happier tears, fueled by the hope that her dresses work. She will go back to her brides and see for herself, find the assurance that she still has some-thing to give, something to believe in.

She picks herself up and hastens through Walthamstow market, through the busy stalls and fabric shops, where once she used to be queen. Her hair is a mess, her cheeks blotchy from all the tears. She has drunk most of a bottle of cheap white wine, triple her usual threshold, and has hit that point of bodily unreality, uncontrolled rivers of emotion spilling all over the place.

Mrs. Rachel Joseph approaches her pink front door. She is dressed in work clothes—black trousers, cream blouse, and navy trench. She has a folder of papers under her arm, a bag of gym clothes, and a takeaway coffee. She is too busy fumbling for her keys to notice Fran approach.

"Rachel?" says Fran, trying to keep her voice level, to hide her inebriation.

Rachel turns, startles, then finds the face. "Oh, I remember you," she says warily. "Francesca, right? You did my wedding dress."

Fran smiles, keeps her distance, a meter from the stone steps that lead up to Rachel's door. The house is immaculate, just as she'd suspected.

"How are you, Rachel? How's…married life?"

Rachel hesitates, observes Fran's disheveled appearance, her tear-stained cheeks and uncombed hair. "It's…it's good, thanks."

"Your house is nice."

"Um, is there something I can help you with?"

Fran's face cracks. She does her best to hold it together. "I just…wondered if you were happy. You seemed so happy on your wedding day. I chose that dress for you because I thought you needed some grounding. You were so caught up in having some huge extravagant wedding, it was as if the actual marriage—the life, the commitment, and everything that comes with it…it was as if none of that was important to you. I thought the dress would help you appreciate the value of simplicity, remind you that love needs nothing other than two people who care. And you felt it, didn't you? On that day? You seemed really happy together. My question is…has it lasted?"

Rachel fingers her door keys. Her eyes search back to the dream-like joy of walking with her new husband in the sun, among all those stupid swans and ponies, laughing at their ridiculousness.

"Elijah and I are great," she says, a smile on her face. "In fact, we're going backpacking. We cashed in the all-inclusive Dubai honeymoon, and we've handed our notices in at work. As soon as the wedding was over, we both said it…*we want an adventure together*. Honestly, it's the craziest thing. We've even bought a *tent*. It just seems…right."

Fran sniffs, wipes her tears. "Oh, Rachel, I'm so happy for you. That's the best news ever!"

Over in Streatham, Melissa West is moisturizing hands in her sister's nail bar. She recognizes Fran immediately but is unnerved by her scruffy demeanor—Fran, who was always so well put together, so dainty and stylish.

"Hey," says Melissa, beaming. "Look, everyone. It's Fran. Fran's the genius who found me my amazing wedding dress."

The sister's eyes narrow to slits. The less said about that scarlet monstrosity the better.

"How are you, Melissa?" says Fran.

"I'm doing all right, you know. Doing good. What about you?" She pauses, a twist of concern on her face. "You all right, Fran?"

Fran nods vacantly, blinded by the floor-to-ceiling shelves of candy-colored polish, all the glitter gels and metallic shellac. "How's married life?"

The sister steps forward, looks protectively over Melissa.

Melissa shrugs. "It didn't work out, Fran. He left me, three weeks after the wedding."

"*You* left him," says the sister.

"No, Jac. He left me. Let's not dress it up like something it isn't."

Fran's eyes widen. Not Melissa. She'd had every hope for Melissa. The Meryl Percy dress had been one of her finest, most potent offerings yet.

"Turns out he was sleeping around," says Melissa. "Guess I should have seen it coming."

"I'm sorry," says Fran, shocked, her tears now flowing uncontrollably, glazing her eyes, blurring the lights. "I've failed you. I'm so sorry. I thought I could help you but—"

"No," says Melissa. "Don't be sorry." She goes to Fran, takes her in her arms. "Don't you see? It's the best thing that could have happened. You, your dress, that dress you picked for me—it gave me back my confidence. Don't you remember? In that moment when I tried it on, you showed me I was beautiful as myself, to hell with other people, to hell with husbands. You've got nothing to be sorry about, Fran. Honestly, you saved me."

"Really?"

"Definitely. I said so, didn't I? Tell her, Jackie." She nudges her sister.

"Yes," says Jackie, forcing a smile.

"Oh, don't worry about her," says Melissa, linking arms with Fran. "She gets moodier every second. I reckon it's the fumes from the polish. But you listen to me, Fran, the wedding joy might not have lasted, but I've got me now. Life's great. I'm working for Jackie and I've moved out, got my own flat. And I'll meet someone else one day, I'm sure, but this time I'll be a bit more choosy. I know my worth now."

The two women hug. Fran declines Melissa's offer of a free mani-pedi and says goodbye, doubtful their paths will ever have cause to cross again. As she walks away, she knows, somehow, deep down, the dresses have done their job.

༄

Later that day, Fran's phone rings. A foreign number.

"Francesca, ciao."

"Fabian?"

"How are you, Francesca? I am so excited to speak with you. I have been doing some thinking. Did you keep it for me?"

"Um…"

"The dress. It has been on my mind since we met. I think the only way to solve this mental pester is…to have it. I have decided. I would like to buy the dress after all."

Fran sinks into the armchair beneath her, eyes the strands of white cotton spilling out of her sewing box.

"Oh, Fabian, I'm afraid it's been very badly damaged. I've repaired it as well as I can, but I expect its value is reduced considerably. You may not want it now."

"But it's still in one piece, no?"

"Just about."

"Its heart still beats."

Fran smiles. "Its heart will always beat."

"You understand me, Francesca. You know clothes the way I do. So you'll understand when I say I want it regardless—not for how it looks and what it's worth, but for what it means. It is the only way, I think, that I can truly come to terms with its legacy. When I have it in my hands, I shall see how I feel and decide what to do. Who knows? Maybe I will put it in a glass case and show it off to my friends. Or maybe…maybe I will destroy it."

Fran flinches.

"If you could ensure that it is packaged well, I will send my best courier right away, then I will deposit £50,000 into a bank account of your choice."

Fran's mouth falls open.

"I believe this is its market value," says Fabian, "unless you think otherwise."

"No, that…that sounds perfectly reasonable," says Fran, her legs trembling in shock.

"Well, in that case, just let me know when the dress is ready for collection. If you need some time to think about it, however…"

"Yes. Yes, I might."

⚜

Fran thinks of the money offered by Fabian. With a windfall like that, she could do so much. She could travel, go hunting for vintage wedding dresses of the world. Or buy a canal boat—she's always wanted a canal boat. She could paint it red, add gypsy-style decor, flowerpots and deck chairs, a little bed, and a bike for shopping and errands. She could call it Alessandra. She could set up London's first wedding dress shop on a barge. How sweet. How hip. But as the daydream unfolds, its sides start to fray and give way. Underneath the idyll, her conscience bulges. While the dress has its complexities, at least its fabric and stitches are something she can relate to. Money? What difference does money make when what she really wants is love?

She stares at the dress now, retraces its journey, remembers how she pulled it from the wardrobe, saved it from a dumpster, spared it from cigarette burns as it was paraded in jest by Janey, how she rescued it from the hands of a half-crazed bride who'd gone at it with a pair of kitchen scissors. After all this, she belongs to it, and it belongs to her—each just as bruised and battered as the other.

She slips off her tea dress and climbs inside the wounded silk, feels the form of the bodice, the lace of the sleeves, and the flow of the train. Despite its injuries and its turbulent history, despite its sad whispers, it sings to her, as though, somehow, it still has a purpose. Suddenly the door rattles. Fran looks up, shocked to see Mimi entering the Whispering Dress, dressed in funeral black.

She glares at Fran's white sparkle, looks her up and down, gives a tight, condemnatory frown.

"Can—can I help you?" says Fran.

"I hope so."

"You want a wedding dress…from *me*?"

"No." Mimi sighs, exhales slowly. "I want you to do something."

"Like what?"

"I want you to reunite with Rafael."

Fran blinks. "But—"

"As his personal assistant of three years, it is my obligation to ensure that Rafael's working life runs as smoothly as it can. I am astoundingly good at my job, Francesca, but I am not so skilled with…affairs of the heart. Right now, Rafael seems to want something of an emotional connection. He told some bizarre story about seeing you in a wedding dress"—she looks Fran up and down again—"and that he immediately knew it was undying love…or something. Either way, as annoying as he was when he was with you, he is worse without. So essentially, you need to get back together. Otherwise, I shall end up throwing things at him."

Fran listens, astounded. Of all the people to be playing matchmaker, she never thought it would be Mimi.

"You genuinely think he still loves me?"

"I know so. Unfortunately for Rafael, he is too proud and perhaps too scared to admit it. He hasn't had a serious girlfriend in all the years I've worked with him. You're the first…the only one that… Anyway, perhaps you'll see to it?"

Fran looks down. "If he wants me," she says quietly, "then he needs to come to me himself."

"Then I shall tell him that," says Mimi.

"Hey," says Fran, a thought crossing her mind as Mimi makes to leave, "you're getting married soon, right?"

"In a week."

"And you have a dress?"

Mimi frowns. "I've scheduled a shopping appointment on Friday afternoon."

"Leaving it late. Any thoughts about style?"

"Style? Why should I be concerned about style? I shall select the kind of dress I usually wear, that my fiancé is used to seeing me in, so that he'll know he's marrying me and not some trussed-up, little bridal zealot in white."

"Not so little, though, since you're tall. In fact…how tall are you? Six foot?"

"Six foot one barefoot, I believe."

Fran grins. "In that case," she says, the hint of a dress match bubbling in her soul, "I think I have the dress for you." She directs Mimi to the window, where the 1930s fishtail shimmers.

"No," says Mimi flatly. "That's not for me."

"Trust me," says Fran, a glint in her eye, "once you've tried this beauty on, life will never be the same again. Mimi, you are about to discover your inner joie de vivre."

They both made mistakes, she knows that. Both allowed their past-made fears of commitment to drive a wedge between them, both failed to empathize, to live a moment in each other's shoes, but perhaps this is love. Confusing. Contradictory. Its dizzying wonders constantly beggared by uncertainties. That evening, still wearing the Alessandra Colt dress, touched with an eerie, billowing lightness, Fran's instincts draw her out of the shop. Before she can question them, her hand reaches up, hails an oncoming taxi. She climbs in.

"Where to?"

"Epping Forest," she says. "There's a house there. It's hard to find, but I'll direct you. It's called Dryad's Hall."

The house is silent, its glossy fringe of rhododendrons shivering in the breeze. The lock on the front door is loose. Fran pushes the door gently and wanders inside, into the ghostly rooms with their sad, soft vacancy. She looks around for memories of Alessandra but feels nothing, almost as though, without its furniture and personal effects, the spirit of the house has deadened. Then a butterfly lands on the dusty window ledge, stops briefly, and flutters away. Fran's senses prickle. There, at the window, suddenly she can see her… Alessandra. Older now, a mature woman, silently gazing across her beautiful garden.

Fran reaches out. "Alessandra," she says, desperate to hold on to what she knows can't remain.

Immediately the imagining fades. Just before it vanishes completely, however, the diminishing face of Alessandra turns. She looks at Fran in the dress, *her* wedding dress, those soft folds of white silk, the sumptuous lace overlay, those delicate beaded, embroidered hummingbirds, symbols of infinity. She smiles kindly, looks back to her garden, then is gone completely.

For ten minutes, Fran stands alone, staring at the empty window.

There is peace now—she can feel it. Alessandra has found peace. Curious, she wanders through the deserted hallway, to the library and the terrace at the back. The door is ajar so she walks outside, makes her way down to the ornamental gardens, to Rafael's bridge, where they stood that evening and talked about how, next time, his troubles would be behind him. Maybe they are, one way or another.

In the soft evening light, she walks to the middle, leans over the balustrade, the wedding dress billowing in the breeze, and vows to be strong for Alessandra. She drops a leaf into the water, turns to go, and then, through the haze, he is there. He comes to the bridge, his tall, fine form as real as the sun. In silence, they lean together, bathed in amber end-of-day light, gazing at the frogs on the water lilies.

"They don't turn into princes," says Fran quietly.

"Nor do they look good in wedding dresses," says Rafael.

They face each other.

"It's a bit of a mess," he says.

"Us or the dress?"

"Let's start with us."

"I'm sorry I let you down," she says, eyes glassy with tears. "I never meant to cause any stress for you or your sister. And I'm also sorry I couldn't explain myself. The truth is, that night at the Café Royal, I saw my ex—or at least a photo of him—on the side of a bus outside the venue. He's an actor in films." She sighs. "He broke my heart years ago, jilted me at the altar. Ruined me. When I saw his image, in that moment, I panicked. I got it in my head that it was a warning, the world's way of saying: *No, Fran, don't let down your guard, don't fall in love again.* The point is, for the past ten years, I've been kidding myself that I'm over the heartbreak, when in reality, all I've done is bury it."

"Oh, Fran," says Rafael, his face touched by sorrow.

"But"—Fran brightens, meets his gaze, and smiles—"I'm letting it go. I've faced it, and now I'm letting it go for good. Finally, I've realized I want to move on. Because I want…I want…" She trembles, heart pounding. "I want to be happy. As you can see"—she looks down at the swathes of lace—"I got the dress back off Karina T. It felt like the only thing I could do. She butchered it. I should have known—she was always the wrong bride for it."

"So who is the right bride?"

Fran smiles. "Actually, I'm not so sure it needs a bride. I'm starting to wonder if maybe…" She runs a hand down the wounded silk, its beauty shining despite its scars. "Maybe it has another purpose."

"Maybe it does," says Rafael, almost like he believes her.

Then he reaches out, takes her hand in his—the first physical contact they've had in weeks.

And it feels like fire.

# epilogue

THE PROPOSAL COMES ONE BLUSTERY OCTOBER AFTERNOON, among the autumn colors of Epping Forest. Owing to Fran's observance that Rachel and Melissa are both, in their ways, doing well after their encounters with whispering dresses, Rafael, always wanting to be a man of his word, honors his bet—and the call of his heart—and gets down on one knee.

Two months later, in the rooms of the Savoy, one of London's most historic grand hotels, Miss Francesca Delaney becomes Mrs. Francesca Colt.

As for a wedding dress, Fran surprises everyone by making her own from scratch, like she'd always wanted to. She is breathtaking in a bright-white halter neck with mermaid skirt, bare shoulders, and a scooped back. She ordered the fabric from Paris, worked six days nonstop. Rafael cannot help but beam at her, his shimmering bride who has hurtled into his life, who he has fought with, slept with, laughed with, escaped with, and told the best and worst of his innermost secrets to. He loves her so much, so completely, so definitively.

Mick gives her away and makes a heartfelt speech:

"You know what my old mum used to say: she said love will find its way. Cliché, I know, but this was a woman who reunited with her childhood sweetheart at the ripe old age of seventy-two, having been widowed for over a decade. Rafael, Fran, all you need to remember is that love finds its way—just stop putting barriers in its path."

Mick is delighted to be sporting an original gentleman's frock coat and top hat, and even more delighted that it has garnered interest from Janey, who, sober, straight-haired, and wickedly playful, seems like a promising new companion, now that Francesca has a husband to hang out with. The occasion is celebrated with many of Fran's old brides, including Rachel, Ella, Melissa, and Kate Fugles, who happens to be pregnant with twins but is still rock and roll.

As for Mimi, fresh from wedding-dom herself, she looks dazzling in a daring orange slip dress and an enormous statement fascinator. She is also, much to Fran's enjoyment, relatively smiley. But the smiliest of all is Fran's mum, who is only too delighted to see her brilliant daughter finally exorcise those actor-related demons and find the marital happiness she deserves.

The Alessandra Colt dress has found its way into one of Fabian Alexia's glass display cases—apart from one loose embroidered hummingbird, rescued and sewn into the hem of Fran's own wedding dress, a secret little token of all the old gown has meant to her. The money from Fabian has gone to the foundation. To Fran, it seemed like the right way to restore all that had been set askew, past and present. A complete circle. For all the suffering the dress has wrought, over so many years, now it can do some good. Although, of course,

Fran will never forget that its true whisper belongs to her and Rafael, a lesson of faith for two damaged hearts, that there can be, if you're open to it, love after heartbreak.

# reading group guide

1. The Colt family has a toxic, hidden history that Rafael tries to outrun. How would you feel if you learned that your family had a dark past? Would you react similarly to Raf? Would you react differently?

2. How would you characterize Janey's personality? Despite her mistakes, do you like her?

3. Flapper costumes, French couture gowns, kaftans, and princess dresses—the Whispering Dress boutique has them all. What kind of dress do you think Fran would recommend for you? Why?

4. Before meeting and falling in love, both Rafael and Fran drown themselves in their work to forget their loneliness. Have you ever worked especially hard to avoid dealing with your feelings? Did it help?

5. Discuss the friendship between Mick and Fran. Would you want to be friends with them?

6. Rafael gets angry with Fran when she embarrasses him at the gala. Do you think his anger is entirely justified? Discuss the importance of maintaining an image in the public eye. Does it matter to you?

7. Fran has the uncanny ability to see into the past of vintage dresses. Do you think this is magic or imagination?

8. Rafael criticizes Fran for her romanticism, claiming she can't hide in the idealized past. To what extent do you think her imaginative nature is good for her? In what ways is it detrimental?

9. From the very beginning, we know that Rafael can be short-tempered and rude. Do you think this behavior is reasonable? Discuss why he acts this way. What factors influence his behavior?

10. Mimi's views on marriage are pragmatic—her marriage won't be a passionate one, but it will allow her to get a visa and have a child. Do you think she'll be happy with this arrangement? Do you think that Fran's influences have changed her?

11. When she goes to check up on her past clients, Fran learns that Rachel is still happily married and that Melissa is divorced but content. Discuss these two kinds of happiness. What kind of joy can be found in a healthy marriage? What kind of joy can be found outside of marriage? In what ways are each important?

12. In the end, Fran chooses not to get married in the Alessandra Colt dress and sews her own gown. Did this choice surprise you? Why? Put yourself in Fran's shoes. Would you have made the same decision?

# a conversation
# with the author

**This book delves into the fashion world. Can you talk a little bit about your research for the story?**

I write content for the Victoria and Albert Museum, the world's leading museum of art and design. The first subject assigned to me was their collection of bridal wear. It was a pinch-me-now moment, being paid to contemplate exquisite, historic wedding dresses. As I got deeper into my research, I realized it wasn't just the dresses that fascinated me, but the personal stories behind them. From demure to ultimate glamour, from the courtesan's sack-back gown to the ever-changing Victorian silhouette, from the thirties to the sixties to the nineties, these dresses were as varied in character as the women who wore them—and it struck me that the spirit of these women seemed very much present, embodied in the fabric and stitches. All my life I've loved clothes but have little experience of making or repairing them, so while I was working on the book, I asked a talented costumer friend for tips and advice on sewing jargon. I also became slightly addicted to vintage clothing websites and blogs!

**What does your creative process look like?**

It always starts with thinking and daydreaming (which can take weeks, months, years even). I can sense when a "good" idea is emerging—it just keeps blooming in my mind and won't stay quiet. Once I've committed to developing an idea, I scribble in notebooks and on big sheets of paper, thrashing out character, theme, and plot ideas. I then pull all of this into something more refined on my laptop (usually in the form of a plot overview) and then, as quickly as I can, I get a messy first draft down. I don't care about finesse at this stage—I just like having words to sculpt. It's a bit like making an oil painting: a blank canvas is daunting, so just cover the whole thing in paint and build from there. I see a lot of parallels between writing and painting. You start with something raw and loose, then layer after layer, edit after edit, the clarity emerges. I'd say my process is roughly 30 percent writing, 70 percent editing. I love to hone and sharpen and see the power of the story come through. I listen to music when I write, often the same song on repeat to set the mood. Fran and Raf have their own theme songs, and I have playlists called In the Wedding Shop, Special Dress Moment, and Encouraging Love!

**In the book, Fran matches each bride with the perfect dress to teach them an important lesson about happiness. What dress would she assign you, and why?**

I love the glamour and sophistication of the thirties, but I think the dress I truly identify with is the good old cotton farm-girl frock. Its down-to-earth honesty makes sense to me. Life's drama has taught me the value of simple, everyday pleasures: a good cup of coffee, the roses in my garden, that tingly feeling when a sentence reads well. I'm happiest hanging out with my family, being creative and outdoors. To me, time matters more than stuff, and I think the Sarah-Anne Bootle dress reflects this. That said…if Fran could find me a dress that once belonged to a talented pastry chef, that would be marvelous! I love cake, but I'm a terrible baker!

**The idea of a wealthy, corrupt family with a charitable foundation is an ironic one. What inspired you to write the Colt family?**

I had a conversation about the nature of altruism with my sister, who is a charity fundraising director in the UK, and it got the cogs whirring. The desire to "give" isn't as straightforward as we might assume. There are many different factors and motivations underlying it, such as having personal experience of an issue or wanting to improve public image. I felt this would make an interesting background for my male protagonist. I was intrigued by the idea of a grand family with a glowing reputation who are hiding all kinds of malfunction. The foundation is their mask, but it's one that does a lot of good, so no one challenges it. For Raf, however, this deception of altruism is complicated. He's had high-status responsibility foisted upon him. He wants to do the right thing with it but is shadowed by his family demons.

**Who are some of your favorite authors?**

As a child, I loved the Finnish author Tove Jansson, who wrote the Moomin books—so much so that I named my daughter after her! I love reading, but I have precious little time to do it, so my policy is to take a chance on whatever comes along. This way, I get plenty of variety, from comedy romance to creepy thrillers to literary epics. I've always had a thing for twentieth-century writers like J. D. Salinger, Daphne du Maurier, W. Somerset Maugham, and Evelyn Waugh. That's true escapism for me. I love reading books about periods of history that were written "at the time," the prose oozing old-style elegance. Jane Austen's another one.

**Fran values clothes with a history. What is your stance on vintage versus modern clothing?**

Vintage all the way. For day-to-day wear, I mostly buy modern, practical clothes (mum of three, lots of running around) and wear them until they fall apart, but for special occasions, I wear vintage. I love floaty, hippyish things from the seventies and regularly raid my mother's collection of original Biba dresses. They're so beautifully designed and cut, it's impossible not to feel wonderful in them. I love the sense of story in vintage clothes—their possible pasts. You can't always know them, but it's fun to imagine. I think vintage clothing, and secondhand clothing in general, has importance for many reasons: story, quality, style, and ethics. The ethical issue is pressing. The current appetite for cheap, disposable new fashion comes at a huge cost to society and the environment.

**Fran's visions bring a touch of magical realism to this book. What made you decide to bring magic into the story?**

Because I could! Or, in other words, because the world of fiction can go places that reality can't and this excites me. This is where my imagination can do cartwheels. In its earliest incarnation, I imagined *The Second Chance Boutique* to be like a fashion-based *Quantum Leap* (an old time-travel TV show). Fran was literally going to travel in time to plunder the dresses of history and bring them into the present, but as the writing evolved, I found myself instinctively pulling back, losing the heavy sci-fi element, and finding a subtle but delectable thread of "time-*sensing*" within Fran's talent. I do think old things have a certain kind of energy within them, but is this magic or sentimentality? The dreamer in me thinks it's a bit of both.

**You work for the Victoria and Albert Museum, researching and writing about archived gowns. Why were you drawn to this kind of work?**

I'm creative to the core. I've always loved clothes. I wanted to be a fashion designer when I was younger, but equally I loved art and writing. At one point, I thought I was destined to become a portrait painter and secured a place at art school, but then I worried I'd miss writing. I traveled and did a bit of soul-searching, then eventually, I decided to combine interests and study art history. I spent a lot of time hanging around the Victoria and Albert Museum and the National Art Library, then became distracted by living the rest of my life, so it was lovely when, years later, the opportunity to write for the museum came along. I immediately felt at home. The museum is known for its fashion and textiles, but I don't just write about gowns. I've covered all kinds of objects and design eras, from art deco to David Bowie memorabilia. There is a secret part of me that still wonders whether I should have become a portrait painter, but hopefully one day I'll have some spare time to explore this!

**You and Fran share a love of vintage clothing. Are there other parallels between you and your protagonist?**

I think we both have a sense of fun and curiosity. We're both optimists and we're both intuitive. I'm interested in psychology, and like Fran, I'm drawn to helping people. Also like Fran, I've made the mistake of focusing too much attention on others while ignoring my own problems. Fran throws herself into finding perfect dresses for other brides, while her own fateful dress lurks in the back of a closet, barely looked at but quietly scaring her away from love. I became happier when I learned not just to listen but to talk, to admit my troubles and let people in. And that's the journey I sent Fran on. She has to confront her fears and insecurities and let Raf in. So, in other words, yes, I think Fran's a little bit of me—but with better sewing skills!

**Rafael, Fran, Janey, Mick, and even Mimi grow in their own ways. Did these characters teach you anything about love and happiness?**

I think Mick says it all when he tells Fran "You have to show yourself, really show yourself." Growth to me is about developing self-awareness. If you know and accept yourself—not just the veneer of you, but the inner you, warts and all—then you're in a much stronger position to have an honest, healthy relationship with another person. Fran tries to achieve this for others through her dresses, but ultimately, she's burying her own head in the sand. She can only move on in her relationship with Raf when she faces her hidden hurt. Likewise for Raf, he is freed by confronting his family demons. Crucially, the Alessandra Colt dress helps them both do this. As for Mimi, well, she's one of a kind, but I think she's quite comfortable in her cold-blooded, pragmatic skin. I like that the thirties dress gets her to loosen up a bit though—the glamour of backless full-length satin is potent.

**You're from just outside of London. Did you choose to set the story in London for any significant reason?**

If I jump on public transport, I'm only a twenty-five minute ride from the center. It's my city. I love it. I know it. The east, where Fran has her shop, is so vibrant. There are lots of vintage clothing stores and markets in the area, so it was fun to shop—I mean research! I wanted my characters to be based in London, with all its frenzy, excitement, and action, but equally, I wanted them to have an escape, somewhere they could be quiet and reflective. We all need a different pace from time to time. Their escape, Dryad's Hall, where Fran finds the dress, is based on an actual house near where I live in Epping Forest. The house was knocked down a few years ago and replaced with something modern. It broke my heart to see such an extraordinary old building, with so much history, suddenly disappear. I guess that got me thinking about the life and stories that inhabit old things.

**What do you hope readers will take away from this story?**

I hope readers will feel assured that inner demons—whether they are doubts, fears, insecurities, or emotional scars—don't have to be a barrier to happiness. I also hope that readers might think a little more about the clothes they wear each day. And if a wedding is on the cards, that they'll think of Fran and go vintage!

# acknowledgments

With thanks to my agent, Sarah Such; to Shana Drehs and the team at Sourcebooks; to Jo Jones for reminding me how much I love the V&A Museum; to Eirian Walsh-Atkins for being on hand with sewing advice and motivational wedding dress photos; and to my family, especially Julian, Tove, Harper, and Emil.

# about the author

Louisa Leaman was born, raised, and now lives near Epping Forest in England. She studied art history at Leeds University before becoming a teacher working with children with special needs. After winning the *Times Education Supplement*'s New Writer's Award, she turned her hand to writing books for children. Louisa currently writes content for the Victoria and Albert Museum in London, but has also been published in the *Guardian*, the *Observer*, the *Independent*, and the *Times Educational Supplement*. Her interest in the arts is often inspiration for her plots, and her first book, *The Second Chance Boutique*, was inspired by the Victoria and Albert Museum's large wedding dress collection and fulfils her dream of writing romantic fiction. When she isn't busy writing or rearing her three lively children, she paints portraits, takes long walks, and spends far too long browsing vintage clothing shops.